THE ISLAND

Books by Peter Benchley

THE DEEP
JAWS
TIME AND A TICKET

PETER BENCHLEY

THE ISLAND

BOOK CLUB ASSOCIATES LONDON

This edition published 1979 by
Book Club Associates
By arrangement with André Deutsch Ltd

All of the characters in this book are fictitious,
and any resemblance to actual persons, living or dead,
is purely coincidental.

Printed in Great Britain by
Richard Clay (The Chaucer Press), Ltd.,
Bungay, Suffolk

for Tracy and Clay

'Romantic adventure is violence in retrospect.'
– adage.

'[In a state of nature] no arts; no letters; no
society; and which is worst of all, continual fear
and danger of violent death; and the life of man,
solitary, poor, nasty, brutish, and short.'

– THOMAS HOBBES, *Leviathan*.

I

The boat lay at anchor, as still as if it had been welded to the surface of the sea. Normally, this far out, there would be long, rolling groundswells – offspring of far-distant storms – that would cause the boat to rise and fall, the horizon constantly to change. But, for more than a week, a high-pressure system had squatted over the Atlantic from Haiti to Bermuda. The sky was empty even of fair-weather clouds, and the reflection of the midday sun made the water look as solid as polished steel.

To the east, a splinter of grey hung, shimmering, suspended a millimetre above the edge of the world: the refracted image of a small island just beyond the horizon. To the west, nothing but waves of heat rising, dancing.

Two men stood in the stern, fishing with monofilament hand-lines. They wore ragged shorts, filthy white T-shirts, and wide-brimmed straw hats. Now and then, one or the other would dip a bucket off the stern and pour water on the deck, to cool the Fibreglass beneath their bare feet. Between them, over the socket where the fighting chair would fit, was a makeshift table of upturned liquor cartons, covered with fish-heads, guts, and skeins of thawing pilchards.

Each man held his fishing hand out over the stern, to prevent the line from chafing on the brass rub-rail, and felt with the tip of a calloused index finger for the tick that would signal a bite, a hundred fathoms below.

'Feel him?'

'No. He's down there, though . . . if the hinds'll let him get near it.'

'Tide's runnin' like a bitch.'

'It is. Keeps takin' my bait up the hill.'

Cooking smells drifted aft, mingling with the stench of sun-ripening fish.

'What's that Portugee bastard gonna poison us with today?'

'Hog snout, from the stink of it.'

In the darkness of the canyon beneath the boat, a fish of some size took one of the baits and ran with it to a crevice in the rocks.

The man was slammed against the gunwale. Bracing himself with his knees to keep from being pulled overboard, he reached out with his left hand and hauled a yard of line, then a yard with his right, another with his left! 'Damn! I knew he was there!'

'Prob'ly a shark.'

'Shark, my ass! That's Moby goddam shark if it is.'

The fish ran again, and the man gritted his teeth against the pain in his hand, refusing to let the line burn through his fingers.

The line went slack.

'Bitch!'

The other man laughed. 'Man, you can't fish. You pulled the hook right out his mouth.'

'Bit it off, is what.'

'Bit it off . . .'

He retrieved the line slowly, careful to let it tumble in a pile at his feet, untangled. Hook, weights, and leader were gone, the monofilament severed. 'I told you; bit it off.'

'Well, I told *you* it was a goddam shark.'

The man tied a new hook and leader to his line. He peeled two half-frozen pilchards from the ball of bait fish, ate one, and threaded the hook through the other – in and out the eyes, along the spine, in and out by the tail. He cast the hook overboard and let the line run through his fingertips again.

'Hey, Dickie.'

'Hey.'

'What time tomorrow, the cap'n say?'

'Noontime. He's meetin' the plane at eleven-somethin'. Dependin' how much crap they got, they should be at the dock around noontime.'

'What kind of doctors they are again?'

'Nelson ... I told you a hundred times. They's neurosurgeons.'

Nelson laughed. 'If that don't beat all ...'

'I still don't see the funny in neurosurgeons.'

'*Head* doctors, man. What's head doctors doin' goin' fishin'?'

'Neurosurgeon ain't just a head doctor.'

'*You* say. All I know is, after that fella in Barbuda hit me up 'side the head with the ballpeen, they sent me to a neurosurgeon.'

'You told me.'

'I baffled him, though, so he sent me to a Czechoslovak.'

'Anyway, no law says a neurosurgeon can't fish, too. Important thing is, cap'n say they pay cash up front.' Dickie paused. 'You 'member how many there is?'

'I never did know.'

Dickie shouted, 'Manuel!'

'Aye, Mist'Dickie!' A boy appeared in the door to the cabin. He was slight and wiry, twelve or thirteen years old. His skin had been tanned umber. Sweat matted his hair to his forehead and streaked the front of his starched white shirt.

'How many ...' Dickie stopped. 'You dumb, scramble-headed Portugee sum'bitch! I *told* you not to wear your uniforms when there ain't no guests aboard!'

'But I ain't—'

'Look at your pants, boy! Looks like you crapped your-self!'

The boy glanced down at his trousers. The heat in the cabin had steamed out the creases, and the legs were spat-tered with grease. 'But I ain't *got* no other pants!'

'Well, I don't care you have to stay up washin' all night, they better be white as an angel's ass by first light.'

Nelson smiled. 'What do *we* know, Dickie? Maybe neurosurgeons like dirty little Portugees.'

'Well now, Nelson, maybe you got a point. What d'you say, Manuel? Sh'we let them nooros fool with you?'

The boy's eyes widened. 'No, sir, Mist'Dickie. Whatever that is, I don't want none.'

'How many bunks you make up?'

'Eight. That's what the cap'n said.'

Nelson sniffed the air. 'What the hell you cookin', boy?'

'Hog snout, Mist'Nelson.'

Dickie said, 'I told you, Nelson. That's all you're good for.'

When Manuel had washed and stowed the plates and pots and pans, and had scrubbed the galley clean, he had nothing to do. He would have liked to shut the outside door, turn on the air conditioning and the television in the main saloon, and lounge on the velour-covered sofa. But the air condition-ing was never turned on except for the comfort of paying guests; there were no signals for the television set to receive; and the sofa – like all the rest of the furniture – was covered by protective plastic shrouds.

There was a bookcase full of paperbacks, and Manuel could have gone to his bunk and read, but his reading fluency was limited to the block letters on packages of frozen food, labels on marine instruments, and place names on nautical charts. He was determined to improve his reading, and he had been studying the captions in picture magazines left behind by previous customers – *People*, *US*, *Playboy*, *Penthouse* and *Yachting*. But he felt he had already gleaned as much as he ever would from the magazines on board.

Dickie and Nelson were still fishing off the stern. Manuel could have rigged himself a line and joined them, and he would have if they were catching anything. But the banter between Dickie and Nelson increased in inverse proportion to the number of fish being caught, and on days this slow it was ceaseless. If Manuel joined them, they would turn on him as a fresh target, and that he hated.

So he washed his clothes and ironed them, and was bored again.

Dressed only in a pair of mesh undershorts, Manuel walked to the stern. The sun was swelling as it touched the western horizon, and the moon had already risen, a weak sliver of lemon against the grey-blue sky.

'Mist'Dickie, you want I should take the covers off the chairs and stuff?'

Dickie did not answer. He was sensing his fingertips, trying to decipher the faint jolts and tugs on his line, to distinguish between the nibble of a small fish and the first tentative rush of a larger one. He yanked at the line to set the hook, failed, and relaxed.

'No. Leave it be. Time enough in the morning. But if you're sittin' around with your thumb in your butt, you might's well fill the booze locker.'

'Aye.'

'And bring us a charge of rum when you're done.'

'Can I turn on the radio?'

'Sure. A touch of gospel do you good. Flush the evil thoughts from your mind.'

Manuel returned to the saloon. In a cabinet beneath the television set was a bank of radios: single side band, forty-channel citizens band, VHF, and standard AM–FM. At this time of day, most of the receive-and-transmit bands were cluttered with conversations between Cuban fishermen discussing the day's catch, cruise-ship passengers calling the States (via Miami Marine), and commercial purse-seiners telling their wives when to expect them home. Manuel switched on the AM receiver and heard the familiar, anodyne voice of the Saviour's Spokesman – an Indiana preacher who taped religious programmes in South Bend and sent them by mail to the evangelical radio station in Cape Haïtien. Most boats cruising in the neighbourhood of latitudes 20° and 22° north, longitudes 70° and 73° west, kept their AM receivers locked on WJCS (Jesus Christ Saviour), for it was the only station that was received without interference and that broadcast regular local weather conditions. US Weather Bureau reports from Miami were reliable enough for Florida and the Bahamas, but they were notoriously, dangerously, bad for the treacherous basin between Haiti and Acklins Island.

'... and now, shipmates,' crooned the Saviour's Spokesman, 'I invite you to join us here in the Haven of Rest. You know, shipmates, for every soul a-sail on the sea of life there is always a small-craft warning flying high. But if you'll let him, Christ will stand beside you at the helm ...'

Manuel rolled back the carpet in the saloon, lifted a hatch cover and dropped into the hold. He took a flashlight from brackets on the bulkhead and shone it on countless cases of canned food, soft drinks, and insect repellent, net bags of onions and potatoes, paper-wrapped smoked hams, tins of Canadian bacon and turkey roll. Crouching in the shallow hold, he moved forward, searching for a case or two of liquor. At most, he figured, three cases: eight people – including four women, who don't drink as much as the men – for a seven-day trip. Thirty-six bottles would be more than enough. And he knew that guests did not order more than they planned to drink. Food was included in the charter price, but liquor was extra, and leftovers remained on board. Those were the rules.

He moved farther forward and shone his light into the bow compartment. It was full of liquor boxes. He read the stencilled letters on the sides of the cartons, and then, conditioned to distrust his reading, read them again: scotch, gin, tequila, Jack Daniel's, rum, Armagnac. In his head, Manuel counted bottles, people, and days. A hundred and forty-four bottles, eight people, seven days. Two and a half bottles per person per day.

Manuel knelt on the deck and stared at the cartons and felt ill. This was going to be a bad trip. There would be complaints about everything: when the guests drank too much, nothing was right for them – not the weather, not the comforts aboard the boat, not the food, not the kinds of fish caught nor the number, and especially not each other. Dickie and Nelson and the captain were immune to churlishness; their age and experience and toughness deterred all but the most reckless of boors. That meant, of course, that the drunks saved their most vitriolic abuse for the young and defenceless Manuel.

He set the flashlight on the deck and tore open the nearest case of scotch. The topside bar could hold two bottles of everything – enough for the first night, at least.

At twilight, the fish began to feed.

'I never could figure it,' Nelson said, hauling in his line hand over hand. 'There's no light down there anyhow, so how's them buggers know when's dinnertime?'

'They got a natural clock inside 'em. I read that.' Dickie leaned over the stern. 'Well, looka that goggle-eyed bastard.'

Nelson reached for the leader and hauled the fish over the gunwale. It was a glass-eyed snapper, rich, reddish pink, six or eight pounds. As the fish had been dragged from the bottom, the air inside had expanded, bloating the fish's belly and popping its eyes. The tongue had swollen to fill the gaping mouth.

'Supper,' Nelson said.

'Damn right. Manuel!'

There was no reply. The boy was in the hold, far up in the bow. From the saloon came the voice of the Saviour's Spokesman, backed by a choir: '... you may say to yourself, shipmate, "Why, Jesus can't love *me*, for I am too grievous a sinner." But that's *why* he loves you, shipmate ...'

'Manuel!' Dickie started forward. 'Goddammit, boy ...' Looking beyond the saloon, through the forward windows, Dickie saw something drifting towards the boat, carried by the swift tide. 'Hey, Nelson,' Dickie pointed. 'What you make of that?'

Nelson leaned over the side. In the half-light, he could barely see what Dickie was pointing at. It was twenty or thirty yards in front of the boat – dark, solid, twelve or fifteen feet long. Obviously, it was unguided, for it swung in a slow clockwise circle. 'Looks like a log.'

'Some robust log. Damn! It's gonna smack our bows dead-on.'

'Not movin' fast enough to do no harm.'

'Scrape the crap outa the paint, though.'

15

The object struck the boat just aft of the bow shear, stopped momentarily, and then, caught in the tide, moved lazily towards the stern.

Below, Manuel heard a dull thump on the port side. He opened a case of Jack Daniel's, tucked two bottles under his arm, and, holding the flashlight in his other hand, went aft towards the hatch. He reached up and set the Jack Daniel's on the saloon deck. He crouched again and moved forward, ignoring the Saviour's Spokesman's exhortation to '... write to us here at the Haven of Rest, and we promise to write you back if you will enclose a self-addressed stamped envelope.'

'It's a *boat*!' said Dickie.

'Go on ...'

'Like a canoe. Look at it.'

'I never seen a boat like that.'

'Get a gaff. The big one.'

Nelson reached under the gunwale and brought out a four-inch gaff hook with a six-foot steel handle.

The object was closing fast. 'Snag it,' said Dickie. 'Wait ... not yet ... not yet ... Now!'

Nelson reached out with the gaff and jerked it towards him. The hook buried in the wood, and set.

It was a huge, hollowed log, tapered at both ends. The tide pulled at it, swinging the far end away from the boat. 'It's a heavy bastard,' Nelson said. 'I can't hold it much longer.'

'Bring her 'round here.' Dickie unlatched and opened the door in the transom used for bringing big fish aboard. He stepped down on to a narrow platform at water level, just over the exhaust pipes.

Nelson guided the log around the stern, into the lee of the boat, out of the tidal flow. The log rocked gently, like a cradle.

Nelson said, 'There's something in it.'

'I see it. Canvas, looks like.'

Nelson hauled the log up to the stern.

Steadying himself with a hand on a stern cleat, Dickie reached out with his left foot and flipped back an edge of the canvas. There, palm upward, as if mendicant, was a human hand.

16

'Holy shit!' Dickie's foot snapped back on to the platform. He held the cleat with both hands.

For a moment, neither man spoke; each listened to his heartbeat. Then Nelson said, 'More of him under there?'

'I don't want to know.'

'Maybe he's alive.'

'What he be doin' out here alive? 'Sides, *smell* the bastard!'

'Won't know till you look.'

'*You* look.'

'*I* can't look. I'm holdin' the gaff.'

Dickie gazed down at the hand, considering. He reached out, drew back, reached out again. 'C'mon, chummy,' he muttered. 'C'mon. Be nice and dead.' He touched the corner of the canvas and lifted it.

He saw a wrist, circled by a crude, green metal bracelet, and part of a forearm.

'C'mon,' Nelson said impatiently. 'He ain't gonna bite you.'

'I can't get a grip on him. Pull him in farther.'

'There ain't no farther. He's hard against the transom now.'

Holding his breath, Dickie leaned away from the stern, reaching with his left hand, clutching the cleat with his right. His fingers wrapped around the lifeless palm. He pulled.

Suddenly, the hand was alive. Fingernails bit into Dickie's wrist and yanked downward, tearing him away from the boat.

The canvas heaved up and flew back.

Dickie's body hit the canoe, and a blur of grey hissed through the air, striking him above the left clavicle. Like a doll dismembered by an enraged child, Dickie's head flopped loose from his body, connected only by threads of skin and sinew. A rush of air burst from his open trachea, blowing bubbles of blood. Nelson heard two splashes as body and head hit the water separately.

The man was aboard before Nelson could unhook the gaff. Frantically, he tried to free it, but the hook was fast in the wood. He dropped the gaff and backed away.

Nelson did not look at the man advancing upon him; he

17

was mesmerized by the upraised axe, a crescent blade drooling with blood. As droplets fell to the deck, they glittered in the twilight. The axe spun in the man's hand, and facing Nelson now was a tapered pick, a curved triangular spike. The pick jabbed at him. Nelson dodged.

His eyes flickered away from the pick and saw – behind the man, behind the stern – the pirogue drifting away. If he could get overboard, if he could swim to the pirogue, then paddle it ... where? Anywhere. Away.

He feinted to his left, and the man swung at him, burying the pick in the bulkhead. Before the man could dislodge it, Nelson sprinted for the stern.

But, in the shadows, he didn't see the pile of liquor cartons until his shins hit them. He tried to stop, skidded on fish guts, and sprawled on the deck. As a last, reflexive defence, he covered his head, helplessly, with his hands.

Manuel had the last of the bottles, two quarts of Armagnac, under his arm. His legs were beginning to cramp from crouching so long in the hold, and he scurried aft, hoping to be able to straighten up before a muscle knotted. Ahead, in the rectangle of light cast through the open hatch, the shadows of the bottles arrayed on the deck above were obscured by the shadow of a man.

'I got the last of them, Mist'Dickie.'

The Saviour's Spokesman was bidding farewell: 'Well, shipmates, the time has come to furl our sails here in the Haven of Rest....'

It was the smell that Manuel noticed first, a heavy, putrid stench. He had smelled something like it once before, when a goat, killed and half eaten by dogs, had lain decaying in a neighbour's field. He reached the hatch and held up the bottles, but no hand took them.

The stench made his eyes water. He looked up, saw feet.

'... until tomorrow, when we'll raise our anchor and cruise together through the shoals of life ...'

Manuel stood in the hatchway, frozen. A drop of blood fell on the carpet before him.

A hand withdrew from a broad leather belt a weapon

18

unlike anything Manuel had ever seen. A thumb pulled back the hammer, and a shudder swept through Manuel's body. He closed his eyes and heard, all in a fraction of a second, a click and a *psst*, then a resonant BOOM.

He fell backward, striking his head on the edge of the hatchway, and collapsed in the bilge. He heard glass break, smelled alcohol and sulphur, felt pains in his head and a spasm in his bowels.

And then he heard: '. . . and remember, shipmates, there's always a fair wind when Jesus is your skipper.'

2

As usual, Blair Maynard was late for work. He was due at the office at ten, but he had stayed up until 2.30 the night before, finishing a freelance piece for one of the airline magazines. He could knock off most such assignments in an afternoon or evening: movie or theatre reviews, celebrity interviews, $750 for 1,000 or 1,500 words. He had struggled over this piece, though, for it was on a subject that interested him – recent discoveries of what were thought to be pre-Columbian stairways and paving stones, underwater in the out-island Bahamas. His conclusions, after analysing the evidence, were unsatisfying: nobody knew, for sure, what the stones were. In all probability, they had been formed and smoothed by nature. But maybe not. And the research into the past, into who might have made the stairways, and why, had been fun.

But even if he hadn't been working, Maynard would have found some excuse to stay up too late, and away from his apartment. Since his wife and son had moved out, taking most of the furniture, paintings, curtains, and carpets, the apartment had become a place he preferred to avoid. When it was furnished and cared for, it had been a characterless, yet liveable, cluster of squares. Now, empty and unkempt, it was a hollow cell, constructed, Maynard concluded, of shirt-cardboards and spit.

In the first two months after his wife walked out, he had spent fewer than a dozen nights in the place. He went instead to saloons, found leggy girls who would listen to him lament about how his apartment was full of unbearable memories. After a few scotches and some fictional anecdotes about his career as a journalist, he usually got an invitation to spend the night with the girl.

But by now, his post-separation impulse to sleep with every female in Manhattan had about run its course. For a while, it had been thrilling to live the life of the clichéd roué, to awaken in strange beds beside women whose names he had forgotten and whose appetites gave full vent to his fantasies. But the thrill had faded with repetition.

If he had been willing to pursue a relationship, something enduring might have resulted with one or two of the girls. But he was not yet ready to make any commitment to anybody, or, really, to anything. And so his life, and his sex life, drifted. Occasionally, he bumped into another drifting vessel, they coupled briefly, and drifted on again.

As Maynard crossed Madison Avenue at Fifty-fifth Street, he glanced downtown and saw the clock atop the *Newsweek* building flick from 10.59 to 11.00. He entered the *Today* Publications building, exchanged pleasantries with the guard who monitored the banks of elevators, and rode up to the eighteenth floor. As he knew he would, he intercepted the woman who sold snacks from the Schrafft's cart just as she was about to enter the service elevator.

Maynard's office was one of a dozen cubicles that overlooked Madison Avenue. Twelve feet square and painted aquamarine, it contained two desks (one for him, one for his researcher), two bookcases, two typewriters, two telephones, and a file cabinet. The only décor on the walls was a dozen *Today* covers, representing the cover stories Maynard had written in his decade at the magazine.

He had had the same office for all ten years, yet his name had never been on the door. When he was entertainment editor, the plate on the door said 'Entertainment'. Then it had said 'Sports'; then (briefly) 'The Sciences'; then (even more briefly) 'The Visual Arts'. For the past three years, the

21

plate had said 'Trends'. When the door was closed – that is, when Maynard was on the phone negotiating for a freelance assignment – a passing naïf might have suspected that within laboured a Madison Avenue Marshall McLuhan, or a budding Tom Wolfe, or, at least, a dynamo with his finger on the pulse of pop sociology. The naïf would hardly have envisioned *Today*'s 'Trends' editor as he was: a lanky thirty-five-year-old who smoked Lucky Strikes, read history, and thought Frank Sinatra was the greatest song stylist of the last quarter-century. He had sold off the gun collection he had inherited from his father only when threatened with imprisonment. He neither knew nor cared what the difference was between the Monkey Hustle and a Pet Rock.

One social phenomenon Maynard *was* interested in, however, was his researcher. Her name was Dena Gaines. She was in her mid-twenties and was, by any generation's standards, stunning. She had high cheekbones, a sharp, positive nose, fair skin, and black hair that hung to within inches of her waist. She was always manifestly clean. Everything about her – her skin, her hands, her clothes, her hair, her scent – was impossibly clean. She was gentle, modest, soft-spoken, intelligent, and hard-working. She was also very fond of Maynard, not sexually (though that side of both their personalities was repressed in the office and neither had suggested unleashing it after hours), but in an affectionate, sisterly, caring way.

None of these qualities had anything to do with Maynard's fascination with Dena. What interested him about her was that she was the only woman (only *person*) Maynard knew who was an admitted, practising, proselytizing (though shyly) sadomasochist. She had been working for him for only two weeks when she first told him, quietly but candidly, that she was a votary of the cult of pain, and periodically since then she had offered to convince him that agony was the true path to sensual awareness and self-knowledge. He had never consented, but neither had he been able to quench his curiosity about the particulars of her life. He justified his more lubricious daydreams by telling himself

22

that it was part of his job to investigate the fringes of American mores.

When he entered the office, Dena was checking a story he had written for next week's issue, examining every fact and underlining each in red pencil when she was satisfied with its source.

'Good morning,' he said as he crossed to his desk.

She looked up. 'Are you okay?'

'Sure. Why shouldn't I be?'

'No reason, I guess. I just worry about you when you're this late. I always think something might have happened to you.'

'Don't worry. The most exciting thing that happens to me is when I have a nightmare and fall out of bed.' She smiled. Maynard took a sip of coffee and noticed that Dena was wearing a high-necked dress and, above the collar, a scarf. 'What's under the scarf?'

Dena blushed. 'Nothing.'

'Come on. You know the only kicks I get in life are from you.'

Dena hesitated, then said, 'Bites.'

'You mean nibbles?' Maynard tried to sound disappointed. 'Everybody gets those once in a while.'

Challenged, Dena turned her head to him and pulled down the scarf. 'Bites.'

Maynard could see distinct puncture wounds. 'Judas priest!' he recoiled. 'That must have hurt like hell.'

'I'll say.' Dena smiled, replaced the scarf, and turned back to her work.

Maynard fetched copies of the *Daily News*, the *Wall Street Journal*, and the *Christian Science Monitor* from the bookcase and spread them out on his desk. He had read the *Times* at home, and now he scanned the headlines in the other papers in search of potential 'Trends' stories. It was always easier to convince his editor that a story was worth doing once it had appeared – even as a parenthesis – somewhere else. Original ideas were suspect, a situation Maynard called the Confirmation Paradox: he was paid $40,000 a year to come up with original ideas for the 'Trends' section, but (so the

23

paradox went) if a story truly merited space in a weekly magazine, surely it would already have been covered by one of the wealthier, better-staffed wire services or daily papers.

A year ago, during a trip to Florida, Maynard had discovered that an outfit specializing in scuba-diving tours was, in violation of all industry procedures, accepting customers who had no training at all. He had suggested the story to his editor, who had turned it down despite evidence that two people had drowned from inexperience and unfamiliarity with scuba equipment. Unwilling to let the story go unreported, Maynard had given all his research to a friend at the *Times*. When the story finally appeared in the *Times*, Maynard's editor had urged him to write the piece for *Today* – using the *Times* story, of course, as his primary source material.

Maynard dumped the *News* into the wastebasket and turned to the front page of the *Journal*.

As inspirational material for 'Trends' ideas, the *Journal* was useless. The long feature stories on columns one, four, and six of the front page were often about 'Trends' subjects, but they were so comprehensive, so exhaustively reported, that there was nothing a newsweekly could add to them. Maynard admired the stories and envied the reporters who wrote them, for they were sometimes detached for up to a month to do a single piece. The *Reader's Digest* might condense a *Journal* story, but *Today* couldn't plagiarize one.

He was about to move on to the *Monitor* when he noticed a short item at the bottom of the 'What's News' column on page one.

'MISSING' said the slug, and the item read, 'A luxury sport-fishing cruiser was reported several days overdue at the Caribbean island of Navidad. The *Marita*, registered in Grand Bahama, was scheduled to pick up its captain and a charter party on Tuesday.

'According to Coast Guard statistics, 610 vessels of 20 feet or more have disappeared in the Caribbean, Bahamas and Gulf Coast areas in the past three years, with a loss of at least 2,000 lives.'

Maynard read the item twice, concentrating on the second paragraph. How could 610 boats just *disappear*?

Carrying the *Journal*, Maynard walked down the hall to the corner office. The door was open, and Leonard Hiller, the senior editor in charge of several sections of the magazine, including 'Trends', was arguing with somebody on the telephone. Maynard hesitated outside the door until Hiller's secretary said, 'You can go in. He's just having one of his fits because they killed the Woody Allen cover.'

'For what?'

'Some civil war, I think.'

As Maynard slouched in the chair opposite Hiller's desk, Hiller raised his eyebrows and puffed his cheeks, conveying the frustration he felt at being thwarted by the people he referred to as 'the Philistines on the seventeenth floor', who ran the magazine.

'I *know* it isn't funny!' Hiller shouted into the phone. 'It isn't *supposed* to be funny! The man is making a serious film. He's a serious artist, probably the only serious artist in American film today.' He paused, listening. 'So what else is new? South Africa's been about to explode for the past twenty years. Who *gives* a damn?'

Maynard stopped listening. It was a routine he had heard time and again, between successions of senior editors and managing editors. The subjects changed, but the complaint was always the same: a back-of-the-book cover story, on which the editor, a writer, several researchers and, probably, two or three bureau chiefs, had worked for weeks, was falling victim to an unforeseen national or international crisis. The back-of-the-book editor thought the crisis was overblown; the national (or international) affairs editor thought the back-of-the-book cover story was irrelevant. The hard-news advocates always won, because the final, irrefutable argument was, 'We're a *news* magazine.'

Though he didn't like Hiller much, Maynard felt sorry for him. He was only thirty-three and had been promoted to senior editor – a dead end for a writer – over the heads of people for whom he had once worked, people who had turned down the job before it had been offered to Hiller.

Maynard had refused it twice, preferring the more relaxed pace of his present job and the opportunity it offered him for unlimited freelancing. Senior editors had a lot of responsibility and little authority, were blamed for much and praised for little, and had to coddle the dozen delicate egos who wrote for them while at the same time placating the three Olympian egos to whom they reported.

When, after the last executive shuffle, it came to pass that Maynard would report to Hiller, he had tried to establish a relationship with him that would demean neither man. But from his first day in the corner office, Hiller had acted the role of boss, claiming for himself vast expertise in each of the news areas for which he was responsible. To Maynard, Hiller had fast become a pain in the ass.

'Okay, okay,' Hiller said into the phone. He had lost, as Maynard knew he would. 'How long do you want it, then?' He ran a pencil down a sheet of paper on his desk. 'I guess so, but that'll mean killing two columns of "Books" and ... I can't kill "Sports". Just a sec.' He looked up at Maynard. 'Does "Trends" have anything that won't wait till next week?'

Maynard shook his head. 'Does it ever?'

'I'll kill "Trends". That'll leave me eight for Woody Allen. Yeah ... okay.' He hung up the phone and said to Maynard, 'Sorry.'

Maynard shrugged. 'What's going on in South Africa?'

'Another riot in Soweto. Christ, they riot in Soweto every odd Tuesday. It'll be another forecast-of-Armageddon cover that won't amount to squat.'

'Did you see this? Maynard passed the *Journal* across the desk. He had circled in red grease pencil the item about the hundreds of missing boats.

Hiller glanced at the item. 'So?'

'*So?* Six hundred and ten boats? *Gone?* Where the hell did they go?'

'It's a misprint.'

'I doubt it.'

'Then they sank,' Hiller said. 'The world is full of idiots who buy boats they don't know how to drive and take them

26

places they don't know anything about. My brother has a big Bertram that he bought just to wreck marinas with. I wouldn't trust him to take me for a ride on a moped.'

'Two thousand people are missing.'

'Fifty thousand people get killed every year on the highways. I don't get your point.'

'My point is,' Maynard said, 'boating has become a huge sport, or pastime, or industry, or whatever you want to call it.'

'So has skateboarding.'

'Yeah, but two thousand people don't disappear off skateboards. There's something going on, and I think it'd make a hell of a good "Trends" cover. How come these boats are vanishing? Where are they vanishing *to*? How dangerous *is* it to cruise the islands? What can you do—'

Hiller interrupted. 'Speaking of covers, have you come up with a broad to put on the fall-fashions cover?'

'You mean a celebrity?'

'We have reason to believe that *Newsweek* will be doing Diane von Fürstenberg.'

'And?'

'And she is one smart-looking lady. I want you to find somebody just as good. If a guy goes to a news-stand, I don't want him to be faced with a choice between Diane von Fürstenberg and a gargoyle. Our whole issue will be down the tubes.'

'So, get Farrah Fawcett-Majors and roll her up in polythene.'

'That's not helpful, Blair.'

'Leonard, I'm trying to sell you on a story I think is important. You're always after me to come up with what you call big story ideas.'

'Yeah, but *fun* ones. Problems they've got plenty of in the front of the book.'

'This story will reach people. It affects a hell of a lot of our readership. It's got romance; it's about the part of the world they used to call the Spanish Main. It's got hard news – a possibility, anyway – and at the same time it's a pure "Trends" story.'

'Boats don't sell magazines.'

'Because they don't have tits?'

'Forget it. Look, this story would cost too much time and too much money, and there's probably a simple explanation for the whole damn thing.'

'Like what?'

'Like ... I don't know. That's your department. Has the *Times* done anything on it?'

'I'll check.' Maynard pressed, sensing that Hiller was weakening. 'If there is something on it, can I do the story?'

'Query the Atlanta bureau.'

'The Coast Guard is in Washington.'

'Coast Guard? All right, Washington, then.' Now Hiller was wearying of the argument.

'They don't like to answer queries from the back-of-the-book. You know that. Half of them think they're Woodward and Bernstein, and the other half are Walter Lippmann.' Maynard stood up. 'I'll check the clips.'

'Just don't forget the fashion cover. I want a real dynamite broad. Like Jackie Bisset in a wet T-shirt, only high-fashion.'

'How about Dena Gaines?' Maynard said from the doorway. 'Wrapped in whips.'

On his way back to the office, Maynard stopped by the *Today* library and signed out folders on 'Boats', 'Boating', and, as an afterthought, 'Missing persons' and 'Disappearances, mysterious'.

Dena had already left for her noontime aikido class. Maynard plucked a telephone message from his typewriter, tossed the library clips on his desk, and dialled his wife's office number.

'Devon Smith's office.'

'Hello, Nancy. It's Blair Maynard.'

'Mr Maynard! How nice to hear from you! How *are* you?'

It was the same question Devon's secretary asked every time he called, posed with the same solicitude, a question loaded with implicit sympathy. What he felt he was really being asked was: how are you surviving without this wonderful woman? Are you bearing up? Isn't it a shame that she outgrew you? Left you behind?

28

Maynard always had to fight the temptation to explain. Devon hadn't actually left him, except technically, geographically. Their separation (which ninety-three days hence would become a divorce) had been agreed upon tearlessly and relatively amicably. After twelve years of marriage, they had simply concluded that they were travelling different roads to different destinations. In fact, Devon had done the concluding, but Maynard had agreed.

For the first few years, they had had a common goal: his success. He had been an eager, talented, and ambitious reporter for the *Washington Tribune*, making $10,000 a year, living in a basement apartment in Georgetown, and enjoying the suspense, the unpredictability, of Washington newspaper work. Every routine story had potential. A traffic ticket could blossom into an enormous political scandal, revealing, say, alcoholism and philandering in the private life of a powerful committee chairman. A plea copped by a low-level white-collar criminal might lead a diligent reporter into a maze of higher-level corruption. (Watergate was still years in the future, but it had its antecedents.)

Maynard had been seduced away from Washington by his own impatience. Analysing his future at the *Tribune*, he saw that if he continued to perform well, in two or three years he might be rewarded with a beat covering a suburban school system. By age thirty, he might be the paper's Anne Arundel County correspondent.

Today lured him away from the *Tribune* with a salary of $15,000 and a job that put him in charge of a major department of the magazine. He was listed on the masthead as a department head. He and Devon were courted by public-relations executives and invited to cocktail parties, dinners, and private screenings. It was a heady time for a man who had just turned twenty-five. If he was no longer required to exercise his reportorial skills (more than half of his stories were filed by bureau reporters), well, that was all right. Now he was a writer – of newsmagazine prose, granted, but he was learning to write tight, lean pieces that told a story quickly and with clarity. He and Devon agreed that after he had had time to hone his skills, he would try to write a novel or a

29

screenplay. A newsmagazine was a terrific training ground, but it wasn't a career.

The day after he turned thirty, he was offered the senior editor's job for the first time. Devon urged him to take it. It was a promotion, it paid more money, and, most important, it would mean change. There was no longer any challenge in writing for the magazine; he could write his whole section in a couple of hours.

He had argued with her. If he took the editing job, any salary increase would be eaten up by the loss of freelance income. Senior editors had no time to freelance. It would mean giving up all hope for a novel or screenplay. Better to stay where he was, make a decent wage for working (in fact) a two-day week, broaden his experience and contacts through freelance work, absorb ideas that could be used later on.

Devon was disappointed, but she continued to support and encourage him, to appreciate his freelance pieces (for they were the work he was proudest of), to help him develop possible story lines for a novel. Not once did she accuse him of settling into a rut of comfortable survival. Not once did she suggest that his novel represented a dream of freedom and fulfilment that he would never attain.

Their marriage had begun to break up four years ago, though neither of them knew it at the time. Their son, Justin, had entered second grade at the Allen-Stevenson School, and for the first time he was away from home from eight until four. Devon took a job at an advertising agency and, to her utter surprise, turned out to be a good copywriter, and then, with practice, a brilliant one. When her boss and two other colleagues left the agency to form a new one, they took her with them. Within a year, she was chief copywriter and a partner in the firm. Her annual salary was $50,000, augmented by a bonus of half again as much.

She loved everything about her work — long hours, hustling new accounts, travelling, entertaining clients, and the challenge of convincing the public to spend money on her products rather than on the competition's.

She built herself a world in which she was happy, while

30

Maynard floated through a world of someone else's making, doing well enough without really doing anything, and not knowing exactly what he wanted to do. He had no particular lust for fame, and a contempt for celebrity: he believed in Andy Warhol's prediction that by the year 2000 everyone in America would be a celebrity for twenty minutes. His one real passion was for history – perhaps, he realized, because of a subconscious dissatisfaction with the present. In his daydreams he lived during an age of discovery (say, the late fifteenth or early sixteenth century), when people did things for the sake of doing them, went places simply because no one had been there before, and lived out (he recalled the quote from a book about the Spanish Main) 'a dream of irresponsibility, lethal larkiness and, above all, mobility ...'

His dream was Devon's nightmare. Finally, they agreed, they faced different futures. She asked for no alimony and accepted a token $500 a month in child support.

'Fine, Nancy,' Maynard said. 'Just fine. Devon called?'

'Yes, sir. She's at lunch. I know she'll be mad that she missed you.'

'Sure. What did she want?' He knew that Devon would have given Nancy the message; she never bothered him without a reason, and there was rarely anything to say that Nancy could not transmit efficiently. For all Maynard knew, Devon was in her office now, but didn't want to make idle, awkward conversation with him. He knew that she had come to regard him as a part of her past; if he was not actually forgotten, he was stashed at the back of a closet, and consulted, along with baby pictures and college yearbooks, only when nostalgia crept in.

'She wondered if you could take Justin for a few days. She has to go to Dallas, and—'

Maynard cut in. 'Sure. Fine. Starting when?'

'Tomorrow. For a week.'

'Okay. Tell him to take the bus down here, and ...' He stopped. 'No, forget it. "Trends" has been killed for this week. I'll pick him up at school.'

Maynard hung up and opened the folders he had brought from the library. Most of the clippings were 'Trend' pieces, dating back to the mid-1950s, about various stages in the boating boom in the US. There were stories about boat shows, new developments in ferro-cement hulls, and inflatable runabouts as a tool for coping with the energy crisis. There were short items about the disappearance or sinking of individual boats. But nothing to corroborate the statistics in *The Wall Street Journal*.

Then he found a note in an information packet from the Coast Guard. He might have overlooked it if it had not spilled on the floor. It was a Coast Guard bulletin urging yachtsmen to take special precautions when sailing in the Gulf of Mexico, around the Bahamas and in the Caribbean. And, more helpful to him, a Xerox copy of a 4,000-word wire-service piece titled 'Peril on the High Seas – Dawn of a New Age of Danger'.

He read the piece once quickly and once thoroughly, underlining as he read, and then walked down the hall to Hiller's office. The door was closed.

'He's editing,' Hiller's secretary said.

Maynard nodded at the secretary and opened the door.

Hiller was hunched over his desk, scrawling changes in the margins and between the lines of a story. He looked up, annoyed at the interruption, but when he saw Maynard he smiled and said, 'Margaret Trudeau'.

'What?'

'For the fashion cover. She's dynamite! Well connected and well put together. She's a natural.'

'Yeah, well ...'

'Think about it. That's all I ask.'

'Listen, I found something on this boat business. In the clips. There *have* been six hundred and ten disappearances – even more by now; the piece is a year old. Nobody knows why. The Coast Guard figures maybe fifty foundered – you know, broke up and sank. Another half dozen or dozen they know were heisted.'

'What do you mean, heisted?'

'Hijacked. Stolen. Say Mom and Pop are going for a cruise. They can handle the boat themselves on the Inland Waterway, but when they get to Florida and want to go to

32

the Caribbean, they need an extra hand. They stop somewhere and hire a crew – one, maybe two guys, who say they'll work for free if they can get passage to one of the islands. A couple of days out of Florida, they kill Mom and Pop, dump them overboard, and take the boat.'

'What for?'

'Two reasons. They can go up north and sell the boat, forge a bill of sale that says they bought it, or fence it to someone who'll change the numbers and the papers and resell it. Even if they get a fifth of its value, that could be ten or fifteen thousand bucks. Or they take the boat south and use it for running drugs up from Colombia. They're known as grasshoppers. Some cruddy old Colombian boat could never get into an East Coast port without being searched, but a clean, US-registered boat returning to its home port – nobody'd stop it. Once they make the drop, these guys take the boat offshore, scuttle it, come back to shore in a dinghy, and wait for another sucker.'

Hiller said, 'Drugs bore the piss out of me.'

'It isn't just drugs,' Maynard pressed. 'That's only a dozen boats. Make it a hundred boats! Add that to the fifty they think sank by themselves, that still leaves more than 450 boats that have simply vanished. Gone!'

'The Bermuda Triangle,' Hiller said. 'Bigfoot got 'em.'

'Leonard ...' Maynard suppressed an impulse to swear. 'Whatever this thing is, it has screwed up the ethic of the sea. Nobody goes to help a boat in distress any more, because they're scared they'll get boarded and Christ-knows-what. A sailboat with two kids on it went down in sight of three fishing boats last July, because no one would help.'

'So, you tell me. What's the answer?'

'I don't know. All I ask is, let me have a look at it.'

'I told you: send a query.'

'That's not good enough.'

Hiller said nothing. He fixed his gaze on Maynard, leaned back in his chair, and formed a tent with his fingertips, making a sucking sound with his teeth.

Maynard thought, he's trying to look like Clarence Darrow.

Still without a word, Hiller got up, walked across the room, and shut the door. Returning to his desk, he looked sombre. 'I suppose this is as good a time as any,' he said, sitting down again.

'Now what?'

'Don't you think it's time you settled down?'

'What do you mean?'

'Made peace with yourself.'

'About what?'

'What you're doing here.'

'I'm earning a living.'

'And in return?'

'I do my job.'

'I agree,' said Hiller. 'But that's all.'

'What do you want?'

'I want you to give me something extra, an enthusiasm, a commitment.'

'You want me to be enthusiastic about fall fashions? You want me to commit myself to TV Tennis, pinball machines?'

'Blair, look ...' Hiller paused. 'Christ, this may sound patronizing, but listen anyway. There's a time when everybody has to come to terms with himself, has to say to himself, "This is what I'm good at, I'm not gonna be President of the United States or win the Pulitzer Prize. I'm gonna be the best damn newsmagazine writer there is." Or whatever.'

'Yeah. I'm still looking for "whatever".'

'You've found it, and you know it, but you won't admit it. Something inside you knew it when you turned down this job.' Hiller slapped his desk. 'You're a newsmagazine writer. That's what you're good at, and that's all you're good at. Maybe ten years from now you'll win a talent contest and be a movie star, but—'

Maynard interrupted. 'You mean I'm mediocre and I might as well learn to live with it.'

'No! I mean you've found something you can do well, and you should be happy with it, just for what it is. Don't overreach. You'll screw everything up.'

'Yeah. I might even lose my dental plan.' Maynard stood up. 'I'm going to Washington.'

'What's in Washington?'

'A Coast Guard guy who looked into this boat business. They pulled him off the job and put him in charge of a bunch of lighthouses. They called him a fear-monger. I want to talk to him.'

Hiller said, 'You were the one who told me the bureau guys think they're Woodward and Bernstein. What does this make you?'

'It's the weekend. I can do what I want.'

'Okay. But think about what I said, will you?'

'You mean about accepting the fact that I'm a loser?'

'Blair, for Christ's sake ...'

Maynard walked to the door. 'I may be a loser, Leonard,' he said. 'But if I'm gonna fall on my ass, I might as well make a big splash.'

3

They had sailed together, in tandem, for protection as well as company.

They were partners in an accounting firm in Montclair, New Jersey, one a tax expert, one a specialist in corporate audits. They had been roommates at Wharton, done their accountancy training at the same firm, and worked together for twenty-five years. They had had their boats built by the same man, to identical specifications: a single mast that would carry a main and a jib; two comfortable bunks amidships and two cramped ones forward; a dry cockpit; a simple, reliable auxiliary engine, state-of-the-art communications equipment. The only difference between Burt Lazlo's *Penzance* and Walter Burguis's *Pinafore* was in interior headroom. Lazlo's wife, Bella, was six feet tall, while neither Ellen nor Walter Burguis was over five-ten.

The Burguises and the Lazlos had sailed together every vacation since 1965. They spent weeks selecting a course, learning about port facilities – where you could get ice and water and fuel, where there were showers open to the public, where decent restaurants were – planning side-trips to inland historical sites. They tried, as best they could, to leave nothing to chance.

This year's trip was their most ambitious, from Miami to Haiti, island-hopping through the Bahamas on the way. As an extra precaution, each boat carried – broken down and hidden in the food locker when they cleared Bahamas customs – a 12-gauge shotgun and fifty rounds of number-four buckshot.

Twice – once at Eleuthera, once at Crooked Island – they had been approached by wharf-rats, young, excessively charming Americans who pleaded for passage south (anywhere south) in return for whatever work needed to be done. But the Lazlos and the Burguises had read the Coast Guard precautions, and they refused.

The wind had been blowing from the east at a steady ten knots all day, and there was no reason to believe – from the radio or the sky or the breeze itself – that it was about to change. So the skippers of *Penzance* and *Pinafore* cruised slowly southeast along the western shore of a low island, searching for a leeward anchorage.

The island was not on the Defence Mapping Agency Hydrographic Centre charts, but such omissions had long since ceased to concern them. Everything about this part of the world was badly charted: shoals appeared where none were marked; deep-water channels separated islands that were, supposedly, one; lighthouses listed on the charts were heaps of rubble; 'submerged reefs' turned out to be whole islands; and named islands were often nothing more than lines of breaking surf. Navigation was based on the principle of 'What you see is what you get.' Consequently, the Lazlos and the Burguises never sailed at night.

A hundred yards ahead of *Pinafore*, Lazlo sat at the helm of *Penzance* and scanned the craggy shoreline. The island was about half a mile long, ten-foot-high cliffs topped with a tangle of scrub and thornbushes and sisal trees. Lazlo noted idly that the sisal trees had been stripped and were regrowing. Once, the sisal must have been harvested, its fibres used to make rope. But, though Lazlo couldn't see into the interior (if there was one), it was obvious that no one bothered with the island now. Nothing lived there. Nothing *could* live there, except birds. And bugs.

'You'd best get the repellent, dear,' Lazlo said. 'I'm afraid tonight will be buggy.'

37

'You're not going ashore,' said Bella, pointing to the desolate island. 'Not on *that*.'

'No, but the water's too deep to anchor out. We'll have to be within fifty yards of shore. And you know what kind of radar those devils have.'

Lazlo saw a break in the cliff line ahead. He took a microphone from the bulkhead. 'Walter, there's an inlet up there. I'm going to head for it.'

'All right,' Burguis' voice came back. 'I certainly can't drop a hook here. I'd never get it back.'

As he drew nearer, Lazlo saw that the inlet was a small harbour, perhaps a hundred yards wide and two hundred deep. At the far end, rusty iron tracks led up the beach into the scrub.

'To haul the carts of sisal, I suspect,' he said before Bella could ask. 'They probably loaded it aboard ship in here.'

Lazlo anchored *Penzance*, while Burguis hung outside the harbour. Lazlo used his engine to manoeuvre his boat as close to dead-centre as he could: at the moment, the tide was running into the harbour; the boat would lay at anchor with its stern towards the shore. But, in a few hours, the tide would slacken and turn, heading out. The boats would need plenty of room to swing with the tide. By morning, their sterns would be pointing out to sea.

As soon as the boat turned away from the wind, the bugs struck, kamikaze mosquitoes and tiny black gnats known as 'no-see-ums' that transmitted no itch or sting when they bit but whose toxin later raised painful welts. Lazlo removed his sunglasses and wristwatch (a substance in the bug spray corroded plastic lenses, first making them opaque and then, weeks later, dissolving them until they cracked and fell apart) and let his wife spray him with repellent from the parting in his hair to the soles of his feet.

Pinafore anchored aft of *Penzance*. The Lazlos hauled in the rubber Zodiac tethered to their stern, climbed aboard, and let themselves drift back until they could board *Pinafore*. While Walter Burguis mixed martinis, Ellen and Bella started a charcoal fire in a hibachi that fitted into slots on *Pinafore*'s stern.

As they ate club steaks and canned *petits pois* and watched the sun set, the water behind the boat came alive with rolling, jumping, feeding fish.

'Jacks,' said Burguis.

'Really?' Lazlo said. 'How can you tell?'

'He can't,' said Ellen Burguis. 'Everything's jacks, unless he's swimming and they bite him, and then they're sharks.'

'That's not so, Ellen,' Burguis said. 'It's true that I have ... well, respect ... for the anthropophagi. Call it a morbid fear if you like. But there is a characteristic way that jacks flail their caudal fins when they feed, not unlike our own bluefish.' He smiled. 'You see, even we pedants sometimes know what we're talking about.'

Lazlo finished his meal and washed his plate off the stern. 'I hope you folks have a wonderful ichthyological symposium,' he said, 'but I think it's time we hit the sack. Tomorrow's a long stretch of open water. Who wants the first watch?'

Burguis said, 'I'll take it. I'm not tired. Ellen can take the second, Bella the third. That'll give you a good five or six hours before your turn.'

'You think we have to stand watches *here*?' Bella Lazlo complained. 'There's no weather, and none forecast, and there's not exactly a lot of traffic.'

'We agreed on the rules,' said her husband, 'and we should follow them.'

'But what could happen?'

'A change in the wind, a freak squall, anything.'

'Even poachers,' said Burguis. 'The book says there are lobster poachers from Haiti and Cuba around here all the time. Believe it or not, they can come aboard and strip you clean while you sleep.'

'We don't have anything they'd want.'

'We don't know what they want. For all we know, they're repellent addicts who'd kill for a squirt.'

'It's basic good seamanship,' Lazlo said. 'We stand watches every night, even in port, and we wake up hale and hearty. There's no reason to break the routine.' He reeled in the Zodiac, hopped aboard, and held it beside *Pinafore* until Bella got in.

As they pulled themselves back to *Penzance*, they heard Burguis call, 'It's eight-thirty now. Ellen will take over at ten-thirty, and she'll wake you, Bella, at half-past twelve.' Bella waved.

Burguis upended the hibachi, spilling the charcoal briquets overboard. He watched as the school of jacks surrounded the tumbling crumbs, circled them, and, when they concluded that the ashes were inedible, sped away into the twilight. He went below and returned with the Remington pump shotgun, which he loaded with three shells.

'You really think that's necessary?' his wife said, wiping the dishes dry.

'If you're going to stand a watch, stand a watch. There's no point in *not* having it.'

With no clouds in the sky to reflect light, once the sun dropped below the horizon the sky grew quickly dark.

Ellen Burguis looked at her watch. 'Well . . .'

'You might as well try. Any sleep is better than none.'

'All right.' She went below and pulled the curtain across the doorway.

Burguis had brought with him a briefcase full of books. At home, he found time to read little more than daily papers and trade journals, and during the year he set aside piles of books to read on his vacation. They were all paperbacks, light, not bulky, and dispensable. Burguis liked to feel free to stop reading an unsatisfying book after twenty or thirty pages and pitch it into the sea. 'Prose pollution', he would mutter happily as he watched the soggy book wallow in *Pinafore*'s wake.

He sat in the stern, the shotgun by his side, using a small flashlight to illuminate the pages of *Dragons of Eden*.

The night was full of nature's noises: ashore, the random hooting and cawing of birds; in the water, the swirls and splashes of fish; and on the boat, below, the rattling of Ellen's breathing through congested nostrils.

Burguis heard a splash close behind the boat – not loud,

40

but more substantial than a rolling fish would make. Curious, he pointed his flashlight overboard and saw a circle of ripples spreading, as if something had been dropped. A fish must have jumped completely out of the water and re-entered head-first. He returned to Carl Sagan's analysis of the R-complex function of the brain.

Suddenly, the stern of the boat seemed to sink – gently, just a few inches. Burguis turned, but before his pupils could dilate to adjust to the darkness, a garrotte had whipped around his neck and the filament of wire had severed everything but bone.

Dragged backward overboard, in his last seconds Burguis felt no pain. There was an instant of perplexity, a sense that something had gone wrong, and then nothing.

The man stood in the cockpit, dripping, listening. He heard snoring. He pulled the curtain back from the doorway.

Ellen Burguis lay on her back, covered by a sheet, breathing deeply through her nose. A drop of water fell on her face and trickled up a nostril. She stirred.

'Already?' She snuffled, to clear her nose, and felt a sting of salt water. She smelled something terrible, as if an animal had died in the bilges.

A figure stood between her bunk and the doorway, blocking the starlight. 'Walter?'

'Ha a prayer, mum?'

'Walter?'

She tried to sit up, but the heel of a hand drove her back against the pillow. A shadow flashed by her eyes.

The figure turned away. Ellen reached for it, and tried to speak, and only then realized that her throat had been cut.

In the stern, the man held the shotgun and examined it, turning it in his hands, aiming it at the sky. The pump slide was alien to him. He jiggled it and pulled it back, startled when a shell ejected from the chamber and spun out over the water. He peered into the open chamber and counted the shells that remained, then pushed the slide forward.

41

Holding the shotgun aloft in his right hand, he slipped over the stern and paddled silently, scissor-kicking with his sodden, hide-wrapped feet, towards *Penzance*.

A few moments later, two shots resounded across the still water and echoed off the rock cliffs.

4

'Oh-oh!' Justin looked up from his magazine, the latest issue of *The American Rifleman*. 'Mom's gonna kill me!'

Beside him, in the aisle seat, Maynard closed the folder in which he carried all the *Today* clippings. 'What'd you do?'

'My piano lesson. I forgot.'

'When is it?'

'Noon. Every Saturday.'

Maynard looked at his watch. 'It's only nine-forty. We'll call your teacher from the airport. She'll be easy.'

'It's a him. Mr Yanovsky. He doesn't believe excuses.'

'He'll believe me. I'll tell him you have a bad case of sunspots.' Maynard smiled, remembering. 'I used that once on *The Tribune* when I had a God-awful hangover. It worked, too. The city editor thought it was a cancer.'

Justin was not placated. 'She's still gonna have to pay him.'

'I'll pay him, okay? A deal?'

'I don't know.' Justin flushed. 'Mom says your cheques bounce.'

'Oh she does, does she? One lousy cheque does not make a habit. I'll pay your piano teacher and the cheque'll be good. Okay?'

'Okay.'

43

'Okay.' Maynard frowned. 'She shouldn't tell you things like that.'

'She says a bad example is the best sermon.'

Maynard laughed aloud. 'First of all, it's "a *good* example is the best sermon." It's Benjamin Franklin.'

'I know. But it didn't fit.'

'Didn't fit what?'

'The jingle she was working on.'

'O, that this too, too solid hair would fall and resolve itself unto the drain.' Maynard laughed again.

'What?'

'It's *Hamlet*. His famous depilatory speech.'

'What's *Hamlet*?'

'A play. You'll know it soon enough.'

Justin returned to *The American Rifleman*. 'Hey, didn't we used to have one of these?' He pointed to a photograph of a Colt Frontier revolver.

'Yup. A rare one, too. A .32–.20. You remember how the holster used to shine? That leather was a hundred years old.'

'They say in here that the single-action Colts weren't accurate. The grips were too small.'

'They didn't have to be accurate beyond about twenty feet. The fighting was all close-in.'

'What about gunfights? You know, when they drew down on each other.'

'I bet that didn't happen ten times in ten years. If a fight came to guns, they shot each other any way they could. In the back, from under a table, behind a door.'

'That's not fair.'

'It wasn't meant to be fair. The point was to get it over with as quickly as possible, and walk away from it in one piece.' Maynard paused and looked at his son. 'No fight makes any sense, Justin. If you get into one, all you should want to do is end it. "Fair" is for the other guy to worry about.'

The seatbelt sign lit up, and the stewardess announced over the intercom that they would be landing at National Airport in a few minutes.

'I wish we could still shoot,' Justin said. Until a year ago, when Maynard's parents had moved to Arizona, Maynard and Justin had spent frequent weekends shooting with Maynard's father, who was called Gramps, on his small Pennsylvania farm. Gramps had been Marine Corps rifle champion during World War Two, and during the Korean War he had tested weapons for the Pentagon. His eighteenth-century stone farmhouse was packed with military memorabilia, from a James I-cipher musket to a Ferguson breech-loading flintlock rifle used at the battle of Kings Mountain during the Revolution, to (Justin's favourite) a rare example of the protean 'Stoner system', which made a one-man battalion out of a modern soldier. They had been good weekends, warm and close and cosy and exciting.

'So do I,' Maynard said. 'We will, someday.'

'When?' Justin looked at him, wanting a promise.

Maynard could not promise. 'I don't know.' He saw the boy look away, disappointed. 'Hey, you remember when we shot skeet that time? You did really well.'

'I got three.'

'Yeah, but ...' It was a stupid thing to bring up. Maynard had forgotten that the shotgun stock had been so long that Justin had had to hold it under his arm instead of against his shoulder. 'I only got three the first time, too.'

'Yeah, but the second time you got nineteen.'

The plane dipped and bounced and slowed as the flaps were lowered.

'Have you decided which place you want to see?'

'The new one. Air and Space, I think it is. You said you'd be two hours.'

'More or less. But don't get excited if I'm a little longer. And for God's sake, don't leave the building.'

'Dad ...' Justin's voice suggested insult and reprimand. His maturity and judgment had been impugned unjustly.

'Sorry.'

'What I still don't get is, why you couldn't talk to this guy on the telephone.'

'The telephone isn't a good way to meet people. They

45

can't get to like you or trust you. I have to make this man trust me.'

'Why?'

'Because I want him to tell me things he's been told not to talk about. My hunch is, he talked about them once already, and it ruined his career.'

'Then he's not going to talk about them again.'

'Maybe, but I hope he will. I hope he's angry.'

They took a taxi from the airport. Maynard dropped Justin at the Smithsonian's Air and Space museum, armed with the phone number of *Today*'s Washington bureau, 'in case the place burns down or something'. Then Maynard gave the taxi driver an address uptown, near the Washington Cathedral.

As the cab cruised along Rock Creek Parkway, Maynard reviewed the questions he planned to ask Michael Florio, the Coast Guard man who had been reassigned after questioning the boat disappearances. On the phone, Florio had been wary. At first, he had refused to speak to Maynard, had insisted on returning the call through the *Today* switchboard. It was an old-fashioned, but usually reliable, way to make sure that the caller was who he said he was – or, at least, that he worked where he said he worked. Then Florio had recited the standard litany of bureaucratic cant: he didn't know for sure why he had been transferred; people were transferred all the time; he did what he was told.

None of these responses surprised Maynard. Florio was within a few years of retirement. Why should he jeopardize his pension just to get his name in a newsmagazine?

The cab turned off Connecticut Avenue and climbed Thirty-fourth Street into a quiet, bosky neighbourhood of old, medium-size, medium-price homes. The driver stopped in front of a grey stucco house with a sagging wooden front porch.

Michael Florio was in his mid-forties, flat-bellied, evidently in good physical shape. His hair was cropped close to his skull. He wore a white T-shirt, and his hands, arms, and

46

face were coated with fine white dust. There were goggle marks around his eyes.

'I appreciate your seeing me,' Maynard said.

'Yeah.' Florio ushered him into the hallway and shut the door. 'Use a beer?'

'Thanks.'

Florio led the way back to the kitchen. Maynard guessed that he lived alone, for cooking in the kitchen would have been impossible: the room was a workshop. The round table was covered with drills and chisels and tiny hammers and pieces of ivory and bone. A vice had been bolted to the edge of the table. The shelves were filled with carvings – whales, sharks, fish, birds, and ships.

'Nice stuff,' Maynard said.

'Yeah.' Florio reached into the refrigerator for two cans of beer. 'Gotta have a trade, for after. Can't sit on the porch and watch the sun go down for twenty years.' He handed Maynard a beer and said, 'I don't do interviews.'

'I gathered.'

'Anything I say ... I mean, *if* I say anything ... is off the record.'

'That's fine.'

'It is?' Florio was surprised.

Maynard sipped his beer. 'Don't take offence, but I'm not really interested in you.'

'Good. I don't want anybody interested in me. Twenty and out and screw 'em all.'

'I don't want to hassle you. I won't even identify you if you don't want me to.'

'That's it.' Florio was beginning to relax. He sat down and motioned Maynard to a seat across the table. A half-carved eagle's head was clamped in the vice, and Florio could not take his eyes from it.

Maynard pointed at the eagle. 'Don't let me stop you.'

'Good.' Florio drained his beer and put on a pair of goggles and attacked the eagle with a slender chisel held between his fingertips. 'They still call me, you know.'

'Who does?'

'The relatives of the missing ones. They know I cared – I

47

did, too – and they think I can help. I can't, but they think I can. It tears you up, seeing how they go on hoping.'

'Can anybody? Help, I mean.'

Florio shook his head. 'The bitch of it is, there's no cover-up or anything; it's not like Watergate. It's just ...' He looked up. 'I don't know *what* it is. It's like the Coast Guard says, "If we can find you easily, we will. If we can't, tough titty. If you send us a radio message that you're in trouble, we'll bust our hump for you" – and I tell you, those guys are magicians when they get their act together – "but if you disappear without a trace, well, good riddance." They're a policeman on a beat, not a missing-persons bureau.'

'Six hundred and ten boats! There's got to be *some* answer.'

'Sure, a bunch of them. You know some; you told me on the phone. There's more: badly built boats that people take where they shouldn't, people who sink their own boats for the insurance and then drown before they can be picked up, freak weather. One boat here, one boat there, they're all good answers. But you're right: more than six hundred goddam boats! How many more, no one knows. Look at *Marita*, just the other day. That one's a good and a bad example, by the way.'

'How so?'

'Good, because she was a sturdy boat, well built and well maintained, sailed by a captain with a master's ticket – by law he was qualified to drive the frigging *QE II* – and manned by a crew of first-rate professionals. She sank, *if* she sank, on a flat-calm day, with a loss of all hands. I tell you, in those conditions a baby could've floated around on a seat cushion for three days and still come out of it okay. She's a bad example because she was a Bahamas-registered boat, and the Coast Guard doesn't give a rat's ass what happened to her.'

'Do they have any theories?'

'Oh, sure. They figure she either hit a reef and sank, or else one of her engines blew up. But you have to *try* to blow up a diesel engine, and if you do, it's gonna scatter trash all over the frigging place. But there's no debris. And if she went up on a reef and sank, why didn't anybody get to shore? They

48

say sharks. Shee-it!' Florio picked up a dental drill, turned it on, and held his breath while he probed delicately at one of the eagle's eye-sockets.

He blew bone-dust away from the eagle's eye and said 'The *Banshee* was a better example. She was registered in Wilmington, owned by a guy who made a bundle in cedar shingles. They had been fishing for a month, dicking around between Puerto Rico and Haiti, trying to raise a record marlin. The owner, he flew home from Port-au-Prince, and the captain started back with the boat. He radioed ahead to Mayaguana that he'd be there by nightfall. That's the last anybody ever heard from him or the boat. Good weather, two mates who'd been with him for fifteen years, no hitch-hikers. The Coast Guard thought maybe the captain had ditched her and split for parts unknown. But look here: the man made thirty thousand a year, plus half the charter fees for when the owner wasn't using the boat, plus free private-school education for his three kids, plus a house in Fort Lauderdale. Man, he could have gone to *Palau* and not found a deal like that.'

'What's your answer ... for either boat?'

'I don't have one. The drug thing is a possibility. They were both long-legged boats, had a range of a thousand miles or more. They'd be prizes for the grasshoppers. But I know for a fact that the skipper of *Banshee* carried guns aboard, so I don't believe he was hijacked. Even if he was – even if they both were – that leaves six hundred and nine others. One boat has been disappearing every other day for three years. That's how it averages out, like the population clock down-town: every so often, bingo!, roll over another one. Tell you the truth, I don't think anybody's ever going to know what happened to those boats. Not to all of them ... not to half of them.'

'Why not?'

'Another beer?'

Florio began with the simple explanations: the difficulty of patrolling vast expanses of open ocean, the ignorance and carelessness of the new breed of sailor, the incomprehensible magnetic disturbances that rendered compasses and radios

49

useless, and the sudden savagery of weather, the full potential of which was still only a matter of conjecture.

'You heard of rogue waves? Some people call them super-waves.'

'No.'

'Waves travel in what are called trains, sequences with different distances between crest and trough. Every now and again, the trains get in step. Three or four of them crest and trough together. The waves they make are monsters. Some of them go a hundred, a hundred and fifty feet high, and they come out of nowhere. They only last for a minute or so – the trains fall out of step pretty quick – but that's all it takes. There's a tanker, say, ploughing along nice and easy through twenty-foot seas. All of a sudden, right in front of him, roaring down on him at fifty or sixty miles an hour, is a ten-storey-high wall of black water. The hole in front of these things is sometimes deeper than the tanker is long, so he finds himself steaming straight down, with a mountain of water – millions and millions of tons of dead-weight water – ready to break on top of him.'

'It breaks them apart?'

'Some. Others can't slow their own momentum. They just keep steaming on down. The ocean swallows them.' Florio took a sip of beer and searched through the rubble on the table for a small, spoon-bladed chisel. 'Then there are collisions.'

'Most of them are reported, though.'

'Really? Couple of years ago, a tanker pulled into Long Beach, California. Easy passage from the Orient, everything fine. One of the longshoremen said, "What happened to your anchor, Cap?" "What do you mean?" says the captain. "Have a look," says the guy. The captain goes ashore and looks at his bows, and wrapped around his starboard anchor is a full set of sails and rigging.'

'They never felt anything? Heard anybody call out?'

'Feel what? A hundred-and-thirty-thousand-ton ship tooling along at twenty-five knots? He wouldn't feel anything, he wouldn't see anything, he wouldn't hear anything – even if he had visual radar lookouts on duty 'round the clock, which

50

he did. On a rough sea on a bad night, a big ship and a small sailboat are pretty much invisible to each other. The sailors never knew what hit them.'

Florio moved on to enumerate a maze of jurisdictional confusions that muddled maritime affairs: the FBI had authority when there was evidence of a federal crime, but precious few facilities with which to investigate crimes committed on the high seas; the Drug Enforcement Administration could act on suspicion of a narcotics violation, but if smuggling was involved, then customs got into the act, too; many boats disappeared in the territorial waters of a foreign power, triggering interest from the State Department and Interpol. Always, the Coast Guard was in the middle, hamstrung.

And more often than not, the result of the interagency squabbling was inaction. After all, on a global scale the loss of an occasional boat and a few lives was not an issue of great public concern.

'Now, if Robert Redford turned up missing, the government might get in an uproar,' Florio said with a chuckle. 'But the average joe, forget it. Besides, there's a neat little hook in the law that makes a boat-owner better off if he doesn't cry wolf and call the cops. Insurance companies usually won't pay off in cases of "capture and seizure". So the guy whose boat disappears, if he shuts his mouth and lets everybody believe it sank, he collects in full. If he goes to the FBI and makes a case that the boat was hijacked on the high seas, he doesn't collect a dime. You got a hundred, a hundred and fifty thousand bucks in a boat, that's a pretty strong reason to close your eyes and blame Neptune. Or the Bermuda Triangle. Everybody wants to believe in the Bermuda Triangle.'

'Do you?'

'What's to believe? Oh, I've read all the books, that it's Atlantis and spaceships and sea monsters and underwater hurricanes. No question, a lot of stuff disappears out there. But if you held a gun to my head and said, "What is it?" I'd have to say that it's a perfect example of man and nature working at cross-purposes. It's a *big* goddam area. There's

51

not much traffic, not much communication, not much decent mapping or weather forecasting. So when Charlie Sailboat leaves Miami to cruise the Bahamas, maybe using an atlas for charts – and some of these idiots *do* that – he's an accident looking for a place to happen.'

'Make a wild guess for me,' Maynard said. 'Off the wall. What happened to all those boats?'

Florio slid his goggles off his eyes and let them hang around his neck. He gazed out the kitchen window, apparently doing figures in his head. 'A third to half of them I'd say just went down, sank: weather, stupidity, whatever. A fifth – say, a hundred and thirty boats – were taken by the grasshoppers and then scuttled or maybe taken into the Pacific. A handful – a couple of dozen at most – were stolen like you'd steal a car and then resold somewhere else. Those are the real crazies who do that, who put their ass on the line for a double or triple homicide just to sell a hot boat.' Florio stopped.

'That still leaves more than a hundred boats.'

'I know.' Florio smiled bitterly. 'And it's those boats that got me put in charge of a bunch of lighthouses.' He looked at Maynard. '*Really* off the record? No bullshit?'

Maynard nodded.

'I think somebody's taking those boats. I don't know who, I don't know why, and I don't know what they're doing with them. But it's the only thing that makes sense. Look . . . this isn't anything new. I got that six hundred and ten figure just by adding. I stopped at 1974 because . . . because I stopped. I could have kept adding, year by year, back as far as you want. Sure, there are more recently, because there are more boats around. But proportionally, that many boats have been disappearing, in one small area of the world, without a trace, without explanation, for as long as people have been keeping records. What is going on down there has been going on for at least *eighty years*.'

'And you think it'll keep going on.'

'I do. Christ, it *is*. There were two more this week, y'know.'

'I didn't see anything about that.'

'No, you wouldn't have. There are no hard facts. The only news is, two boats didn't show up where they said they would. Two New Jersey couples. They may turn up yet, but, knowing where they were sailing, I wouldn't bet on it.'

'Where was that?'

'A pocket between longitude . . .' Florio stopped. 'Screw it. Showing you's easier than telling you.' He stood, and led Maynard upstairs to his study, a small, snug room lined with books and filled with ships' paraphernalia – a bell from one ship, a binnacle from another, a set of crossed belaying pins, a brass porthole. The walls were papered with marine charts. Florio knelt behind his desk and ran his finger across a crescent-shaped chain of islands. 'In here. Around the Caicos Banks.'

Maynard searched the chart for broad reference points, but found none. 'Where are they?'

'Caicos? Southeast of the Bahamas, northeast of Haiti. They're a British colony. Full name is the Turks and Caicos Islands.'

'What's down there?'

'Shipwrecks, mainly. In the early days, the Spaniards had to pass through Turks Passage, here, or Caicos Passage, here, on their way home. The place is a mare's nest of shipwrecks. The Banks are a real nasty trap: you're in deep water and suddenly – bang! – the bottom shallows up to four or five feet. Bermudans used to come down and rake salt in Turks, and for a while there was a sisal industry in some of the Caicos group.'

'Hold on.' Maynard was recalling something from his reading. 'I once read an argument about where, exactly, Columbus had landed in the New World, the first time. One guy said San Salvador . . .'

'Yeah. That's up in the Bahamas.'

'. . . but the other guy kept insisting it was in what he called "the Caicos group". I didn't know what he meant.'

'There's not much to know. It's a God-forsaken place. And God's the only one who knows how many boats have gone poof down there – hundreds, for damn sure.'

'Nobody's kept track?'

'No way to do it. And nobody gives a damn, anyway.'

'How do you get down there?'

'By air? From Miami, when there's an airline flying. The route changes hands about every six months. They haven't killed anybody recently, but I'd guess that's because the planes fly so slow.'

'You ever been there?'

'No. What I hear, the most attractive thing about the place is the scorpions.' Florio looked at Maynard and perceived that something was going on in the back of Maynard's mind. 'What do *you* know about the tropical islands? First-hand, I mean.'

'I've been to Nassau. I fished at Walker's Cay once, and I scuba-dived off Eleuthera. But that was years ago.'

'I don't know what you're thinking of, but the Caicos isn't Nassau. It's about as much like Nassau as Entebbe is like New York, and just about as civilized.'

'I'm not thinking of anything,' Maynard said.

'Yes, you are. But that's your own business.'

It was one-thirty when Maynard returned to the Air and Space museum. He had been gone nearly three hours. Justin was not on the steps outside the museum, nor in the lobby.

Maynard found him in a line of people waiting to enter the movie theatre. He called to Justin from behind the velveteen rope barrier.

Justin left his place in line and ducked under the rope.

'You can see it if you want. We're not in any rush.'

'No, I saw it already. It's about the history of flying. It's neat. I almost puked.' Justin pointed through the glass doors, to a building across the mall. 'Can we go over there? A kid told me there's a neat gun exhibit.'

'Sure. The plane doesn't leave for an hour and a half.'

As they crossed the avenue, Justin took his father's hand. When they reached the green on the other side, Maynard released his grip, but Justin held on. At first, Maynard felt a twinge of discomfort; he was not accustomed to holding hands. But then, recognizing his feeling, he felt sad. In the months of separation from the boy, he had lost touch with him, had not been exposed to his son's daily worries and needs. He had ceased to regard him as a child: Justin was a person Maynard saw every other weekend, whose company he enjoyed and with whom he had civil, entertaining, but not intimate, conversations. Now the boy seemed to want to re-establish contact. Maynard was touched and flattered and grateful. He squeezed Justin's hand.

'That was a cool museum,' Justin said.

'Good.' Maynard wanted to say more, but he didn't know what or how.

They skirted the sunken sculpture garden by the Hirshorn Gallery and headed for a gabled brown-brick building.

'What's the exhibit?'

'The centennial something.'

'You mean *bi*centennial.'

'No. Centennial. That's what the kid said.'

As part of the bicentennial celebration, the Smithsonian had reassembled a hall of exhibits that had been shown during the centennial celebration in 1876. It had been scheduled to close in early '77, but had proved so popular that the institution had let it run.

There were cases of clothing, machinery, housewares, ships' fittings, foodstuffs and medicines, and, in the rear of the building, an assembly of every weapon known to mid-nineteenth-century man: camel-mounted Gatling guns, mortars, tomahawks, Bowie knives, Derringers and cannons. On a wall, in an enormous glass case, was a presentation set of Colt firearms.

Justin stood before the case, his eyes consuming each weapon, his imagination carrying him to battlefields and Indian camps and cattle drives.

Maynard's mind wandered backward, to his conversation with Michael Florio. He repeated to himself questions and answers, recited numbers. Every question for which there was a satisfactory answer led inevitably to the one for which there was not even a credible hint.

'That's my favourite,' Justin said, pointing to a percussion rifle with a six-shot revolving chamber. 'I've never seen one of those before.'

55

'They're rare. They didn't last long.'

'Why not? They fired six shots. The others only fired one.'

'Yeah, but Winchester came along with their repeater that used cartridges instead of cap-and-ball. The trouble with the percussion rifles was that when one chamber went off, it sometimes set off all the others. People kept losing eyes and blowing off their left hands.' Maynard looked at his watch. 'Let's go.'

There was no traffic on the road to National Airport, and they arrived with twenty minutes to spare. On their way to the Eastern Shuttle gate, they passed a National Airlines lounge where a crowd was boarding a flight to Miami. Maynard stopped.

'What's the matter?' Justin asked.

Maynard didn't reply. His mind was a mess of impulses and doubts and hunches and rationalizations. Common sense commanded that they return to New York, shelve the boat disappearance story. Think it through. Talk to Hiller. That was the way of safety and self-preservation. But somewhere in his mind he was driven by the thought that what he would return to in New York might not be worth preserving. The choice was not between safety and risk; it was between reaching for something and resigning himself to nothing.

He took Justin's hand. 'Come on.' He turned into the National lounge.

'That's not our plane!'

'It is now.'

'Why?'

'Why not? You ever been to Miami?'

'I don't even know where it is!'

'Twelve years old, and you don't know where Miami is? Well, it's time you learned.'

Justin allowed himself to be pulled along. 'Chee! Mom is gonna *kill* me!'

'Why do you keep saying that? She's never killed you yet. Besides, we'll have you back before she knows you're gone.'

Maynard took his American Express card from his wallet and approached the ticket desk.

56

5

'I don't even have a toothbrush.'

'We'll buy you one. People in Florida brush their teeth.'

It was the tenth objection Justin had raised, and Maynard had answered, so far during the flight. The objections were not serious or considered, Maynard was sure; Justin was excited, and also was seeking reassurance by verbalizing every conceivable problem that might arise from a spontaneous departure from established routine. As his father solved, or explained how he would later solve, each problem, the boy grew more at ease.

'What're we gonna *do* down there, anyway?'

'Fool around. See a few people. Ask a few questions. Maybe go sightseeing.'

'When are you gonna grow up, Dad?'

Startled, Maynard said, 'Hey, that's not you talking, is it? That's good old Mom.'

Justin blushed.

'Never mind. Why'd you ask? What makes you think I'm not grown up? I saw an ad for *Playboy* the other day, and they think I'm over the hill. After thirty-four, you're not even worth market research.'

'Grownups don't do things like this.' Justin gestured at the plane.

'Grownups can't have fun?'

'Mom says you don't like yourself very much any more. That's why you stay at *Today* and do "Trends".'

Maynard tried to think of a snappy, jocular response, but he couldn't. He felt embarrassed and angry – angry especially, because he and Devon had agreed never to speak disparagingly of one another to their son. 'Now look, Justin . . .'

Justin reached over and, tentatively, took Maynard's hand. '*I* like you. Don't you like yourself? *I* like you.'

'Hey, buddy . . .' Maynard patted Justin's hand and looked away. After a moment, he said, 'I'll tell you. I work at *Today* for a lot of reasons. They pay me well, and we have to eat. I'm good at what I do there, as good as anybody can be, and that's something. It's not a bad job. There are a lot of people who'd *love* to write for *Today*.'

'Do you want to do something else?'

Maynard smiled. 'You mean, when I grow up?'

Justin looked sheepish. 'Yeah.'

'I don't know. I think about it, and sometimes I try not to think about it. It's easier to think about what you are than what you're not. If there's one person in the world I'd like to be like, it's Samuel Eliot Morison.'

'Who's he?'

'He travelled everywhere and saw everything, and what he couldn't see because it was in the past he read about and tried to relive, and then he wrote books telling everybody else about what he'd learned.'

'You want to write stories.'

'True stories. That's one reason we're going to Florida.'

Justin nodded, apparently satisfied with the explanation.

'What do *you* want to be, Mr Inquisitor?' Maynard asked. 'Do you ever think about it?'

'Sometimes. When I was young, I wanted to be bionic, but now I'm not so sure.'

As soon as they landed in Miami, Maynard dispatched Justin to buy some comic books and an evening paper. He was hoping there would be details about the missing New Jersey couples. Meanwhile, he went to a counter labelled 'Courtesy Desk'. An ebullient young woman – with dyed

58

blonde hair, a Barbie Doll face, and aspirations to a Dolly Parton figure – smiled at him and announced, 'Hi! I'm Ginny! How can I help you?'

'Can you tell me how to get to the Caicos?'

'Yes, sir! Is that on the Beach?'

'No, ma'am. It's a country. The Turks and Caicos Islands.'

'Oh sure! Let's just have a look.' She opened her airline guide and thumbed through the T's. 'Golly, sir, I guess there isn't any.'

'Isn't any what?'

'Turks or Caicoses.'

'I see. Would you try Navidad for me?'

'Sure thing.' She flipped through the pages. 'Here we are! Navidad. You can't get there from here.'

'Right. Then where can I get there from?'

'Nowhere, I guess. See?' She turned the book around so Maynard could see the listing. 'Air Sunrise: cancelled. Out-Island Air: annulled. Tropicair: discontinued.'

Maynard said, 'But people do get there.'

'Yes, sir. If you say so.'

'But *how*?'

The girl shook her head. 'Isn't that something?'

'Perhaps somebody charters?'

'Could be. You could ask Reliable.' She pointed to the Reliable desk at the end of the corridor.

'Thanks for your help.'

'It's been my pleasure, sir. Come see us again.'

Maynard waited for Justin, who scurried towards him with an armful of comic books. Together they walked to the Reliable desk.

A thin, leather-faced man behind the desk was filling out ticket forms, writing as slowly and carefully as a calligrapher. After every word, he licked the tip of his ballpoint pen and held his breath before attacking the next syllable. His tongue was smeared with blue. Maynard guessed that the man was on the edge of illiteracy.

He waited for him to complete a ticket, and then said, 'Excuse me, can you tell me how to get to Turks and Caicos?'

'There's no lights on the runways. Try to find the goddam place at night, you're like to end up in Africa.'

'How about tomorrow?'

'If they feel like flying.'

'Who's "they"?'

'Arawak.' The man smiled. 'We call 'em Air Whacko.'

'Reliable doesn't go down there any more?'

'Gov'ment pitched us out. Claimed we weren't givin' 'em regular service. How the hell you're supposed to be regular when half the runway is full of potholes and the other half is underwater, well, that beats me.'

'D'you charter?'

'Sure. I'll take you down there myself. Seven hundred and fifty bucks. Twin Beech.'

'Where's the Arawak office?'

'Ain't one. Fella does his business out of the bar.'

'What's he look like?'

'Can't miss him.' The man sniggered. 'Unless he's on his back on the floor by now.'

The bar was crowded and dark, but the white T-shirt with 'ARAWAK' stencilled on the back was clearly visible from the doorway. Maynard parked Justin in an empty seat beside the T-shirt and ordered him a Coke. Justin angled his *Archie* comic so that it caught the pinpoint of ceiling light, and started to read.

Maynard leaned forward, over Justin's shoulder, and spoke to the Arawak man. 'Pardon me. I gather you fly down to the Caicos.'

'Uh-huh.' He glanced at Maynard and returned to his piña colada.

'When's the next flight?'

'I got a food plane going down tomorrow.'

'Can I book a couple of seats?'

'Nope.'

'Oh. You're full?'

'Can't take passengers. Only pilot rated for passengers goes on Wednesdays. Or Thursdays. Depending.'

'Oh.' Maynard thought, to hell with it. He said to Justin, 'Drink up. We'll see if we can catch a plane to New York.'

Justin slurped the last of his Coke and slid off the seat.

The man said, 'I didn't say you couldn't go.'

'Yes, you did.'

'Nope. I said you couldn't book passage.'

Maynard took a deep breath. 'I see. So how do we ...'

'I have to take you down for free.'

'Oh ... well, that's very nice of you.'

'"Course, there's nothing to stop you from contributing to the cost of the fuel.'

'Sure. What's a ... fair contribution?'

'Fifty bucks a head. Cash. In advance.'

'You got it. What time?'

'Seven o'clock. Won't wait for you.'

'What gate?'

'Gate? Shit.' The man tipped his head towards the runways. 'Out there, on the apron.'

'What's the equipment?'

The man looked at Maynard, and lowered his voice to a mocking basso. 'Well, captain, I tell you: the equipment is whatever freakin' bird feels like starting in the morning.'

The only civil thing Maynard could think of to say was, 'Okay.' He took Justin's hand and led him away from the bar.

The girl at the Courtesy Desk reserved a room for them at the airport hotel and directed them to the Courtesy Bus that would take them there.

In the little van, Maynard said to Justin, 'Anything you want to do tonight?'

'I don't care. Watch TV?'

'Hey, buddy, we're in Miami. You should have a look at it.'

'Okay. We going somewhere tomorrow?'

'Maybe. I have to make a couple of calls.'

'I have school on Monday.'

'Monday may be a holiday. You never can tell.'

'What holiday?'

'Let's wait and see.'

. . . . .

According to the overseas operator, there was only one phone line into the Turks and Caicos Islands. Usually, it was either busy or out of order. Most messages were received by radio and transmitted, at leisure, via the island grapevine. Furthermore, she argued, there was no point in trying to call the government on a Saturday night.

Maynard pleaded with her to try any number. He had to get a message through to the government. He wasn't sure the islands *had* a government, but the argument seemed to work. The operator said she'd call back.

They watched the evening news – no mention of the New Jersey boats – and, at Justin's insistence, 'The Brady Bunch'. Maynard was about to call the overseas operator again, when the phone rang.

'I've got the Caicos for you,' the operator said. Behind her voice, Maynard heard a loud hum and a flurry of crackles.

'Who am I talking to?'

'I don't know. I kept trying numbers till one answered.' There was a click, and the operator was gone.

'Hello? Hello?' The hum on the line pulsed, swelling and fading, swelling and fading. 'Hello?'

'Same to you, then.' It was a woman's voice, faint and far away.

'Who am I talking to?'

'Who you ringin'?'

Maynard spoke slowly, trying to enunciate every word clearly. 'My name is Blair Maynard. I am from *Today* magazine. I am trying to contact someone in the government.'

'Birds,' said the woman.

'I'm sorry.' Maynard didn't know how, but evidently he had offended the woman.

'Birds!' the woman repeated.

'What's birds?'

'*He*'s Birds. He the commissioner 'round here. Birds Makepeace.'

'Do you know where he is?'

'Not here. He got no truck with Evvy.'

'Can you get a message to him for me?'

'What you want with Birds?'

'I would like to see him tomorrow. Can you tell him that?'

'I reckon he be around, 'less he fishin'.'

'Where are you?'

'Where am I?' The woman was puzzled. 'I'm here. Where're you?'

'No. I mean, are you in Grand Turk?'

'Grand Turk? What I be doin' in Grand Turk?'

Maynard tried to recall the other large islands in the Caicos group. 'Great Bone? Are you on Great Bone Cay?'

'I hope so,' she giggled. 'Last time I looked.'

'And where is he? Where is Birds?'

'Not with me. I told you.'

'I under*stand* that. But where ...?'

A high, piercing whistle interrupted the connection. It was followed by three unhealthy-sounding snaps, and the line went dead. Even the hum was gone. Maynard hung up.

Justin was watching a 'World of Survival' show about apes. 'Did you get the appointment?'

Maynard laughed. 'My application is being processed.' He picked up the phone and dialled *Today*'s New York number. At 7.30 on a Saturday night there would be only one editorial employee on duty, sitting in the telex room, keeping watch for any crises that might occasion a change in a major story. By now, next week's issue of the magazine had been closed for several hours, and nothing short of a presidential assassination or the outbreak of a major war could interfere with the press run.

'Campbell.'

'Ray, this is Blair Maynard. Can I give you a message for Hiller?'

'I'll give you his home number.'

'I don't want to bother him at home. I'd save it till Monday, but I'm not sure where I'll be.' Maynard didn't want to speak to Hiller. Hiller might refuse to let him go: the islands were the territory of the Atlanta bureau or, on an unproven story like this one, of a Miami-based stringer, and bureau chiefs were sensitive to intrusions from New York.

Furthermore, Hiller would argue, Maynard had no right to abandon his department. But if Maynard went ahead, without first checking with Hiller, the worst that could happen on his return would be that Hiller would refuse to sign Maynard's expense-account voucher for the trip. There were countless ways to pad subsequent expense accounts to make up for out-of-pocket costs. 'Just tell him I've got a lead on the boat story, and I'll call him when I can.'

'Okay.'

'Thanks, Ray. G'night.'

Maynard disconnected Justin from 'Star Trek', and they went downstairs. In the lobby they bought a small satchel which Maynard filled with toilet articles, underwear, and bathing suits. 'We may go swimming,' he explained to Justin. 'You don't want to go to the beach in your jockey shorts.'

They took a taxi from the hotel, and Maynard asked the driver to cruise along Collins Avenue in Miami Beach. 'No one should be allowed to die before he sees the Fontaine-bleu,' he told Justin. 'It may have gone the way of the dinosaurs, but it represents a critical step in the evolution of man.'

'It's gross,' Justin said as the cab passed through the blue miasma that surrounded the Fontainebleu. And, at the end of the strip, he stated flatly, 'They're all gross.'

'So much for culture.' Maynard leaned forward and said to the driver. 'Let's go downtown.'

'Where downtown?'

'I don't care. Show us the sights.'

'Sights.' The driver grunted. 'They're standing on every street corner. Only question is, d'you want Cuban or black or po' white trash.'

It was after eight. Maynard was hungry, and Justin looked sleepy. 'You want some food?'

Justin yawned. 'Sure. Let's go back to the hotel and have room service. Room service is cool.'

The driver took a right and started back towards the airport.

Justin suddenly sprang forward. 'Hey, look!'

64

Ahead, on the right, Maynard saw a flashing neon sign: EVERGLADES SHOOTERS' SUPERMARKET. 'What the hell is that?' he asked the driver.

'What it says. A supermarket. They sell guns. Got a range out back. Like a bowling alley.'

'C'mon, Dad. Let's stop.'

'I thought you wanted food.'

'I just want to have a look.'

'Okay.'

Without being told, the driver pulled over to the kerb. 'How long you be?'

'Couple of minutes. You don't mind waiting?'

'I should ask for security, like your watch or a double saw. But that's okay.'

It was, as advertised, a weapons supermarket, half a block long and a full block deep. There were four aisles, each marked with directional signs: on the left, 10-, 12-, and 16-gauge shotguns; on the right, rifles calibre .30–.06 to .44–.40; this way to handguns, automatic; that way to handguns, revolver; aisle number four for military rifles, to the rear for black-powder. A placard proclaimed this weekend's specials: a Marlin Golden 39A .22 lever-action rifle for $125, a Hammerli .45 Frontier revolver for $175. Buy two and get a box of bullets free. Each gun was in its own locked glass case. Green-jacketed salesmen patrolled the aisles, master keys chained to their belts.

There were six check-out counters, where clerks examined identification cards, took money, and wrapped purchases.

'It looks like an automat,' Maynard said.

'What's an automat?' Justin didn't wait for an answer. He darted ahead.

Maynard caught up with him at a wall case filled, on one side, with AR–15 combat rifles and, on the other, with similar-looking weapons called Valmets.

'Man!' Justin said. 'Are they cool!'

'Can I help you?' A salesman had come up behind them. He was in his mid-forties, bulky, built like a cabin trunk with legs. He wore rimless glasses; his hair was slick with pomade, and he reeked of Aqua Velva.

65

'I didn't know you could sell those,' Maynard said, with a gesture at the combat rifles.

'AR–15s? Sure. Of course, they're not full-automatic. These are the sporters.'

'They can be changed over, can't they?'

'Not by us. What a gunsmith does to them after they leave here, that's not our affair.' The salesman extended his hand. 'Stan Baxter. Call me Bax.'

As Baxter's blazer moved, Maynard caught a glimpse of the butt of a revolver snugged against his belly in a small holster. 'Maynard,' he said, and he shook Baxter's hand.

'And who might this be?' Baxter reached for Justin's hand. 'You look like a gun person to me.'

'Yeah.' Justin pointed at the Valmets. 'They're cool. What are they?'

'Finest military rifle ever made. Finnish design. They took the best of the AR–15 and married it to the best of the AK–47 and gave birth to the Valmet.'

'What's so good about it?'

'Simplicity. Very few moving parts. Almost never jams, even in mud and sand. Much more reliable than either of its parents. Uses 7.62 NATO ammunition, interchangeable with almost every rifle in Eastern and Western Europe. That .225 the AR–15 uses does a fine job of tearing a man up, but it isn't good at any distance. And sometimes the tumbling bullet'll torque and stray on you. Valmet gives you a clean kill at great distance.'

Maynard said, 'I thought these were "sporters".'

'That they are.' Baxter winked. 'But sport is always in the eye of the sportsman, isn't it?'

Justin had moved down the aisle. He stood at a case filled with pistols. 'Dad! Look at this.'

Baxter smiled at Maynard. 'Looks like your boy's found a friend.'

Justin was excited. 'That's the James Bond gun!'

'Right you are, son,' Baxter said. 'Walther PPK. A real fine starter gun.'

'Starter gun!' Maynard said. 'When I was a kid, we started with single-shot .22 rifles.'

Baxter nodded. 'But when you and I were boys, all you had to know how to shoot was rabbits and your odd snake. You didn't have to worry about when they were gonna come over the hill.'

Maynard did not ask who 'they' were.

A shot exploded, then another, then a third. Maynard grabbed Justin's arm, prepared to throw the boy to the floor and fall on him.

Baxter laughed. 'It's just folks practising out back. An in-house range lets the customer try out the merchandise before he buys it. Saves us a lot of hassle in returns.' He turned to Justin. 'Would you like to shoot that PPK, youngster?'

'Boy, would I!'

'Hold on ...' Maynard said.

Baxter was already unlocking the case. 'Comes to about a dime a round. You won't find a better buy anywhere.'

'That's not the point.'

'Oh, don't worry. There's no obligation.' Baxter winked again. ''Course, when you squeeze off a few with a PPK, it's like eating potato chips. It takes will power not to keep on squeezing. This gun *talks* to you.' Baxter pulled the slide back, checked the chamber, released the clip, and replaced it. 'What did you say your name was, youngster?'

'Justin.'

'Well, Justin, why don't you carry this for me?' Baxter passed the pistol, butt-first, to Justin.

Justin grinned uncontrollably. He looked up at his father.

Maynard smiled reluctantly and nodded his head. He had been sandbagged.

Baxter took a box of bullets from a drawer and led Maynard and Justin to the shooting range behind the store.

Baxter was an expert instructor – deliberate, explicit, and patient. He watched Justin shoot five shots at a target fifty feet away. Four missed the target altogether, the fifth was low and away from the scoring ring. Then he showed Justin how to correct his grip, how to aim, when to hold his breath and when to release it. Of the second group of five shots, three were on the target.

By his sixth group of five shots, Justin was putting all five in the scoring ring, and three in the two-inch black circle at the centre.

Maynard shot ten rounds slow-fire – all ten on the target, four in the black – and ten rapid-fire – six on the target, two in the black.

'Not bad,' Baxter said.

'Rusty.' Maynard was pleased with himself, despite himself, and proud of Justin, and surprised at how easily he had been seduced by the sensations of shooting: the smell of potassium nitrate and silicone preservatives, the feel of the textured grips on his palm, the sight of the holes appearing, magically, in the target at the exact instant he pulled the trigger.

Walking back into the store, Baxter took Maynard's arm. Maynard recoiled, but Baxter pressed closer. 'That boy is a natural.'

Maynard nodded. 'He did well.'

'*Well*? That PPK was made for him!'

Maynard said nothing. He was amused to feel himself consumed by an adolescent itch to own the pistol. Gramps had raised him with guns, had taught him to use them and respect them. Of all the fatherly things Gramps had said to him over the years, Maynard was proudest of a note that had accompanied a target pistol Gramps had given him for his eighteenth birthday: 'I'd trust you with a loaded pistol any day before I'd trust half your friends with an automobile.'

Maynard knew that what he was feeling was a combination of nostalgia and atavism – here was his son learning the rituals of firearms, preparing himself for manhood. If there was something primitive, tribal, about the sensation, it was nonetheless genuine. Maynard knew all the arguments for gun control and agreed with most of them, though he was convinced that, on a national level, gun control was a hopeless crusade. But he had never agreed with those who claimed that guns were good only for killing. Maynard had killed nothing in his life except rats and diseased rabbits. A gun was one of the few pieces of machinery that could impart to its operator challenge, satisfaction, pride and dismay.

There were not many experiences more frustrating than to sight in on a beer can nestled in the sand a hundred yards away, to squeeze the trigger, to see the can still sitting there. And there were few things more fun than seeing that same can rise from the sand and spin through the air with a ping and a whir.

Justin came alongside Maynard and took his hand. 'Man, it sure would be neat to own that pistol!'

Since Maynard was sure there was no way he could meet any of the legal requirements for purchasing a handgun, he thought it safe to agree. 'It sure would.'

'Well!' Baxter beamed and patted Justin's shoulder. 'It appears that Master Justin has got himself a gun.'

'I do?'

'Not a chance,' Maynard said.

'No?' Baxter stopped. 'Why not?'

'We don't live in Florida.'

'That *is* a problem.'

'I knew it.' Justin was crestfallen.

'Even if we could buy it, buddy,' Maynard said, 'we couldn't own it. Not in New York.'

'We could keep it at Aunt Sally's. It's okay in Connecticut.'

Baxter was not willing to lose the sale. 'You don't happen to have a Florida driver's licence?'

'No.' Impelled by mischief and curiosity, Maynard decided to lead Baxter a step or two further. 'I don't drive. Only licenced drivers can buy guns?'

Justin's eyes registered the lie, but he kept silent.

'No. If you have proof of.residence, that's enough. A rent receipt, for example.'

Maynard took his wallet from his pocket. 'Let me check. I just might have one.' He went to a nearby counter. Justin followed, but Baxter hung back, ostensibly to search through a drawer for a box in which to pack the pistol.

Leaning on the counter, with his back to Baxter, Maynard tore a blank page from his pocket diary. He printed in block letters: 'Received from Mr Maynard the amount of $250, in full payment of rent for the month of May on apartment 206.'

He added the date and a fictional address and signed the paper, in a florid script, 'Molly Bloom'.

'I found one,' he said to Baxter.

'Terrific!' Baxter took the slip of paper and, without looking at it, stuffed it in his pocket. 'I'll take care of the paperwork later.'

'You'd rather I didn't use a credit card.'

'It might be awkward.'

'A cheque?'

'Fine. But make it out to cash. Simpler that way. A round number.'

Maynard smiled. 'How round?'

'Let's see ... the pistol, plus, say, a hundred rounds of ammo ... make it out for two hundred. I'll make change.'

Maynard started to write the cheque. 'Uh-oh. I forgot one small detail. We have to get on a plane tomorrow.'

'To New York?' Baxter said. 'No problem. Put it in your checked baggage. They don't X-ray.'

'No. To Turks.'

'Turks!' Baxter laughed. 'No *problem*! Here.' He reached in a drawer and produced a shoulder holster. 'Carry it with you. There's no security on those flights.'

'What about customs?'

'They'll search your bags, but unless they think you're smuggling something, they won't touch your person. Here's a piece of advice: take some contraband, and declare it at the airport.'

'Like what?'

Baxter leaned close and whispered in Maynard's face. It was an effort for Maynard not to back away from Baxter's sour breath, and he barely heard Baxter's suggestion. But he nodded as if he had heard every syllable.

6

Katherine stepped outside to ring the dinner bell. It was a beautiful evening, sparkling clear, with enough of a southerly breeze to keep the bugs down. She scanned the sky for clouds but saw none. There had been no rain in two weeks. The cistern was low, and all water, scooped up in buckets, now had to be boiled, for it had a greenish cast and was populated with living things.

Still, with the dry weather her arthritis had bothered her less than it had in years, and for that she was grateful. Feeling grateful, she felt selfish, and, feeling selfish, guilty. She resolved to pray for greater strength.

The sun had touched the horizon and was moving down quickly, squashing into a swollen pumpkin. She reached for the bell cord, then withdrew her hand, deciding to wait for a few more minutes. Tonight would be a perfect night for the green flash: the horizon was a straight line, free of clouds. In a year here, she had seen the green flash only twice, both times on nights like this. None of the others had seen it, and she knew they thought she had had a private experience, a revelation intended for her alone. Perhaps she had, though she had read mariners' accounts of seeing the green flash.

The sun was almost gone. Katherine widened her eyes to thwart a blink: the green flash was quicker than a blink. The

71

last of the yellow light vanished, and then – there and gone –
a brilliant pinpoint of emerald.

Now light drained from the sky, spilling over the western
horizon, leaving a mantle of blue-black speckled with stars.

Katherine smiled, wanting to interpret the green flash as a
good sign. If the weather held and the cargo was worthwhile
and the engine was sound and the captain was sober, the
paquebot would be along in a few days and would collect
the people. She would have two weeks alone before the
next group came. No one to listen to, no one to instruct
or bandage or cook for. Again she felt guilty for her
thoughts.

This was a good group, really, pleasant and more self-
sufficient than most. But after a month of scrub and briers
and bags and guano and heat, the children were restless and
ornery. Prayer might soothe the adults, but it was not
enough for the children.

She rang the dinner bell and turned to go back inside. She
glanced downward, and suddenly she shrieked and leaped
backward on to the sand. A scorpion crouched on the top
step, its hooked tail stabbing forward and back, exploring for
something into which to inject its venom. Katherine threw a
handful of sand at the insect, and it scuttled away into the
brush.

She shuddered. She would never get used to scorpions,
God's creatures though they might be. They were nasty,
ugly, unpredictable vermin. Their sting was beyond painful:
it was sickening and sometimes – to the allergic or the old or
the very young – fatal. Two of these children had been stung,
and one had proven to be severely allergic. Had it not been
for Katherine's pharmacopoeia, the child might well have
died.

She saw two children running along the beach towards the
building. She went inside.

They were all members of a breakaway sect of the mystical
fundamentalist religious sect. Some were polygamists; some,
like Katherine, were single and ascetic. They came from the
States and Great Britain. This was (for the polygamists
especially) their only safe haven. They applied a year or

more in advance, and, in turn, they were granted a month at the retreat.

The retreat had been built twenty-five years earlier, and it was still the only building on the islands. It was a concrete blockhouse, fifty feet across and shaped like a five-pointed star. One point was occupied by the resident matron. It was divided down the middle into a small bedroom and a private chapel. In each of the other four points a whole family could live – four commodiously, six comfortably, and ten or twelve in cramped, suffocating misery, which served to increase the speed with which the parents became irritable and the children impossible.

This group was manageable. Counting Katherine, there were twelve people resident in the star: two couples, each with two children, and a woman with identical twins.

Katherine was glad there were no practising polygamists in the group. For all their piety, they tended to be a difficult lot – sensitive to every nuance, always ready to take offence, masters of the imagined slight. Suggestions were received as criticism, criticism as condemnation.

The centre of the star was a large circular room, divided in the centre by a rattan rug. On one side were half a dozen bamboo chairs, two kerosene lamps and a bookcase filled with Bibles and other religious material. The other side was the kitchen, which consisted of a driftwood table and a huge, walk-in cooking fireplace. The sole electrical appliance in the star was a refrigerator, powered by a gasoline-operated generator, which was used to store drugs and milk.

Three women stood at the table, preparing a conch chowder. The men, who had dived up the conch from a wooden skiff, sat on the cement floor and, with hatchet and knife, removed the animals from their shells and cleaned and sliced them and passed the edible pieces to the women.

The children straggled in, one by one.

By the time the chowder was ready, the only light in the room came from the embers of the cooking fire. One of the men lit two kerosene lamps and placed them on the table.

'Everyone here?' Katherine said as she placed bowls of chowder on the table.

A child's voice replied, 'Josh and Mary are still outside.'

'Doing what?' asked a man.

'They were getting eggs.'

A woman said firmly, 'They heard the bell. They know the rules.'

'There's plenty to go 'round,' Katherine said cheerfully. 'They won't go to bed hungry.'

'Serve them right if they did.'

Holding hands around the table, they said grace.

They ate noisily, gnawing the rubbery conch and soaking up the juices with balls of bread.

The door swung open, and a boy stood framed in the doorway, panting. 'There's a boat coming!' he said.

Katherine froze. Boats did not cruise this shore, certainly not at night. Blades of surf-chiselled rock stuck out from the land for hundreds of feet, many of them inches below the surface. In daylight, it was a dangerous course for a cruising boat; at night, it was suicidal.

'So what?' said a man.

'A fisherman, I imagine,' said another.

The boy's mother commanded, 'Come sit down.'

Katherine said to the table, 'Shush!' Then, to the boy, 'Is it passing by, Joshua, or coming this way?'

'This way, ma'am. Right for the cut.'

A man said, 'I'll have a look,' and he stood up.

'Stay there,' Katherine said. 'I'll do it.'

'I don't mind.'

'Stay *there*, I said!'

The man did not argue. He sat down.

Katherine went to the boy and whispered, 'Where's Mary?'

'We were gathering eggs. She found a baby bird. Said she wanted to find its nest and put it back.'

Katherine passed the boy and went outside. She looked towards the cut, a narrow slash in the rocks that ended in a pocket of beach no more than twenty yards wide. She could see the island's skiff careened on the sand.

74

The boat was a couple of hundred feet offshore, a dark smudge against the black water, angling slowly in towards the cut.

It could be a local boat, Katherine told herself, a fisherman caught at sea by an adverse breeze. Or a Haitian poacher, looking for a place to hide for the night.

But then the boat moved into a shaft of moonlight, and her hopes died. It was the same boat.

For the past ten months, she had striven – through force of will and devotion – to convince herself that the boat had not been real, that what had happened had not really happened. It had been a test, a grotesque metaphysical nightmare designed to further forge her faith. She had come almost to believe that. Now, the only thought that came to her was, have I sinned so much?

As she watched, the pirogue turned into the wind. The lateen sail luffed and was lowered. Paddles poked out from bow and stern and swept the water.

Katherine sprinted to the nearest corner of the star and searched the darkness for the missing child. She did not dare call out.

She went back inside and shut and locked the door.

Her heart was pounding. She took several deep breaths and said, as calmly and sternly as she could, 'Listen to me, all of you. You must do exactly as I say. No time for questions. I'll say only this: anyone who disobeys is telling God, "The time has come to take me."'

She pulled back the rattan rug. Underneath was a wooden trapdoor, flush with the cement floor. She lifted it and set it aside. A ladder led down into a black pit.

'Empty the table into here,' she said. 'Everything.'

The table was cleared quickly and silently. Bowls and plates and cups made little sound as they landed in the sand at the bottom of the pit.

'Now ... everybody down there. Fast. Don't fall.' She helped a child locate the top rung of the ladder.

A man muttered testily, 'I think we have a right to—'

'Shut your mouth!' Katherine said. 'Unless you want to die, get in the hole.'

'But where's Mary?' a woman whimpered.

'She's in the brush. When you get down there, pray to Almighty Merciful God that she stays away.'

When they had all descended into the pit, Katherine knelt on the floor and spoke to them. 'Be very still. No coughs or sneezes. If you pray, pray silently.' She shut the trapdoor and replaced the rug.

She checked the table one last time, brushing away bread-crumbs and mopping up drops of chowder with the hem of her dress. Then she unlocked the front door and stood on the rattan rug, her hands folded in front of her, praying.

Footsteps crunched on the sand, then scraped against the concrete steps. The door was pushed open.

There were two of them, black silhouettes against the starlit sky.

She could not see their faces, so did not know if they were the same ones who had come before. A breeze blew through the doorway, carrying their smell, and she trembled at the memory.

They did not speak.

As she knew they would, as they had the last time, they forced her on to the table and raped her, once each. They were not gratuitously brutal. Her feeble resistance was quietly accepted and easily overcome. The knife held to her throat was more a gesture than a necessity. She closed her eyes, so as not to see them, held her breath (as long as possible) so as not to smell them, and let her mind shout prayers so as not to hear their grunts.

It was all very matter-of-fact – they might have been service men come to read her meter – and when they were done, they helped her to her feet.

She grasped the edge of the table, swallowing bile and trying not to faint.

'Mercury,' said one.

She nodded. The last time, she had not known what they meant, and they had, as seemed to be their custom, tortured her while trying to explain. They had slashed the inside of her thighs with the point of a knife and had rubbed lemon juice and pepper into the incisions. Finally, by piecing together words and phrases, she had understood.

She led them to the refrigerator. The bottles of drugs were in boxes of twelve. She brought out a box of penicillin and two syringes. 'This will spoil if it isn't kept cold,' she said. 'How many are sick?'

'Many.'

'Take it all.'

'Rum,' said the other.

'I have no rum.'

The man shoved her aside, reached into the refrigerator, and brought out a plastic quart bottle of isopropyl alcohol.

'Don't drink that,' Katherine said. 'It'll make you very sick. I use it for ear problems.'

'I hear you not. I have an ear problem.' The man laughed aloud. He unscrewed the bottle cap, splashed alcohol in his ear, then took a great swig from the bottle. A tremor shook his chest. He coughed and sputtered. 'Aye, that's a noble tot.' He closed the bottle and tucked it inside his shirt.

'Go now.' Katherine shut the refrigerator door. She heard a sound – faint, indistinct. She could not tell where it came from, whether from the pit beneath her feet or from outside. She shuffled her feet noisily on the sandy floor.

'Aye. Good night, lady, and Lord love you.'

She waited, expecting them to depart.

Instead, they stood, listening.

And then she heard what they were hearing: light footsteps running in the sand, and a happy girl's voice calling, 'Look what I found!'

Katherine released a visceral wail of despair.

Mary was in the room before she saw the men. 'A baby bird!' She cradled it in her hands. 'Look ... Oh!'

'Leave her be!' Katherine cried. 'She's a baby!' It was absurd, and Katherine knew it: Mary was twelve, tall for her age, and robust. But there was hope. It had been only ten minutes since the men had taken Katherine.

Mary backed against the wall. 'Who are you?'

'A good question,' said one of the men. 'Who are you?'

Mary whimpered, 'Miss Katherine ...'

Blindly, thoughtlessly, Katherine hurled herself at the nearest man.

Barely troubling to look at her, the man stiff-armed Katherine in the throat and knocked her to the floor. He grabbed the bird from Mary's hands, crushed it, and cast it aside, then took Mary's elbow and led her to the door.

Mary panicked. She cried and struggled until the man slapped her across the face and said, 'Be still, or as God is my judge I'll cut your tongue out. You'll come with us.'

From the floor, Katherine called, 'Leave her, I beg you!'

The man holding Mary stopped at the door. 'Leave her, missus? Aye, if you will.' He pulled Mary's hair, yanking her head back, and put his cutlass to her throat. 'In how many pieces, pray? In steaks or fillets?'

Both men laughed and, pushing Mary ahead of them, left the house.

Katherine lay on the floor and listened to the child's shrieks recede into the night.

7

The plane was an ancient, ramshackle DC–3, the pilot an albino named Whitey. He had white curly hair, pink irises, and chalky skin. Because he could not endure sunlight, he wore long white trousers, a long-sleeved white shirt, a wide-brimmed hat and sunglasses. Even this early in the morning, with the sun barely risen, he supervised the loading of the plane from the shade beneath the port wing.

Whitey directed Justin to the co-pilot's seat and unfolded a canvas camp chair for Maynard. He set it on the deck just aft of the cockpit.

'No seatbelt?' Maynard said.

'If you don't carry passengers, you don't need seatbelts. Chickens don't have to be strapped down.'

Behind Maynard, the plane was packed – crates of fruit, cases of canned goods, lockers of frozen meats, three cages full of live chickens and one comatose pig. 'You have to really knock them out,' Whitey explained. 'I had a sow on one trip that woke up halfway down the Bahamas. The bitch began to root – you know, with her snout. She rooted up a bunch of deck plates, damn near rooted us into the drink. I finally shot her.'

'You carry guns aboard?'

'Heavens no!' Whitey smiled at Maynard. 'But you never

know what you'll find if you look around an old crate like this.'

At the leeward end of the runway, Whitey revved his engines and checked his gauges and released the brakes. The plane surged forward.

Halfway down the strip, the plane was still on the ground. Gentling the stick back, Whitey talked to the plane: 'Come on, honey . . . haul ass, baby . . . let's go . . .' The plane did not rise. 'Goddamn it, get up!' Whitey said, and he jerked the stick back.

Slowly, laboriously, the plane left the ground, as the end of the runway flashed by.

Maynard looked at his palms, which glistened with sweat. He wiped them on his pants. Off to the right, in a marsh, he saw three or four crumpled airplane carcasses that had been bulldozed together in a pile. 'What are those from?' he asked.

Whitey said, 'We call 'em surprises. You're going down the runway, and you think you're gonna get off okay, and, surprise! You don't.'

Whitey banked to the left, eastward, into the glaring sun. He said to Justin, 'There's a thermos at your feet. Pour me a cup of coffee, will you?'

When Justin handed him the coffee, Whitey took his hands from the controls and said, 'Hold her steady for me, that's the boy.'

Justin obeyed happily, clutching the stick and craning to see out over the nose of the plane.

Whitey took a flask from his pocket and splashed liquor into the cup. He offered the flask to Maynard. 'Eye-opener?'

Maynard smelled bourbon. He shook his head. 'You always fly . . . like this?'

'Gotta fly high, man. It's a boring goddamn trip.'

Whitey replaced the flask and took a map from a pouch beneath his seat. He leaned back, put his feet up on the instrument panel, and opened the map. 'Now . . . let's see if we can find this bitch. From up here, they all look the same.'

Maynard took a deep breath and let it go. He said to Justin, 'You okay?'

'Sure. This is neat.'

They flew across the Gulf Stream, to Bimini and Cat Cays, turned south over Andros and continued down the Bahamas chain. The day was clear and cloudless, the water a dozen shades of blue and green: turquoise in the flats near shore, flecked with brown on the coral reefs, a warm blue seaward of the reefs, and dark – almost black – above the abyss.

Three hours out of Miami, Whitey leaned forward and squinted at the southern horizon. The line was unbroken, save for a single cloud that seemed to hover over the water. 'That should be the Caicos there,' he said.

Maynard saw no land. 'Where?'

'Under that cloud. The heat from the land rises and hits the cold air and makes a cloud.'

Soon a thin grey line appeared, shimmering. As they drew nearer, it solidified into the shape of an island.

Whitey nudged the stick forward, and the plane's nose dropped. The altimeter needles spun slowly, in units of a hundred feet, from eight thousand feet down to four thousand. They passed over the barren island at three thousand feet.

Looking over Justin's shoulder, Maynard saw a star-shaped building below. 'What's that?'

'Jesus freaks,' Whitey said.

'What do they do in this God-forsaken place?'

'Freakout, I guess.' Whitey banked the plane to the right, and the island slid away behind them.

Miles away, to the east, Maynard saw several large islands. Remembering the chart, he guessed that one was Navidad, one North Caicos, one Grand Caicos. There were countless smaller islands to the west, uninhabited, covered with scrub, pounded by surf. Directly beneath were the Caicos Banks, an endless plain of sand and grass, no more than six feet deep. The western edge of the Banks ended abruptly, shelving to forty feet, then shearing down to five thousand feet.

Maynard recalled something Michael Florio had said: in the days of sail – especially the days of the cumbersome, unmanoeuvrable square-rigged ships – the Caicos Banks were among the most treacherous in the hemisphere. Ships storm-driven off course would seem to be in the relative safety of deep water. Their sounding leads would find no bottom. And then someone would hear, above the howl of the wind, a strange thunderous roar. It sounded like surf, but it couldn't be surf, not in the open ocean. They would proceed ahead until, at last, a lookout – his eyes stinging from a film of salt – would see the impossible, an explosion of towering breakers dead ahead. It was too late. There would be recriminations and keening and prayers. The ship would hit the rocks and, within minutes, be gone. Most of it would be scattered across the Banks. Some pieces would float, and some survivors might cling to the floating pieces. Twenty-seven men had survived one such wreck, Florio had said. They had ridden a section of decking thirty miles over the Banks and had washed ashore on Grand Caicos. Twenty-one had died of thirst or exposure. Four had committed suicide, driven mad by bugs. Two had lived.

An airport lay ahead: Great Bone Cay. Whitey finished off his flask and banked hard right, then hard left, lining the plane up with the runway. 'Flaps down,' he said to himself and pushed a switch. 'Flaps down.' The plane slowed. 'Wheels down.' Another switch. A light blinked on. 'Wheels down.'

The plane hit the runway too hard, bounced, hit again, and settled. Whitey taxied up to a rectangular concrete building, where two pickup trucks and perhaps a dozen people, including two who carried clipboards and wore epaulets on their starched white shirts, were waiting.

Whitey shut off the engines and said to Maynard, 'If you got any grass, dump it now. They are friggin' *lunatics* about grass, and the jail got no screens on it.'

'Not me,' Maynard said, feeling a rush of adrenalin and perspiration. He checked to make sure his jacket was buttoned, and he held his left arm close to his side. He slung his satchel over his left shoulder.

'You want to go back today?'

'If you are.'

'Damn right.' Whitey looked at his watch. 'It's eleven now. It'll take 'em an hour to unload, then an hour for lunch, then another hour to load her up again. We'll leave here at two.'

'We'll be here.'

'I won't wait for you.'

'Where will you be till then?'

Whitey pointed at the building. 'Inside. Cyril's Conch and Turtle Palace.' He smiled and put on his hat. 'It's out of the sun.' Completely covered in white, his face hidden by hat and sunglasses, Whitey looked like the Invisible Man.

Maynard said kindly, 'This climate must be terrible for you.'

Whitey shrugged. 'Don't feel sorry for me. Us freaks get all the kinky broads.' He squeezed down the aisle between crates and cartons and opened the door.

Maynard and Justin walked across the apron and into the building, following a man who had been the first to meet the plane and had taken from Whitey a single copy of Sunday's Miami *Herald*. Inside the building, the man sat on a bench and read the comics.

A young police officer, his uniform impeccably clean except for a coating of dust on his black shoes, stood behind the customs desk. He held out his hand to Maynard. 'Passport, visa, return ticket.'

Holding his satchel close to his body with his left hand, Maynard used his right to fish for his wallet and thumb through it until he found his *Today* identification card, which he passed to the officer. 'We're not staying,' he said, as if explaining everything.

The policeman examined the card and held it up to Maynard's face. 'You come to a foreign country with *this*?' he said. 'What you think we are?'

Maynard was sweating. 'You see, I called last night from Miami, and—'

'What you think we *are*!?'

Unnerved, Maynard hurried to deflect the policeman's

outrage before it could lead to an arrest and, ultimately, a search. He leaned on the desk and said confidentially, 'I think you're smarter than you're letting on.'

'What?'

'Listen . . . you know what a press card is. I'm down here on a story for *Today*. I'm trying to keep it kind of quiet, so I'd appreciate it if you wouldn't say anything.'

'What story?'

'Just between us?' Maynard raised his eyebrows and looked furtively from side to side. 'We hear from a pretty good source that an American millionaire is about to buy up a whole island down here. Wants to turn it into a health spa. A lot of folks could get rich, but only if everyone can be kept honest. That's what I'm here to see to.'

Maynard had been thinking so fast that by the time he was finished, he had forgotten most of what he had said.

The policeman seemed impressed. 'And how long this take?'

'Just till two o'clock. See? No bags, no nothing.'

'And who's that?' The policeman pointed at Justin.

'My researcher.' Maynard added in a whisper, 'He has a glandular problem. Don't say anything to him; he's sensitive.'

'That so?' The policeman looked perplexed.

'Anyhow, I called last night to make an appointment with Mr Makepeace, but I'm not sure he got the message. How can I find out?'

The policeman turned to the man sitting on the bench. 'Hey, Birds.'

'Hmmmmm?' The man didn't look up from the comics.

'This the fella. He been feedin' me some line about a story.'

'It's no line!' Maynard said.

'Sure. You got anything to declare?'

'Well . . .' Remembering Baxter's advice, Maynard tried to look abashed. 'Yes, now that you mention it.'

'Like what?'

Very carefully, Maynard reached into his satchel. 'I had no idea it was illegal until the pilot told me.' He handed over

84

a copy of *Hustler*. 'I hope you don't think I meant to violate your laws.'

'You lucky you told me,' said the policeman. 'If I'd've found it in your bag, would've been a fifty-dollar fine.'

'Yes, sir,' Maynard said.

The commissioner finished reading the comics, unfolded his lanky frame from the bench, and stood up. He was roughly Maynard's age and height, and he was built like a fork. If Maynard was correct in thinking of himself as slender, then Makepeace was emaciated. His face was a skull wrapped in black skin, his hands a gathering of bones. He wore his hair in an enormous Afro; Maynard thought that if the Afro were ever caught in a crosswind, it would surely capsize the man.

'How do you do, sir? My name is Blair Maynard.'

Makepeace extended his hand gingerly, as if fearful that a too-hearty greeting would snap his fingers. 'Burrud Makepeace,' he said. 'Birds is easier.' He looked at Justin. 'Your researcher?'

'Justin.'

Makepeace shook hands with the boy.

'Evvy didn't tell me your business down here.'

'I didn't have a chance to tell her. The line went dead.'

'Press isn't always welcome.'

'Oh?'

'They can come. Don't misunderstand. But we don't go out of our way any more. A few times we did, and all we got was a slap in the face.'

'I can't believe ...'

'Believe it. They come down here, all friendly and polite, like you, and tell us they're going to write a story about this unspoiled paradise – like each one is discovering us for the first time. They take free food and free boat rides and free you-name-it, and they go back and write a story about poverty and bugs and pickaninnies. To hell with them. They can go to Nassau.' Makepeace checked his anger. 'So, reporter man, what's your story?'

85

'First,' Maynard said, 'I'm not doing a tourist story. Second, I don't want anything for free.'

'The only way you can make me believe that,' Makepeace said, and he smiled, 'is if you buy me lunch.'

They rode in Makepeace's open Jeep. The road had once been paved, but by now it was arguable whether there were potholes in the pavement or splotches of pavement surrounding dirt-filled potholes. Whenever a car passed in the opposite direction, the Jeep was covered by a swirling cloud of dust.

Makepeace turned off the main road and followed a pair of parallel ruts up a hill to a complex of bungalows identified by a sign as the Crow's Nest Motel. The largest of the bungalows advertised a bar and dining-room.

Makepeace led them through the dining-room to an outdoor terrace that overlooked a half-moon cove. 'I thought your ... researcher ... might like a swim.'

Maynard said to Justin, 'What do you say?'

'Sure. Can I have a cheeseburger?'

Maynard handed him the satchel.

'Changing room around the corner,' Makepeace said. 'Rafts on the beach.'

When Justin had scurried away and they had ordered drinks, Maynard told Makepeace why he had come to the islands. He recited the figures about the missing boats and the explanations offered by the Coast Guard. Finally, he said that of the more than a hundred vessels still unaccounted for, most seemed to have finished in the general area of Turks and Caicos. 'And nobody has any idea how or why.' Wary of giving offence, Maynard decided not to repeat Florio's supposition that someone was taking the boats.

Makepeace was neither surprised nor concerned. His interest was polite. 'That's a riddle, all right,' he said. 'I can see that.'

'What do you think the answer is?'

'Me?' Makepeace was amused that the question was put to him. 'Why ask me? I have no idea.'

'It doesn't bother you?'

'Should it?'

'You're getting a reputation ...' Maynard paused, then added carefully, '... not *you*, but this area ... as a dangerous part of the world. That can't do any good.'

Makepeace laughed. 'We have been dangerous for three hundred and fifty years. We have had rumrunners and gun-runners and pirates and poachers and now the drug people. *We* have not changed; the yachtsmen, they have changed. They think this is a playground. Well, they are damned fools. I can give you a simple answer to your question: the boats are gone and the people are dead.'

'Don't you care how?'

'No. It makes no difference how you die. You are dead. It's like asking me if I care whether Russia and the States go to war. Why should I care? I can do nothing about it, and it will affect us in no important way. If the States blew up tomorrow, a lot of us would starve. We have starved before. Somebody always survives.'

'But it's your responsibility ...'

'What is? To see that a man in a sailor suit has a nice holiday? No. I am in charge *here*. One tiny island.' Makepeace tapped his foot on the floor. 'Like the flies are in charge of the dungheap. That's what we are, you know, a dungheap. Most of the world doesn't know we exist, and the ones that do think we're ignorant jungle bunnies. It's not our fault. We came here as slaves, and they kept us slaves and beat it into us that that is our destiny. I escaped as a boy; my mama sent me up to Nassau, to learn. I learned. I learned that the best job I could hope to get was as a waiter or a bartender or a taxi driver or, if I had influence, a construction labourer. Then the Bahamas got free and everybody got hope. Hope!' Makepeace smirked. 'White-power people were replaced by black-power people, who had to prove how proud they were, how independent. They nearly sank the whole country.

'So I said to myself, "Birds, you go back to the Caicos and show them how it can be done." I came back and rounded up some chummies. We threw Molotov cocktails here and there, and the British they said "Good-bye". So here I am, a commissioner chief fly on one small patty. I have a few hundred people. Most can't read. Them that don't work for the government, they fish – so many that the grounds are being fished out, and in a few years that will be gone, too. They got no hope of anything better, not ever, not anywhere. We give them the vote, and they vote, but they got nothing to vote for. They got all the freedoms they want, but you can't eat freedom.' Makepeace paused. 'And you would have me care whether some fat-ass Yankee gets himself killed?'

'Tourism,' Maynard said. 'It's an old answer, but you *can* eat off that.'

'It is happening, a little bit, but we don't have much to offer. Loneliness and clear water. Bugs. We are a hundred years in the past.'

'People will pay for that, that alone.'

'I know,' Makepeace smiled. 'We get a few. And there is always talk of the big Yankee companies coming down and building golf courses and tennis courts and beach clubs. If it ever happens, there will be money for a little while, and then someone will take over the government and kick out the Yankees and put locals in charge of everything. In five years, it will be a dungheap once again.'

'You have a cheerful perspective.'

'Realistic. This place has no business being populated, let alone being a nation. Nature didn't populate it, except with bugs.'

The waitress brought their food – fish chowder and conch fritters and, for Justin, a thin grey square of chopped meat topped with a smear of cream-cheese and enveloped in bread.

Maynard looked to the beach and saw Justin appear around a corner of the cove and paddle a rubber raft swiftly towards shore. He whistled through his teeth, and Justin waved.

'You won't get answers about your missing boats,' Makepeace said, 'not down here. Most everybody either don't know or don't care to know. It does not pay to ask about things you cannot do anything about. I don't say that a few folks might not suspicion, but they got no reason to talk to you. If a couple people *do* know something, they know

88

because they got a stake in it, whatever it is, and they get nothing from telling you. Personally, I doubt there is anything to know. Things happen. Good things, bad things, things no one understands. They happen.' Makepeace shrugged. 'Life goes on.'

Justin came to the table wrapped in a beach towel. He gazed, horrified, at the slimy puck on the plate before him. He whispered to his father, 'What's *that*?'

'You asked for a cheeseburger.'

'It's *gross!*'

'Eat.'

'I'm gonna starve to death, and it'll be your fault.'

'Eat.'

'I'll probably get diarrhoea.' Justin prodded the doughy bread. He looked at Makepeace. 'What's the boat down there?'

'I don't know. Where?'

'Around the corner. There's a boat half-buried in the sand.'

Makepeace called the waitress to the table. As he spoke to her, he let his diction slip into the singsong cadence of the out-islands. 'What de boat down de beach?'

'Don't know, mon. Been dere month or more.'

'Anyt'ing good on 'er?'

'Stripped clean, mon. Must be t'rowed-away boat.'

'Nobody t'row boat away.'

'Somebody t'row dat one away. Beat her up and t'row her away.'

'Okay.' Makepeace dismissed the waitress and said to Maynard, 'We can look at it.'

After lunch, they walked down to the cove and picked their way across the rocky promontory to a long, straight stretch of white sand.

The wreckage of the boat was above the high-water mark, jammed into the dunes. The surf had washed it ashore broadside and buried its keel in the sand. It lay on its side, its deck tilted towards the sea. Once, it had been a thirty- or thirty-five-foot sailboat, with a deckhouse (now gone) and a single mast (gone, too). The forward hatch had been torn away and the deck around it splintered by an axe – by scavengers, Maynard assumed, after the boat had come to rest on the beach.

Maynard brushed sand from the cockpit. The steering wheel was gone, all the brass and chrome fittings had been removed, and even the cleats had been unscrewed from the deck. The hull was pocked with screw holes. Maynard turned away, but his eyes flickered over something irregular, and he looked again. One of the screw holes was larger than the others and was not empty. He said to Justin, 'Got your knife? See if you can get whatever it is out of there.'

Justin knelt in the cockpit and dug in the wood with his jackknife. It took him a few minutes to widen and deepen the hole and a few more to pry the object free from the wood. He worked steadily and patiently, never trying to do too much too fast. 'It's a ball,' he said, and he dropped it in his father's hand. 'It's heavy.'

Maynard nodded. 'It's lead.' He turned to Makepeace. 'What are your laws about firearms?'

'Simple. You can't have them.'

'What about antiques? Flintlocks, percussions ...?'

'It's never come up. Why do you ask?'

'This is a bullet,' Maynard said, turning the ball between his fingertips. 'Home-made; you can see the mould marks on it.'

'What does that tell you?'

'By itself? Not much. Just that somebody took a shot at the boat, or at somebody in the boat, with an antique pistol.'

Makepeace looked at his watch and said, 'I should get you to the airport.'

As the Jeep turned into the airport, Maynard saw the DC–3 on the runway, baking in the midday sun. The door to the cabin was open, but the cargo hatches were closed, and there was no activity around the plane. 'Why aren't they loading the plane?' he said. 'Whitey said it would take an hour to load it up.'

For a moment, Makepeace seemed confused. Then he laughed. 'He told you that? All they load here is a packet of

mail. He picks up his cargo in Navidad. Frozen conch.'
Makepeace laughed again. 'He meant it takes an hour to
load *him* up, and an hour to sleep it off.'

'What?'

'He has friends here. They get together at Cyril's and
drink rum and tell lies. He feels at home here. Back in Miami
he's a misfit. Call him Kid Clorox or Bleach Boy or, some of
them, the White Nigger. He once did the Bahamas run, but it
was worse there; they treated him like a leper – too white to
be white, too coloured to be coloured. The blacks there think
he's bad luck. Here they accept him for what he is, another
piece of human garbage, like them.'

'When's the next plane?'

'Tuesday, but that is to Haiti. Don't worry. Whitey is
careful enough. He always sleeps before he flies.'

Justin noticed the stricken look on his father's face, and he
said, 'Don't worry, Dad. He showed me how things work. I
think I could do it if I had to.'

Maynard smiled wanly and patted Justin's shoulder.
'That's comforting.'

They waited beneath the wing of the DC–3. Whitey came
out of the terminal building, yawned and adjusted his sunglasses.

'See? He's been asleep,' Makepeace said. 'He'll be fine.'

With an envelope of mail tucked under his arm, Whitey
walked to the plane. His pace was straight and steady.

A bit *too* steady, Maynard thought. He's concentrating on
every step.

'How you doin'?' Makepeace said to Whitey.

'Top form, chief.' Whitey ushered Maynard and Justin
towards the door. 'Let's get out of here. That sun's like to
suck all the juices out of you.'

Makepeace waved to Maynard and said, 'Come back and
see us.'

Maynard waved back. At the door to the plane, he hesitated.

'Move it, man!' Whitey said. 'Want to get home by dark.'

Reluctantly, Maynard helped Justin up the stairs and
followed him into the empty fuselage.

Unburdened by cargo, the plane rose quickly off the runway.

'Flaps up,' Whitey said. He did not flip the switch. 'Flaps up!'

Justin looked at Whitey, then at his father, then at Whitey again. 'Me?'

Whitey flipped the switch. 'Wheels up.'

There were four switches in a row, and Justin didn't know which one to push.

'Dammit, boy!' Whitey said, bringing up the wheels. 'How long you been flying?'

The plane levelled off. 'Now, where we going?' he said as he reached forward to set the autopilot. 'Navidad? Yeah, Navidad.' He set a compass course and pushed a button. 'Keep a sharp eye out for Fokkers,' he said to Justin. 'I hear the Red Baron's looking for the White Knight. But don't let 'em fool you. Some of them Fokkers is Messerschmitts.' Giggling at his little joke, Whitey grunted and shut his eyes to sleep.

Justin looked back at his father. He was scared. 'What'm I supposed to do?'

'Nothing. I think it'll fly itself.' Maynard searched the sky for clouds. 'Let's hope there's no weather.'

The plane droned northward. Even at four thousand feet, it was cold in the unheated, unpressurized cabin. Each of Whitey's deep, noisy snores brought forth a cloud of steam that fogged the side window. Maynard saw Justin shiver. He removed his jacket and wrapped it around the boy.

Justin pointed to the pistol in the holster under Maynard's arm. 'What about that?'

'That should be our only worry,' Maynard said, wondering what he would do if Whitey would not wake up.

Justin sensed his father's anxiety. 'If we turn to the northwest, at least we know there's land there.'

'I know. We're fine.' Maynard forced a smile. 'You'll have a few things to tell your buddies at school.'

'They won't believe me.'

Maynard reached into his shirt pocket and found the lead bullet. 'Give 'em this. They'll have to believe you.'

'Yeah.' Justin was pleased. 'Did you do what you wanted to?'

'Sort of; not really. But what the hell: we had an adventure, right? More fun than piano lessons.'

'For sure. What'll you tell *Today*?'

'That there isn't any story. Not yet, anyway. They're used to that.' Still, Maynard cautioned himself, you'd better come up with somebody for the fall fashions cover. Anybody. Even if you fabricate enthusiasm for Margaret Trudeau, that'll show you've been thinking. Hiller will sign the expense voucher.

The plane was over the centre of the Caicos Banks. To the left, Maynard could see the religious retreat on West Caicos. Navidad was rising ahead. He could make out an X-shaped clearing: the airport.

He shook Whitey's shoulder. Whitey awoke and cleared his head and ran his tongue over his coated teeth.

Maynard pointed. 'Navidad.'

'First-class.' Whitey blinked and yawned. He turned off the autopilot and took the controls.

The wind was from the north, giving Whitey a straight shot at the runway. He looked around, to make sure the air was free of other traffic, and pushed the stick forward. The nose dropped.

The plane was at two hundred feet, and dropping, when the tiny figure of a man dashed out on to the runway and waved his arms, warning Whitey off. Whitey pulled the stick back and poured power to both engines, and the plane rose and roared over the field.

'What's up *his* ass?' Whitey said. He circled the field twice, looking down at the runway. 'No wrecks, no donkeys.'

'Why don't you ask the tower?' said Maynard.

'Good idea. You find me the tower.' Whitey chuckled. 'Nothing down there but a hot-dog stand and a coon with a load of conch.'

Whitey positioned the plane for another approach. The man was still on the runway, still waving wildly. Whitey shook his head. 'Guy must have lost a few dots on his dice.'

Whitey aimed the plane down the runway and reduced

power. The man waved once more and then, seeing that the plane was going to land, broke and ran. Whitey laughed and called, 'Up you, Charlie!'

The plane fell slowly, centred on the runway. A perfect landing.

Justin's eyes darted across the instrument panel, and suddenly he knew what was wrong. 'The wheels are still up!' he screamed.

It took Whitey a full second to absorb the information, and by then it was too late. The engines were without power. The ground was rising, gently but inexorably.

Whitey said softly, 'I'll be goddamned.'

Maynard lurched forward and flung his arms around Justin, pinning him to the cushioned seat.

The tail wheel hit, and for a second the landing was normal. Then the fuselage bellied down on the runway. Metal scraped on crushed limestone rock with the shrill protest of a dull axe being ground on a rough wheel. Rivets were ripped free, plates peeled back.

The plane dipped to the right. A wingtip caught, wrenched the fuselage into a turn, and tore away. Wheeling in a lazy circle, the plane righted itself and dipped to the left, crushing the port wing.

Maynard clung to the boy and to the seat, fighting against the yawing centrifugal pulls. He heard the wing tear away and drag along the fuselage. He smelled fuel.

The plane rolled towards its wingless side. The nose struck and ploughed chunks of rock from the runway. The windshield shattered.

Maynard felt a blast of heat. He smelled hair burning.

The plane skidded to a stop. There was a whoosh sound and a flash of light.

Maynard did not look back. He was driven forward by the heat. He fumbled with Justin's seatbelt, unlatched it, and pushed the boy before him through the windshield frame.

Justin slid off the nose of the plane and fell to the runway.

'Go!' Maynard yelled. 'Run!'

Maynard squeezed himself through the windshield,

insensible to the shards of jagged glass that raked his butt and thighs. He dropped to the ground and ran after Justin.

When he felt that they were a safe distance from the burning plane, Maynard stopped and looked back.

Whitey was caught in the windshield frame. The flames had consumed the after section of the plane. The skin was melting away, and the skeletal ribs were glowing red.

It was like watching a snake swallow a rabbit: inch by inch, the plane disappeared into the fire's gullet.

Whitey was caught around the waist. He pushed with both arms, and his body twitched as he kicked from below.

Maynard ran back to the plane. He thought no noble thoughts, felt no courage. His only thought was: maybe if he pushes and I pull, he'll come free.

He crawled up the nose of the plane and grabbed Whitey under the arms.

Whitey pushed, and Maynard pulled, and Whitey's body popped out of the windshield frame. Maynard fell backward, with Whitey on top of him, and they tumbled on to the runway.

They stood with Justin – panting, exhausted, lightheaded – and watched the plane's nose succumb to the fire.

Justin was still wearing Maynard's jacket. He took it off and hung it over his father's left shoulder, concealing the holster. Maynard reached out and hugged him.

With a rumbling sigh, the plane collapsed in a puddle of flame.

'Surprise!' Whitey said. 'We're still alive.'

8

The investigation took an hour, and consisted of dozens of questions directed mostly at Whitey by Sergeant Wescott, the senior (of two) policeman on Navidad.

Sergeant Wescott resented the plane crash. It was an unwelcome intrusion on his orderly routine. It would bring officials from Grand Turk who would criticize the way he had filled out the accident reports, who would exceed their authority and look into things they had no business looking into. As Whitey explained when Wescott was out of the room searching for more forms, the sergeant collected all customs duties and all fees for all permits, and he reported only a fraction of the revenue. He was an established bureaucrat – proud of his position, arrogant about his power – who had been able to write his own book on procedures on the island.

It seemed to Maynard that Wescott's appearance was, by itself, evidence of corruption: he was grotesquely fat, wore a gold watch on each wrist, and reeked of exotic fragrances.

'You cause me a great ruckus here,' he told Whitey petulantly. 'I not forget it.'

'It's worse than you think, Wescott. I had a case of Drambuie on board for you.'

Maynard assumed Whitey was lying, for he had lied in response to every other question: the crash had been caused by hydraulic failure; the indicator light had told him that the wheels were down; he had seen the man trying to wave him off but had been forced to land because he was low on fuel; Maynard and the boy were not passengers, they were guests of the Chief Minister in Grand Turk and were being rushed back to Florida (a mission of mercy) because the boy had to see a doctor.

'And who gonna pay to get that junk off my runway?'

'Arawak'll pay.'

'Arawak never pay for nothin'.'

'Arawak's insurance company. Get your brother-in-law to bulldoze it off into the brush. You can write the ticket yourself.'

Wescott nodded. 'Bulldozer don't come cheap, that's a fact.'

Maynard put a hand on Justin's arm and expanded on one of Whitey's lies. 'We do have to get to a doctor. When can we get out?'

'Wednesday – Thursday.'

'Tomorrow!' Maynard insisted. 'I'll pay for a charter.'

Wescott paused, calculating the skim he could exact from the price of a charter flight. 'I call in the morning.'

'Call tonight.'

'Hey!' Wescott snapped. 'Who you anyway? Come to my island, crash a plane on my runway, and tell *me* when it's time to leave? You leave when I say you leave.'

'I'm sorry,' Maynard said. 'I'm upset ... the boy.'

Justin eyed his father quizzically, but said nothing.

'Okay,' Wescott said, relenting. 'Take my advice. If he sick, maybe he get better. If he don't, maybe he die. If he die, maybe you have another kid. That's life. Besides, no phone tonight. She broke.'

Whitey had a girlfriend on Navidad who worked as a chambermaid at Chainplates, the island's only functioning inn. She was married, Whitey said, but her husband worked as a crewman on an out-islands supply ship and was seldom home. Unlike her friends in similar circumstances, she refused to share her favours with native men, for such liaisons always created social problems. By servicing drop-in trade like Whitey, she was able to achieve satisfaction and yet remain emotionally faithful to her husband.

Whitey used Wescott's CB radio to call the girl, and she arranged for Maynard and Justin to have a room at Chainplates for the night.

The cab they took to the inn was a battered Corvair, kept alive beyond its time by parts cannibalized from other cars, construction equipment, and outboard motors. No two of its tyres were the same size, and it limped along the dirt roads like a cripple.

Despite the bouncing and the noise of the unmuffled engine and the dust that clogged the air, Justin put his head in Maynard's lap and slept.

Maynard carried Justin to the room – half of a two-family bungalow perched on a hillside overlooking a primitive marina – and tucked him into bed.

The boy did not awaken to questions about food or drink, did not stir when Maynard swabbed the caked dust from his face and lips with a wet washcloth.

Maynard kissed him on the forehead and walked up the hill to the bar.

The bar was a square, wood-panelled room decorated – perfunctorily – with fishnets and pot buoys and slapdash 'native' landscape paintings. The bar itself was a stained, unfinished plywood counter that ran the length of one wall. The plastic-and-chrome bar stools were cheap, mail-order merchandise.

A jukebox, turned cacophonously high, poured forth a jumble of unrelated tunes: reggae, Johnnie Ray's 'Cry', Elvis Presley's 'Heartbreak Hotel' and songs by Patti Page, Jo Stafford, Kate Smith and The Big Bopper.

The room was packed with dancers, all young and all black. Some wore motorcycle boots, some sandals, some mod platform shoes. There were miniskirts and short-shorts and caftans and slacks. Hairdos were Afros and ringlets and pomaded ducktails.

It was a kaleidoscope of cultures and periods and, at the same time, no culture at all. They were generations removed from their African heritage and isolated from all other cultural patterns. There were no models to emulate, no fads to follow. Taste was determined by the supply brokers in Miami. What refuse from the marketplace they could buy in bulk for next to nothing they would ferry to the islands at exorbitant markups. It was a couple of hundred years in time, but only a step in commerce, from the days of trade beads and blankets.

Maynard made his way through the crowd, to the bar. Through a forest of black hair he saw Whitey's platinum curls. He elbowed his way down the bar towards Whitey, but stopped when he saw that Whitey was preoccupied, locked in a boozy kiss with a girl.

The only empty seat at the bar was beside a white man with a long mane of silver hair. Maynard sat down and ordered himself a double scotch.

He felt the man staring at him. It was not furtive or subtle; the man had swivelled on his stool and was staring. Maynard tried to look away – down the bar, at his drink, at the ceiling – but he felt uncomfortable.

He turned and faced the man and said, 'Hello.'

The man raised his eyebrows. 'A veritable phoenix, risen from the ashes.'

'What?'

'Cleansed by fire. You have seen the eye of God and lived to tell of it.'

'*What?*'

The man smiled. 'That was a hairy escape today.'

'You heard about it.'

'*About* it? I heard it. It was a clarion of excitement amid the deafening din of tedium that is our lives. Let there be blood so we can have horror, death so we can feel fortunate, souvenirs for the children to gather. Dullness begets ghouls.'

'Sorry to disappoint you.' Maynard drained his glass.

'Lucky for you. Unlucky for us. Back to fish chowder and onanism. How long are you here for?'

'Tomorrow, I hope. If I can get a charter out.'

'If you're dependent on Wescott's grace, your tomorrow will be the last syllable of recorded time. He'll wait till he can find a pilot from whom he can euchre at least a jolly C-note.

Wretched Nubian.' He thumped on the bar, and the bartender poured his glass full of gin. 'And one more for my shipmate here.'

Maynard demurred. 'Thanks. I should get some sleep.'

'Tush, lad. There'll be time enough for sleep when the journey's done. Pour the man a drink, Clarence, and I'll pick his sodden brain for news of the lido.'

Maynard pushed his glass towards the bartender. 'Thanks,' he said to the man. 'I'm Blair Maynard.'

'I know that. And you work for *Today*. The drums tell all.' He smiled.

The man seemed to have no intention of introducing himself, so Maynard said, 'And who are you?'

'Who am I?' He feigned offence. 'I am the Colourful Island Character, the one you expect to see on the two-dollar tour of out-island speakeasies, the rum-soaked relic of broken dreams, the sun-struck sage who, for the price of a drink, will spin wondrous webs about what might have been, had not Fate – that fickle strumpet – struck me down in my prime. Am I boring you? Pray, be not afear'd: my style is full of poises. Get it? That's a pun, chum, and not a bad one, either.'

Maynard laughed. 'What's your name?'

'Name? What's in a name? He who steals my name steals trash, but he who steals my purse ... aye, there's a thief. Label me as you will, and let your fantasies fashion my persona. My safari shirt speaks volumes: here is a man who fancies himself an adventurer, a vagabond of the veldt. Is he a true romantic, or did he send a money order to L. L. Bean? My white ducks – redolent of a past of leisure and lucre, or pantaloons plucked from the food plane? My sandals – sabots of sorrow, a beachcomber's brogans, or just the cheapest shoes I could find? My name? It's Windsor. And thereby hangs another enigma. Am I really a distant relative of Her Britannic Majesty – a black sheep shunted off to the colonies to avoid embarrassment – or did I make it up, am I a swart Levantine trying to pass as Kraut royalty? Is there substance to the shadow, or is it all a balloon full of bullshit?'

100

'You tell me,' Maynard said.

'And spoil your fun? It's up to you to decide. What is real, and what is schticklied o'er with a pale cast of naught?'

Trying to smile, Maynard said wearily, 'To tell you the truth ...'

Windsor raised his hand. 'Say no more. I've done it again.' He banged his glass on the bar. 'Clarence! Another cordial. And one for my benighted victim. He'll accept if I promise to pay. None of your sly looks, you mongoose! I said I'll pay, and I will. My word is my bond, you know that.' Windsor fished in his pocket for a wad of crumpled bills, which he spilled on the bar. He turned to Maynard. 'Usually, I can tell: by the time I bore myself, my audience is comatose. But it has been so long since I've discoursed with a man of quality ...' He stopped, and grinned. 'God, I sound sincere!'

Maynard laughed quietly. 'Is that so rare?'

'For me? Unheard-of. Colourful Characters are supposed to be mysterious, and mystery involves a lot of lying.'

'Is your name really Windsor?'

'I think so. I mean, yes. It's what I've been going by for so long that it is, even if it isn't, if you follow. I blather so much that I sometimes come to accept my fictions as truth. But that one's so oft repeated that I'm pretty sure it's true. There used to be a precedent Norman, but I suppressed it. "Norman Windsor". What dizzy dam would name her foal "Norman"?'

'How long have you been here?'

'I was born here. People are, believe it or not. White people, I mean. I went away, for a decade or two, to seek my fortune. But Dame Fortune turned her back on me. Or, rather, my students turned their backs on me. So I returned to this sceptred septic system.'

'You were a teacher?'

'I was a pedagogue; I remain a pedant. I took honours in anthropology – raise your eyebrows if you like, but it's a fact – and I thought to share my wisdom with the young. The wonders of the Maya, the primal beauty of the Tasaday, the craft of the Sumerians, the genius of the druidical cults. There is such arrogance in the present. We

101

assume – outrageous hubris! – that what *is* is better than what has ever been. The evolutionary fallacy that growth and change mean improvement. Tumours grow and change, too. That's how civilization has progressed. Simple, efficient societies are festering with the tumours of innovation, justified by political placebos like "democracy" and "human rights" and the "dignity of man". The dignity of man! Where is the dignity in a greedy, solipsistic animal whose only goals are survival and the fulfilment of every sensory itch? The sensible man, the worthy man, recognizes other men for what they are and indulges his so-called social conscience to the same extent that he pulls his pud: till that particular itch is sated.'

'I can see why you ran into trouble as a teacher,' Maynard said, smiling. 'It's "in" to be a born-again Christian. It's not "in" to be a born-again Machiavel.'

'Machiavelli be damned!' Windsor shouted. 'Dumb dago hack didn't have the balls to practise what he preached. Nobody has. I venture that you can't name me one society that functions properly, where everybody gets what he deserves and nobody feels like hoisting somebody else on a plutonium petard.'

Maynard pondered for a moment. 'What about the Amish?'

'The Amish!' Windsor snorted. 'Not even close. Prisoners of some cockeyed version of the Christian ethic. No. In all the world, there are precisely three and a half pure societies. The half is a group in the deep woods of the Ozarks who still speak Elizabethan English. The reason they're only a half is because the Elizabethan England they hark back to was a fairly organized society. Civilized, if you will.

'The two purest are in the Philippine jungles. One is the Tasaday, who were discovered in 1971 – living in the Stone Age. The other was discovered last year – the Taotbato, a cave people whose primitive society has survived unchanged for God knows how many hundreds, or thousands, of years. Discovery will ruin them both. It always does.'

'And the other one? You said there were three and a half.'

Windsor gazed at Maynard for a moment, then took a

draught of gin. 'It's not important. I'm blathering again. Anyway, I had tenure, until some collegiate counsel built a calumnious case against me.'

'What do you do now?'

'This and that. Catch a fish. Rent a boat. Lie beneath a tree and wait for my one-way ticket to the undiscovered country. What journalistic jewels did *Today* dispatch you here to recover?'

'I thought the drums told all.'

'Sometimes they stutter. A hot story? A Navidad profile? Carnival in Caicos? Sewers in paradise – the offal truth?' Windsor winced. 'It must be getting late. Never mind. Don't tell me if you don't want to. Secrets are baggage I can do without.'

'Hardly a secret,' Maynard said. 'I wish I knew enough to *have* a secret.'

He told Windsor about the missing boats, about his conversations with Florio and Makepeace. He edited details only for brevity. 'The frustrating thing is,' he said at the end of his recital, 'I don't believe there *is* a cover-up of any kind. I think it's a case of people not knowing and not caring.'

'You're right.' Windsor nodded emphatically. 'My ebon fellows are not capable of a cover-up. Somebody's tongue would come unleashed, just for the fun of seeing a rival at the gibbet. What you have here, I warrant, is a poacher here, a sinking there, a bit of drug-foolery over there, until it all adds up to a hearty rollcall. Not very satisfying, but very true.'

'You sound convinced.'

'I'm convinced,' Windsor said. 'I learned long ago not to look for substance behind every shadow. Now,' he drained his glass and slid off his stool – 'I must away to the embrace of Morpheus. I'd say "Au revoir," but you'll be off in the morning. And so, "Adieu." '

'Thanks for the drinks.'

'My great pleasure.' Windsor took a step, and then something checked his departure, something he could not resist. 'In thy orisons by all my gins remembered.' He cackled.

Maynard laughed and saluted with his glass.

103

Windsor patted him on the shoulder. 'A pity you're leaving. I so enjoy being appreciated.'

Maynard was drawn from the depths of his dream by Justin shaking his shoulder and whispering, 'Where's the pistol?'

'Under my pillow. Why?'

'That policeman's at the door.'

Maynard climbed out of bed and opened the door. Sergeant Wescott stood on the doorstep, sweat coursing down his puffy cheeks. Gnats circled his head.

'I have your plane,' Wescott said.

'Terrific. What time?'

'Eleven o'clock ... tomorrow.'

'What's the matter with today?'

'Couldn't get nobody to come.'

Maynard wanted to argue, but he knew it would be useless. 'Okay. But I'll have to make a call today.'

'No calls. Phone still broke.'

'How did you call to get the plane?'

'Fella come through the airport this morning.'

'There was a plane here this morning and you didn't come get us?'

'Fella didn't want to take you.'

'You mean he wouldn't meet your price, right?'

'Hey! Who you think you are? I try do you a favour ...'

'*I* would have met your price.'

'Too late now. Give me a hundred dollars.'

'What for? The plane won't be here till tomorrow.'

'Good faith. Or the fella won't come back.'

'Sergeant ... go suck your thumb for good faith.'

Wescott reached out and took Maynard's elbow. 'I think maybe I put you in jail till the plane come.'

Maynard looked down at Wescott's hand, then up into his tiny eyes. 'If you don't take your hand off me,' he said evenly, 'I'll break your goddam neck.'

Wescott released Maynard's arm. Maynard stepped back inside the room and slammed the door.

'You shouldn't've done that,' Justin said. 'Now there'll never be a plane.'

104

'There'll be a plane. That pig wants his hundred bucks.' Maynard shook off his anger. 'Now ... you heard it all, buddy. What do you want to do today?'

'Don't you under*stand*, Dad?' Justin seemed about to cry. 'Mom's gonna *kill* me!'

'Justin ...' Maynard hugged him. 'Don't worry about your mom. Don't worry about anything. You want to go fishing?'

'I don't even have a pole.'

'We'll find one. You've got your knife; we'll make one. Maybe we'll rent a boat. Did you ever catch a barracuda? Do they fight!'

After breakfast, Maynard took Justin to the front desk and inquired about fishing. A frayed, mould-stained cardboard placard on the desk advertised charter fishing trips aboard the *Mary Beth*.

Maynard pointed to the sign and asked the clerk, 'How much is a half-day?'

'Nothing.'

'Oh ... maybe I can contribute to the fuel.'

The clerk chuckled. 'Don't cost nothin' 'cause he don't go nowhere. Boat broke and all his rods broke, so he quit and go home.'

'Why do you keep the sign there?'

'Public relations.'

'I see,' Maynard said patiently. 'Where can I rent rods?'

'Can't.'

'All right. I'll jury-rig a couple. How about a boat? A Whaler. Even a Sailfish.'

'Got none. Doc Windsor, he got some, but he don't rent 'em no more.'

'He said he did. Last night.'

The clerk shrugged. 'Maybe he does, then. Things change around here too fast for me.'

'Where does he live?'

'Down the road.'

'What road?'

'*The* road. Only one road.'

'How will I know his house?'

'You'll hear it.'

'I'll hear it?'

The clerk nodded. He reached under the counter. 'If you going, take a dose of this.' He handed Maynard a can of Deep Woods OFF.

'Thanks.' Maynard doused himself and Justin with the bug spray and returned the can to the clerk.

'You got fifty cents?' asked the clerk.

Maynard smiled. 'Fifty cents a dose?'

'Twenty-five. You took two.'

Maynard reached in his pocket. He had no change. 'I don't. I'm sorry.'

'Hard darts on me, then.' The clerk shook his head. 'Coulda used that fifty cents.'

The road was a dirt swath cut through the tangle of scrub, cactus, prickly pear, and sea grape. Mosquitoes swarmed in clouds that swooped up from hidden fens and darted across the road. The thick, oily bug spray was effective: the mosquitoes charged the pedestrians and hovered a few inches from exposed skin, deciphering chemical signals exuded from the repellent, and then, on some silent cue, buzzed off over the brush. The foliage was alive with noises – hums and clicks and whistling bird sounds.

They walked for half a mile or more. The sweat that ran down their faces was beginning to wash away the spray, and single mosquito scouts were growing bolder.

Maynard was on the verge of turning back when he heard a sound not of the pattern of the insect noises – high-pitched, insistent, mechanical. It was an electric motor. The sound was coming from the right. Maynard stood on tiptoes and looked over the underbrush. He saw nothing.

'There's a path up there,' Justin said.

A convention of gnats surrounded them, plunging into their ear canals, flitting up their sleeves and into their under-arms, strafing their scalps in search of unsprayed spaces. They scratched and slapped and ran, hoping that frantic activity would make them inhospitable hosts.

All that was immediately visible at the end of the path was a steel cube, a generator house from which the loud whine

106

was coming. In the distance, over a ridge of dunes, a few boats were moored to a rickety pier.

Windsor's house was below ground, buried in the sand to its flat cement roof. Bulwarked stairs led down to a huge teak portal adorned with a polished brass ring. An intercom speaker was set in concrete beside the door. Maynard raised the brass ring and let it fall against the teak.

Windsor's voice crackled over the intercom. 'Get away, you Ethiopian! I'm in conference. If you're selling, I'm not buying. If you're buying. I'm not selling. Neither purchaser nor vendor be. Scram!'

Justin listened to the diatribe and said to Maynard, 'He rents boats?'

Maynard smiled and pushed a button on the intercom. 'I have a telegram here for a ... rum-soaked relic.'

'Is that you, Mencken?' Windsor shrilled. 'What news of Sacco and Vanzetti? Keep heart. We'll spring those guineas yet.' The intercom clicked off and, a few seconds later, the door swung open.

Windsor was dressed in a kimono and pointed silk slippers. 'Come in! Come in! I was just fantasizing about a picnic with all the catamites of Macedon.' He saw Justin. 'Forgive me! You brought a catamite of your own.'

Maynard introduced Justin to Windsor. Wide-eyed, Justin shook hands and said, 'What's a catamite?'

'Nothing, lad, nothing. You've heard of a catamaran? Same phylum. Come in! I'll pour you a draught of mead, and we'll salute the divus.'

The house was a single room, thirty feet by forty, panelled in teak and lavishly furnished – in sections, separated by style. The dining area was Louis XV, the living-room area Spanish colonial, the sleeping area Danish modern, the kitchen a horseshoe of stainless steel and butcher block. There were oil paintings in gallery frames, antique documents in sealed glass cases, archaeological artifacts lacquered and preserved against time and wear, mahogany cases crammed with books.

Insulated by sand, air conditioned by the generator, the house was maintained at sixty-eight degrees.

Maynard gazed around the room, admiring.

'My little haven in the pits of hell,' Windsor said. He waved his arm. 'You see before you my life. The palace of a pack rat.'

'Very nice. For a Colourful Island Character, you've done okay.'

'I've been frugal. I started with a little money and that made money, and as we know, the money money makes makes more money. But alas – here now my tragic mask – I'd trade it all for a good woman and a warm hearth.' He laughed. 'So tell me, messenger, what news on the Rialto?'

'We can't get off till tomorrow.'

'I'm not surprised. Wescott is worthless. But your delay is my good fortune. We'll lunch, and I'll enchant you with tales of my years before the mast.'

'Thanks, but we want to rent a boat.'

Windsor stood still. He looked at Maynard, and frowned, and looked away. 'What for?'

'We thought we'd go fishing.'

Justin said, 'Dad says we can catch a barracuda.'

'Impossible.'

'Why?'

'Nothing worth catching out there. It's too hot.'

'We'll fish deep, where it's cool.'

'I have no boats.'

'Come on,' Maynard said. 'I saw a bunch of boats down by the pier.'

'They're not seaworthy.'

'Look ... a couple of hours fishing, and we'll come back and tell you lies about what we almost caught.'

Windsor looked at Maynard. His amiable mask had disappeared. 'No.'

'Okay,' Maynard said, perplexed. 'Sorry to bother you.' He turned to Justin. 'Come on, buddy. We'll see if Whitey can scrounge something up for us.'

'No!' Windsor snapped. Then he softened. 'Please ... leave it alone.'

'What's wrong?'

'It's dangerous! You're the one who was telling *me* about all the boats that have vanished. Why do you want to take a chance?'

'I'm not asking you to charter me a schooner. I don't want to sail to Cuba. I want to go a mile offshore and throw a line overboard, that's all. Besides, I can take care of myself.'

'That I doubt.'

'Don't.' Challenged, impelled by silly bravado, Maynard raised his shirt-tail above the waistband of his bathing suit and revealed the butt of the Walther.

'You're a fool.'

'I can get a boat from Whitey.'

'All right,' Windsor sighed. 'I'll give you a boat. At least I know it'll float. What Whitey would get for you I would not send Vlad the Impaler out on. But you must promise me you'll check in every half hour on the radio.'

'A deal. We'll catch you a grouper, and you can whip up a luau.'

Windsor was not amused. Muttering something about fools walking in darkness, he led them out of the house.

At *Today* in New York, Dena Gaines was sorting the morning mail – a dozen invitations to cocktail parties 'in honour of' new leisure-time products, portentous press releases about a 'revolution' in men's fashion that would spell the resurrection of the narrow necktie, a free sample pair of electrically heated underpants ('Bunny Warmers') – when the phone rang.

'Trends.'

'Mrs Smith's office, calling for Mr Maynard,' said Devon's secretary.

'He's not here just now. May I take a message?'

'Hold a minute.' Dena was put on Hold.

A moment later, Devon came on the line. 'Where is he?'

'He's ... out of the office,' Dena said protectively. 'Can I give him a message?'

'Where is he? Do you know?'

'Not really, no.'

'Miss Gaines, a few minutes ago my son's school called. He isn't there.'

'Yes, ma'am.' Dena's other phone began to ring.

'Let me speak to Blair's editor.'

'Yes, ma'am.' Dena transferred Devon to Hiller's office, then punched up her other line. '"Trends."'

'Mr Maynard, please. Michael Florio calling.'

'He's not here just now. May I take a message?'

'Do you know where I can reach him?'

'No, sir. I wish I did.'

'I think I may.'

'I beg your pardon.'

'I'm with the Coast Guard. I talked to him over the weekend.'

'If you don't mind, Mr Florio, I'll switch you to Mr Maynard's editor. I know he'd like to speak to you.'

Dena transferred Florio, hung up, and walked down the hall.

Hiller was still talking to Devon. Another phone button was alight and flashing, indicating that Florio was waiting on 'Hold'. Dena sat in the chair opposite Hiller's desk.

'I wouldn't be, Mrs Smith,' Hiller said, 'not yet. He'll probably be in later on. There may be a foul-up with the shuttle from Washington ... I *don't* know for sure. It's just the last thing he said to me last week ... I understand that, but one day's school isn't the end of the world ... Yes, as soon as I hear. I promise.'

Hiller hung up the phone and said to Dena, 'What does she think I am, a den mother? The kid misses half a day's school and she wants me to call out the Marines.'

Dena smiled. 'They're on your other line.'

'What?' Hiller pushed the flashing button, spoke his name, and, for several seconds, listened to Florio.

'And you think he actually went down there?' Hiller said. 'No, I didn't send him ... Yes, he works for me, and yes, he was looking into the story, but I wanted him to use the bureaus. That's what they're paid for ... He's a big boy, Commander ... I know, but if anything, having the kid along should make him more careful ... You're kidding! I'm not

110

the Coast Guard. *You're* the Coast Guard! I don't have a boat to send if I wanted to, and I have no reason to want to ... Listen, Commander ... four years ago we had a sports editor who didn't show up for work. All we found was a note that said, "I'm going out the door before I go out the window." His wife didn't know where he was; his kids didn't know; nobody knew. We spent six months and God knows how much money trying to find him, and we never did. For all I know, Maynard's flipped out and gone native on me ... What's *that* supposed to mean? He works for me, that's all. He's not my brother, thank God. Yeah, fine ... by all means ... please do.'

Hiller hung up and shouted, 'Jesus Christ!' He shuffled a heap of papers on his desk.

'Where is he?' Dena asked.

'Coast Guard guy thinks he's in some country called Turks-and-something. All Maynard told *me* was he might go to Washington. What *is* it with him? I told him not to go. I told him to stay here and do his job. But no, that's not good enough. He's got a *Man of La Mancha* complex. Well, he better goddam well come back and do his job, or he won't have a job.' Hiller rooted through the papers on his desk and pulled out a newspaper clipping. 'You want a boat story?' He pushed the clip towards Dena. '*There* is a boat story.'

'What is it?'

'Brendan Trask is retiring, gonna take off and sail around the world for a year. It's a cover, that's what it is. The man who practically invented television news turns his back on the electronic age and returns to nature. What a comment on society!'

'I bet he just wants a raise.'

'Trask doesn't play games like that. Read it yourself. They told him he had to read commercial lead-ins. He said that violated his contract. They insisted; he split. He's already gone.'

Dena was not interested. 'You said we have three columns to fill for early-close. How are we going to close it today?'

'You've gotta help me out.'

111

'I'm not a writer,' Dena said sweetly. 'I'm a researcher.'

'Help me out this week, and we'll see what we can do about that.'

'All right.' Dena smiled again. 'I suppose I can rework that gay story.' She stood up.

'Fine.' Hiller paused. 'You know there's only one writing spot open.'

'What's that?'

'"Trends" editor.'

'It isn't open yet,' Dena said. 'He'll probably be in after lunch.'

9

They had been fishing for more than an hour, trolling slowly in the blue-green water just beyond the line of reefs. They had caught nothing, had had no bites, and Justin was bored. He sat beneath the canopy that covered the midships of the 22-foot Mako, and rested his rod on the gunwale.

Maynard stood at the steering console. 'It's probably too shallow here,' he said. He ran a finger along a small mariners' map of the Navidad area that had been laminated to the wooden console. 'According to this, if we go around that point, the dropoff comes right in close to shore. We should have real deep water. That's where the monsters live. What do you say, buddy?'

'If you want,' Justin replied dully.

'Shape up.' Maynard smiled. 'Fishing wouldn't be any fun if you caught something every five minutes.'

'Okay.' Justin reeled in his line. 'But is once an hour asking too much?'

Maynard brought his own line aboard and nudged the throttle forward. The outboard motor, its innards clogged with carbon, hesitated and coughed and then, with a burst of black smoke, flushed itself clean and pushed ahead. The bow rose and settled down, and the boat planed across the surface of the calm water.

Breeze and tide met in conflict at the point, and the water

was churned into a white froth. The line of reef extended due west from the point. To the left, inside the reef, the water was greenish-white, flecked with coral brown. The dropoff outside the reef was precipitous, the water a uniform, gun-metal blue.

When he reached still water, Maynard slowed and let out the two fishing lines. He checked his watch, turned on the radio, and spoke into the microphone: 'Mencken to Relic... Mencken to Relic ... just checking in.'

'Where are you?' Windsor's voice came back. 'I can't see you.'

Maynard traced his route on the map. 'It says here Mangrove Pass. Pass to what, I don't know. There's nothing anywhere. Nothing by land, nothing by sea.'

'That's far enough. Turn around and head back this way.'

'Nothing to worry about here. Looks like the end of the world.'

'That's not the point. The radio won't reach much farther. If the engine quits ...'

'No problem. Check you later.' Maynard replaced the microphone and turned off the radio.

He continued westward, trolling in the deep water. Half a mile to the southwest, the barren land – a sliver of white sand topped with grey-green scrub – appeared to shimmer as heat was sucked into the clear air.

'Help!' Justin yelled. A fish had taken his lure. The butt of his rod was jammed between his legs, the tip – jerking wildly – rapped against the transom.

'Keep the tip up!' Maynard throttled down to neutral. 'Don't give him any slack, or he'll shake it!'

'I can't hold him!'

'Yes you can!' Maynard put out a hand to brace Justin's rod, but withdrew it. 'Lean back, bring the tip up ... that's the way ... now, go forward with him and reel!'

'Look!'

The fish broke water behind the boat – a writhing blade of silver that sparkled in the sunlight.

'Reel!'

'My fingers are cramped!'

114

'Then rest with it ... but don't let the tip down.'

Leaning against the gunwale, Justin held the rod upright with his left hand and flexed the fingers in his right. 'What is it?'

'A barracuda. Fifteen, twenty pounds.'

The rod heaved, and Justin lurched forward. The fish was running, stripping line from the reel.

'Let him take it,' Maynard said. 'When he turns, reel like stink.'

Justin strained against the rod. His stiff fingers skidded off the crank. 'You take it!'

'Hell no! He's your fish. You're doing fine. Just don't give him any slack.'

'I can't!'

'Yes you can!'

'He's gonna get away.'

'Maybe.'

The tip snapped up; the line went slack.

Justin said, 'I told you.'

'Reel, dammit! He's not gone!'

Justin reeled frantically, and the line tautened.

Maynard leaned over the stern. 'He's coming to the boat. Easy ... easy.' The wire leader cleared the water. Maynard grabbed it and flung the fish over the transom on to the deck. 'Now, there is one sweet piece of fish.' He turned to Justin. 'Good for you!'

Justin was gleeful. 'Look at his teeth!'

Maynard found a pair of pliers on a shelf beneath the steering console and dislodged the hook from the barracuda's mouth. 'Good for you!' he said again.

'Can we stuff him?'

'You want to give him to your piano teacher?'

'To Mom. She won't *believe* this.'

They laughed together.

Maynard turned east and trolled back towards the point, then turned west again. They followed a flock of feeding sea birds, but the larger fish that were forcing the bait fish to the surface were not interested in the shiny steel 'spoons' trolled behind the Mako. A porpoise surfaced and rolled playfully in the boat's bow wave. A small shark basked on the surface until, alerted by the sound of the approaching motor, it thrashed its tail and disappeared.

At one o'clock, Maynard checked with Windsor by radio. He reported Justin's catch and promised to return within the hour.

'I'm hungry,' Justin said.

'So am I.'

'Thirsty, too.'

Maynard nodded. 'To hell with it; let's go in. Maybe the phone's fixed.'

While Justin brought in the lines, Maynard looked out over the water. He saw something ahead, to the west: a small brown dot that lay low in the water. He made sure the rods were secure in their holders, put the boat in gear, and headed west.

'I thought we were going back,' Justin said.

'We are. In a minute,' Maynard pointed at the dot.

'What is it?'

'I don't know. A turtle, maybe, or a shark. We'll check it out.'

'What for?'

'Just because . . .' Maynard smiled. 'On Seventy-eighth Street you can go days, weeks even, without seeing a shark. Admit it.'

The dot took shape very quickly. 'It's a boat,' Justin said.

'More like a canoe.'

'How'd it get there?'

'Must've drifted up from there . . . West Caicos.' Maynard gestured at a grey lump on the western horizon.

The boat was a hollow log, tapered on both ends. Maynard circled it slowly. It was empty, save for a single, rough-hewn paddle.

'Look!' Justin pointed. 'Over there.'

Maynard squinted. The sun was high, the flat surface of the sea a mirror. 'What d'you see?'

'Someone swimming.'

'Sure.' Maynard was still blinded by the brilliant curtain of sunlight. 'Driftwood, I bet.'

116

'Driftwood doesn't wave.'

Maynard crouched beside Justin, beneath the canopy, and shielded his eyes. He saw a tiny silhouette. An arm, waving. 'I'll be damned. Must've fallen overboard.'

It was a young girl, buoyed by an orange kapok lifejacket. She was waving, but in a manner that struck Maynard as peculiar: there was nothing frenzied about her wave, nothing desperate. Her arm moved back and forth as regularly as a metronome. And she did not shout or cry out or say a word, even when they drew near.

Maynard put the boat in neutral, letting it coast up to the girl. 'Are you hurt?' he called.

She said nothing, but she shook her head: no.

He turned off the engine, to eliminate the possibility of an accident with the propeller. He knelt in the stern as it glided to the girl and held his hand out for her to grab. 'Glad we came along. You could float out here for a week without seeing anybody.' His fingers touched her wrist. She was fair-skinned and blonde and, he guessed, no more than twelve or thirteen years old. 'How'd you get all the way out here?'

He gripped her wrist, braced himself against the transom, and pulled. Something was wrong: she was too heavy. And in her eyes was a flash of panic, of terror. 'What's the ...?'

She was yanked downward, out of Maynard's grasp. He saw a rubber tube protruding from her dress, behind her head.

There was a splash, a burst of water, a blur as something flew at his face. He fell backward, and an axe buried itself in the deck.

Maynard backed away from the stern and scrambled to his feet. The girl was gone, and now a man crouched in the boat, panting, drooling water from his mouth and nose. His long hair was plastered to his head and shoulders. Bits of seaweed dripped from his beard. His shirt was torn and stained, his trousers tattered. His feet were wrapped in uncured animal skins that were lashed to his legs by rawhide thongs. He had no teeth.

Holding the axe above his head, never taking his eyes off

Maynard, the man reached behind him and bent down. He hauled a boy aboard – dark-haired, skinny, with black, darting eyes.

The man passed the axe to the boy. 'Now, lad' – he pointed a finger at Maynard – '*Do* him!'

'Justin?' Maynard snapped his head around. Justin was cowering behind the steering console. 'Stay there!'

The boy held the axe clumsily.

'*Do* him, I say!' the man shouted.

The boy did not move.

From his belt the man withdrew a slim, double-edged dirk. He poked it under the boy's ear, drawing blood. 'You Portugee bastard! You do what you been taught!'

Maynard reached under his shirt and drew his pistol. He chambered a bullet and pointed the pistol at the man. 'Drop it.' The pistol trembled in his hand. He had never pointed a loaded gun at another human being. His upbringing, his training, his experience, had conditioned him to avoid pointing a weapon at a living thing. If you ever point a gun at another man, his father had said, you'd better want him dead.

He cupped his left hand under his right, steadying the pistol.

The man coiled into a compact ball, weaving from side to side like a cobra, shifting the knife from hand to hand.

Maynard sighted along the top of the pistol barrel, trying to hold the muzzle at the man's open mouth.

The man screamed and sprang, and Maynard shot him in the face.

The .32-calibre bullet was too small and too fast to knock the man down, so though he died in mid-air – the bullet entered his left eye and exited behind his right ear – he kept coming. His corpse hit the gunwale and bounced on to the deck at Maynard's feet.

Maynard was appalled. He stared down at the upturned face, at the one blank eye and at the oozing cavity where its partner had been. Seconds ago, this had been a man. Now it was carrion. He had caused this metamorphosis by moving his finger an eighth of an inch.

Justin screamed, 'Dad!'

In the instant it took the warning to penetrate the muddle of Maynard's mind, the dark boy was upon him like a gibbon – legs locked around his waist, a hand clawing at his face, an arm wildly swinging the hand-axe, teeth snapping at his face and neck.

Maynard could not see. He tried to pull the boy away, but the wiry limbs were like tentacles: as soon as one was disengaged, another would scratch or kick or slash. The pistol fell from his hand.

Maynard staggered backward. He reached up and grabbed a handful of hair, but before he could pull, the boy turned his head and bit Maynard's fingers to the bone. The axe dug at his back – short, slicing blows that lacerated the flesh. A hand clawed at his eyes, fingers probing to uproot his eyeballs. He stopped one hand, then the other, then felt teeth fasten on the skin of his cheek and tear away. He released a hand and punched at the biting mouth, and the hand he released drove a pointed fingernail deep into his ear.

His brain shrieked: overboard! Get in the water and he'll have to let go. Blindly, he stumbled a few steps, took a deep breath, and flung himself into the air.

He heard a strange, yet vaguely familiar, sound – a hollow, explosive roar, like the sound when the school bus he was riding in had skidded on ice and hit a tree. The sound subsided into a hum, and he was at a going-away party for someone at *Today*. Why was there a hum at the party? Someone tried to speak to him, but the voice was muffled by the hum. Then the party was outdoors in the wintertime, and he was so cold.

Then the hum faded, too, and there was nothing.

The boy squirmed out from under Maynard and left him on the deck, with his head sloshing in the drain beneath the outboard motor. On the motor itself, a patch of hair-tufted scalp hung from the steel brace Maynard's head had struck. The boy leaned over the stern and helped the girl aboard. She shivered from long immersion in the sea. She reached behind her head to remove the rubber tube from her dress,

119

but she could not grasp it. The boy put his hand up her dress and pulled the tube from below. It was in the shape of an inverted 'Y'. He and the man had clung to the girl's legs, breathing through the arms of the 'Y'.

Justin stood behind the console and looked at his father's body. Blood from the wound in Maynard's head dribbled down his neck into the drain, mixed with a puddle of oil and water, and ran out through a hole in the stern. Justin wanted to run to his father, to soothe his wound and beg him to awaken. He wanted his father to sit up and smile and say it had all been a joke. He shook, though he was not cold, and his teeth clacked together.

The radio was on the console, beside his right hand. He slid his hand a few inches to the left, turned the radio on, and removed the microphone from its bracket. He ducked down and pressed the 'Talk' button on the microphone. 'Help!' he whispered. 'Help! They've killed my dad!' He looked up, in time to see the skinny boy's fist descending in a wide arc. He tried to dodge, but the fist hit him behind the ear and sent him sprawling across the deck.

'Nobody help you now,' said the boy. 'Nobody help you ever again. You on you own, sum'bitch!'

The boy retrieved the dangling microphone. 'Hey, Mary, let's sing 'em de song.'

Windsor stood at his kitchen counter, listening to the radio. The reception was faint and scratchy, but he had no difficulty deciphering the words. There were two voices, both high and young and very gay. They sang:

> Him cheat him friend of him last guinea
> Him kill both friar and priest – O dear!
> Him cut de t'roat of pickaninny,
> Bloody, bloody buccaneer!

Windsor did not wait for the laughter he knew would follow. He turned off his radio and said sadly, 'May the wind sit in the shoulder of your sail, my friend.'

120

10

Why were they pulling him? He told them he didn't feel like dancing, but they wouldn't listen. Now they were forcing him on to the floor, dragging him by his arms and legs. They were hurting him, but they didn't care. The more it hurt him, the more they cheered. Please, something to drink. So thirsty! Just a sip. Then he would try to dance. Promise.

The dancers left, the dream faded, and all that was left was the pain – a sharp throbbing in his head and, worse, the sensation that his arms and legs were being wrenched from their sockets.

His eyes opened, and he saw the sky. He was on his back, but he felt nothing beneath him, only the agony in his shoulders and hips. He cocked his head forward, put his chin on his chest, and saw his feet – ropes around his ankles, suspending his legs from two wooden posts. His head lolled back, and he looked up at his hands – hanging from ropes to two more posts. Each rope led to a spoked wheel.

He was on a rack.

He turned his head to one side, then the other. He was in a small sand clearing, surrounded by brush. Alone.

He heard radio music, an orchestra and chorus, a hymn: 'His love is greater than the shining sea, greater than you and me, greater than the power of love, and He's with you, like a hand in glove.'

121

The hymn ended. A voice began, 'And now, shipmate . . .' The voice stopped, and another – closer, alive – intoned: 'The souls of the righteous are in the hand of God, and there shall no torment touch them. Thus has our comrade, Roche Sansdents, a righteous man and true, gone to the lap of God. All men have one entrance into life, and the like going out. When shall we see him again? Who can number the sands of the sea, and the drops of rain, and the days of eternity?'

A murmur of 'Amen' from a sombre crowd.

A new voice, resonant, commanding: 'Goody Sansdents, by covenant you are heir to Roche's goods, and they shall pass to you. Likewise by covenant, you shall receive food from the common store, apparel as you shall have need, and the tenth part of the finest prize next taken. Likewise by covenant, to you shall fall the disposition of him who caused Roche to pass from this world.'

A woman wailed a fierce, vengeful cry.

Maynard tightened his stomach muscles and, holding his breath to prepare for the pain, arched his back and shot his arms upward, hoping to put enough slack in the ropes so he could wiggle his hands free. He failed and fell back, and the fibres in his shoulders were stretched to anguish. He screamed.

'He wakes!' called a voice as the crowd approached the clearing.

'Only to sleep again,' said another. 'I'd sooner make the whole passage asleep.'

'But when you reached the other side, you might be lost.'

'Aye, but awake you have to see the face of death, and that's a fright, they say.'

'No more a fright than the face of your woman.'

They filed into the clearing and stood on its perimeter.

Maynard hung from the rack and looked at them. He was afraid, but pain and confusion had partly detached him from his fear. It was as if he was floating above himself, observing his own terror.

They were all men, all tanned and filthy, their clothing

122

stained with blood and grease. Some carried cutlasses, some axes, and all had at least one knife.

When the ring around the clearing was complete, the men fell silent. The ring parted, and three people walked across the sand towards Maynard.

The leader was a tall man, with a broad chest and a narrow waist, in his late thirties or early forties. His brown hair was sun-bleached and parted in the centre of his head. A waxed moustache hung down on either side of his mouth. He wore a dirty white linen shirt with billowed sleeves and hand-sewn hide trousers that stopped just below his knees. His knobby, leathery feet were bare. Two bandoliers crossed over his chest. Each held a flintlock pistol.

Behind the leader was an older man whose greying hair was tied behind his head in a pigtail. He wore a grey robe, cinched at the waist by a wide leather belt, and rubber foul-weather boots.

Several paces behind the men shuffled the semblance of a woman. Her face was smeared with charcoal; her hair waxed in a Medusa cap. She wore a black overcoat, which she clutched tight around her middle. Her eyes were fixed on Maynard – moist, frenzied eyes that did not blink.

The woman scuttled between the two men, leaned over Maynard, and spat in his face. Her breath reeked of rum.

The tall man smiled at Maynard. 'You wake.'

'Who are you?' Maynard's voice was a raspy croak.

'Give him water,' the older man said. 'You must never kill a thirsty man. He appears before God without communion. It is written.'

From somewhere behind him, hands reached over Maynard's head and squirted water from an animal bladder on to his face and into his mouth. He licked his lips and swallowed, and the ligaments in his shoulders complained at the minute motion. He looked at the tall man and asked again, 'Who are you?'

'Jean-David Nau. Tenth in a line.'

'Where is my son?'

'With the others.'

'Please,' Maynard begged. 'Let him go. He's a baby.'

'Let him go!' Nau laughed. 'Indeed!'

'Don't kill him?' Maynard felt tears leak from his eyes. 'Do anything to me, but don't kill him!'

'Kill him?' Nau looked perplexed. 'Whatever for? Do I kill a soldier before he is old enough to fight? Do I kill a beast of burden before he is old enough to pull? No. He may have a short life, but it will be a merry one, and his end will be of his own making.'

'And me?'

'You,' Nau said flatly, 'you will die.'

'Why?'

The older man replied, 'It is our way.'

'To hell with your way. Tell me what I can do. Anything, I don't want to die.' Hearing himself speak, Maynard was surprised at how calm he sounded.

'Do you fear death?' asked Nau. 'Death is an adventure.'

As quickly and illogically as calm had come upon Maynard, it deserted him. He screamed, 'No!'

'What kind of man are you? Are you craven? You should meet death with dignity.'

'You be dignified. I've got one purpose in life, and that's to stay alive.'

'What do they call you?'

'Maynard.'

'Maynard! A noble name! A warrior's name!'

'Bullshit. It's a name. Who are you?'

'I have answered that.'

'No ... I mean who *are* you? What are you?'

Nau raised his voice so the men around the edge of the clearing could hear. 'Hear me! This man is Maynard. Is there man among you who does not know his blood?' The men murmured to one another. 'It was his forebear that felled the mighty Teach, called Blackbeard.'

Maynard did not argue. He had no idea who his ancestors were, beyond his great-grandparents, but if survival lay in assuming a false genealogy, he was prepared to claim descent from Jesus of Nazareth or Genghis Khan.

'Your blood is good,' said Nau. 'So must your heart be.'

'In that case ...' Maynard said.

Nau held up his hand, to silence Maynard. 'Manuel!'

The skinny boy hurried into the clearing.

'Bring the lad.'

'Aye, l'Ollonois.'

Maynard said to Nau, 'What did he call you?'

'L'Ollonois. It is what the children are trained to call me. Like my father, and his father before him. Back and back and back to the first, who settled this land in the time of the second Charles.'

Maynard knew the name. 'He was a psychopath! He used to eat people's hearts.'

Nau smiled proudly. 'Aye. He brooked no silence from prisoners.'

'Indians cut him to pieces.'

'Aye, and so fearful were they that the pieces would join again and come back to haunt them that they burned and scattered them to the four winds. *There* was a man who knew how to die!'

The skinny boy returned to the clearing, leading Justin on a rope leash. Justin's hands were tied behind him.

Maynard turned his head. He expected Justin to be hysterical with fear, but the boy was glassy-eyed, numb. 'Are you okay?' Maynard said.

Justin did not answer.

'Hizzoner,' Nau said to the older man, 'tell him.'

The man put a hand on Justin's head and said, 'There is a time to live and a time to die. The sire dies and the son carries his name. A man may die, but his name lives on. A man may die, but his deeds are sung forever. You will witness the rite of passage, and when it is done your name will reflect the glory of the past. You will be Maynard Tue-Barbe.'

Nau raised his arms. 'Maynard Tue-Barbe!'

'Tue-Barbe, Tue-Barbe, Tue-Barbe ...' The chant swelled among the men around the clearing and dissolved into a cheer.

The noise seemed to awaken Justin. He looked at his father, and then at Nau, and he said softly, 'Don't kill him ... please.'

'Hush!' Nau said. He bent down and scooped Justin up and swung him on to his shoulders.

'He is not yet a man,' said Hizzoner.

'Soon.' Nau spoke to the woman. 'Goody Sansdents, how would you it were done?'

Maynard screamed, 'I don't want to die!' He looked up and saw his son teetering on the shoulders of the tall man. Justin gazed down at him and wept silently.

The woman slurred, 'Woold him!'

'Nay!' Nau laughed. 'I'll not woold a noble man.'

'I'll woold him myself, then. Give me the strap. And for a favour, I'll eat the eyes when they pop free.'

'I say I'll not have him woolded. He cannot face death without his eyes. He must see his destiny. Build a fire on his belly, and see what kind of man he be.'

The woman argued. 'He tore the eye from Roche.'

'Aye, but Roche was not of good blood. A stew of Portugee and zambo.'

'If he be so noble, let me keep him. I need my service.'

'There are catamites for the likes of you. Service is yours for the taking.'

'Catamites!' The woman spat in the sand. 'This one can give me what Roche could not: a noble son.'

Nau's grin faded. 'He is to die.' He looked to Hizzoner for corroboration.

Hizzoner nodded. 'That is the way.'

The woman snatched a dagger from Nau's belt, dodged around behind the big man, and stood beside Maynard, the knife poised over his groin. 'The covenant says the disposition is mine. Thus I dispose.' The woman's hand flew downward.

Maynard closed his eyes, awaiting a pain he could not imagine.

With a single stroke, the woman slit Maynard's bathing suit from waistband to crotch. She grabbed his genitals. 'This I will have!' She glared defiantly at Nau, then at Hizzoner. 'I will breed a line for the future to sing about. It is my right.'

The clearing was silent.

Maynard's pulse beat against his eardrums. The pains came and went in waves. He saw the woman's hand buried in his crotch, but he felt nothing from her tight grip: the burning in his shoulders and hips overwhelmed all other feeling.

Hizzoner spoke first. 'The covenant rules. It is her right.'

'But the way ...' Nau began.

'The way is custom, the covenant is law. The covenant says she can dispose.'

'But dispose does ...'

'... does not mean kill, not by the strictest letter.'

Nau was not pleased. With one hand, he removed Justin from his shoulders and dropped him to the sand. He said to the woman, 'He may live until the day you are adjudged to be with child. He is your chattel. If he once transgresses, the curse will be on you. With these hands' – he held his fists before the woman's face – 'I will rip your womb from your body and cast it into the sea.'

Made bold by rum and by her triumph, the woman shook Maynard's genitals. 'And if this performs ill service, I will cast *it* into the sea.' She laughed, and a ripple of relieved laughter spread through the clearing.

'You do not die well,' Nau said to Maynard. 'What did you do in life?'

'I write.'

'A scrivener? Perhaps you'll do double service, then. There has been no scribe since Esquemeling.'

'Esquemeling? You know about Esquemeling?'

Hizzoner interrupted, waving an admonitory finger in Maynard's face. 'Ye must know that woman has dominion over you. Do right to the widow. Esdras, 2:20.'

'Cut him down,' Nau said, and turned away.

Justin did not follow. He stayed by his father as two men cut Maynard's bonds and lowered him to the sand.

From the edge of the clearing, Nau commanded, 'Come, lad! He's your father no longer. He lives only as catamite to the hag.'

Barely conscious, Maynard saw Justin hesitate, sensed his dilemma. 'Go,' he whispered. 'Do anything. Roll with it.

127

Stay alive.' Maynard resisted the fog until he saw Justin obey. Then he fainted.

He did not know how long he slept, for his sleep was restless and bothered by dreams of mayhem terrifying in their realism. At times he was hot, and he felt his face bathed by liquid and his nostrils stung with the smell of vinegar; at times cold, and he felt the scratchy texture of coarse cloth against his raw skin.

He awoke during a night, naked on his back on a mat of woven grass. He was in a grass and mud hut, an eight-by-eight-foot hemisphere. When he tried to move he felt restraints, and he saw that his arms and legs were covered with vegetable poultices. The pain had subsided into a dull ache.

The woman sat beside him, cross-legged on the dirt floor, stirring something in a bowl. She had changed from the black coat into a grey poncho, had washed the charcoal from her face and had cut off her waxed hair. What remained was a soft inch or two of brownish-blonde turf. Maynard could not tell how old she was. Her angular face was creased and cracked from salt air and sun. Her fingers moved stiffly, arthritically, and her knuckles were swollen. But in a humid climate, arthritis often came to the very young. Her breasts – what little he could see of their outline beneath the poncho – were high and firm, and the flesh on her legs was lean. Allowing for the probability that weather and primitive living had aged her beyond her years, he guessed she could be thirty or thirty-five years old.

The light in the hut came from a rubber-covered flashlight that was propped between two bricks on the floor.

He pointed at the flashlight and said, 'Where'd that come from?'

'A prize. Roche took it. A rich one it was. Two whole boxes of repellent. Peaches. Nuts, too. And rum! He was hot for a week. They all were.'

'What happens when the batteries die?'

'They die. Like all things. Others come along.' She passed food to him. 'Eat.'

It was a slab of fish, raw, salted and dried, but still slimy.
'You don't cook food?'
'You're mad. You think I want to lose my tongue?'
'I don't understand.'
'Fires are dangerous. A green-wood fire during the day merits a flogging. For a fire at night, they cut your tongue.'
'Why are fires dangerous?'
'You are ignorant as well as craven. They would see us.'
'Who's "they"?'
'They,' she said. 'The others.'
Maynard raised the piece of fish to his mouth. He held his breath and tried to chew it. It was rubbery and caked with grit. He couldn't swallow. He picked the fish from his mouth and dropped it in the dirt. 'I'm not very hungry.'
'I thought as much,' she said. 'I'll fix that by and by.'
Maynard lay back and moved his limbs. The pain was ebbing. 'What's in these?' He patted one of the poultices.
'Spirea.' She poured liquid from a clay jug into the bowl in her lap and continued to stir.
Spirea, Maynard thought. Where had he read about spirea? Morison, Ernle Bradford, Homer? None of them, but Homer triggered the mnemonic. Spirea was a shrub whose bark was used by the ancient Greeks as an analgesic. Nowadays its extract was known as salicylic acid. Aspirin. Where had she learned about spirea?
With careful casualness, he asked, 'Is this a ... religious retreat here?'
'What?'
'Are you folks ... you know ... members of a cult of some kind?'
'What?'
Maynard abandoned indirection. 'What the hell is this place?'
'You're still sotted from the pain.'
'Who are these people?'
'This place is our home,' she said, as to a small child. 'These people are my people.'
'How long have you been here?'
'Always.'

129

He looked into her eyes, searching for a hint of a lie or a joke or a tease.

She smiled at him, hiding nothing.

'Were you born here?'

She hesitated, apparently unsure. 'I have always been here.'

'How old are you?'

'I have been a woman a hundred times,' she said. 'It was celebrated.'

'What do you ...?' Maynard stopped. Perhaps she was referring to menstrual cycles. A hundred periods, a hundred months – a little more than eight years. She had her first period at, say, twelve. She was, maybe, twenty.

'You have no children.'

'I had two, but they were killed.'

'Why?'

'They were poorly. It was seen.' She stopped stirring, and set the bowl on the ground. 'Roche provided, but he was always poxed.' She spat. 'Pig.' She reached for something behind her, in the darkness. It was a pewter canister, about a foot long, with a wooden plunger on one end. 'You are my last chance.'

'For a child?'

'A good child.'

'If you don't ...?'

She fitted a nozzle on to the open end of the canister and screwed it tight. 'I cease being a woman. I join the sisterhood.'

'Of what? Nuns?'

'Nuns!' She laughed. 'Prostitutes.'

'They force you to become a prostitute?'

'There is no forcing. It is the way.' She dipped the nozzle into the bowl and pulled back the plunger, drawing the thick liquid up into the canister. 'Roll over. On your knees.'

Maynard didn't move.

'Roll over!'

'What are you doing?'

'You are not well. You will not eat. You have poisons.' She brandished the canister. 'This will clean you out.'

Maynard slid backward, against the wall of the hut. 'You want to put that ... Oh no, thanks anyway.'

'You need a physic.'

'You're not sticking that thing ...' In the shadowy darkness, he did not see her move until she was on him. Her bony knee pressed into his sternum. She held a short-bladed knife under his chin and forced his head back.

'You are alive because I suffer it,' she said. 'The others would have you dead. You do well to remember. I need you, but I can take you to the edge of death, and bring you back, and take you to the edge again. I can teach you pain.' She moved off him. 'Roll over.'

Slowly, he rolled on to his stomach and brought his knees up under him. 'What's in that thing?' he asked weakly.

'Fish oil and medicines.' She raised his hips and spread his cheeks. 'The elders say it cures everything – shuffle-foot, strabismus, even pox.' She chuckled sagely. 'But their ways are old-fashioned. A clyster gives a good cleansing and relieves the poisons. Nothing more.'

Maynard closed his eyes and squeezed his temples. The sharp, cold nozzle slid up his rectum. It jabbed his prostate, and he felt a burning surge in his penis. As the nozzle probed deeper, the gratitude he had felt to the woman, the relief at being alive, began to wane.

She pushed the plunger. Maynard's insides flooded.

'There,' she said when the pump was empty. She slapped his butt, and he collapsed on to the mat.

He lay, gasping, with his face in the dirt. A fleeting vision of Dena Gaines crossed his mind. Did she do this? For *fun*?

His bowels cramped, rejecting the fish oil. He struggled to his knees. 'Where ...?'

The woman had anticipated his need. She stood at the entrance to the hut, holding back the skin that covered the doorway. 'Follow me.'

Clutching his stomach, struggling to keep his sphincter closed, Maynard staggered out into the night. He followed the woman through the underbrush until she stopped and pointed to an open trench, two feet wide, twenty or thirty feet

131

long. A symphony of bug sounds was broadcast from the trench.

Maynard did not know how to use the trench, but he had no time to ask questions. He straddled it and squatted, and his intestines erupted.

The woman stood beside him, hands on hips, admiring.

Dignity, Maynard thought, as, through a mist of nausea, he regarded the woman. Die with dignity but live like a pig. His bowels heaved in spasms, and he groaned. A burst of air exploded from his guts.

'Now you're fit,' the woman said.

'I think I'm gonna die.'

'Not yet. You've yet to serve your purpose. Come.' She took his hand and pulled him away from the trench.

'You're kidding,' he said. Oil oozed down his legs.

She led him through a maze of narrow, overgrown paths. The bugs followed. Mosquitoes swarmed on his back; flies buzzed around his legs and settled at the corners of his mouth, where they drank from his drool. He was too weak to brush them away. He heard voices in the distance – subdued, conversational – but saw no one.

They emerged from the underbrush on to a beach. She led him into the water and bathed him, rubbing wet sand over his soiled legs, rinsing him in salt foam.

She took him back to the hut and ordered him to lie on the mat. She pulled the animal skin across the doorway, trapping myriad gnats inside the hut. 'No wind tonight,' she said. 'The wind is all that keeps this land from bedlam.' She scooped a handful of something from a pot and knelt beside Maynard.

Alarmed, Maynard asked, 'What's that stuff?'

'Hog grease.'

'Where are you gonna put it?'

'Everywhere.' She laughed. 'It's all I have to keep the bugs at bay. Roche could have taken a ration of repellent from the last prize. He had a good choice. But he chose rum.'

She removed her poncho and, naked, smeared the grease all over her body. Her skin glistened in the flashlight beam.

To Maynard, the pork fat smelled like childhood Sunday

132

mornings, when his father would cook bacon and sausage and fry eggs in the residue.

'Where is my son?'

'With the other boys.'

'Are there many?'

'Now, only two. And the girl, Mary. The number changes.' She sat back and swabbed grease on the insides of her thighs.

'What will they do with him?'

'Do? Nothing. They will teach him to do for himself.'

'Are there others like me?'

She shook her head. 'You are the only one, the only one ever alive.'

'Why?'

'The covenant says, a grown man, a grown person, is corrupt. Only the young are pure.'

'What covenant are you talking about?'

'You will learn ... if you live to.' She filled her hand from the pot and began gently to rub grease on to Maynard's face. She greased his neck and his chest and his legs and his feet and between his toes. She missed nothing. Her fingers were soothing, and as she kneaded his thighs, he drifted towards sleep. He snored.

She snapped the back of her hand across his mouth. Her knuckles opened cracks in his parched lips. She glanced at his startled eyes, then scooped more grease from the pot and slathered it on his genitals. 'You'll not sleep yet.'

'But ... I couldn't!'

'Yes, you can. I'll show you.'

'Are you ...?'

'Ripe? No. But we must prepare for the day.'

I I

'It looks like mush,' he said, gazing into the earthenware bowl.

'It *is* mush. Cassava-root mush and mushed bananas. Good for you.'

'I'm not very ...' He stopped, for he saw that she had put down her sewing and was reaching for the clyster pump. He ate. She smiled and resumed sewing.

The cassava was white and pasty and tasteless; the bananas were overripe, almost pure sugar. What taste there was in the mush came from ground nutmeg.

If the mush was palatable, her sewing was nauseating. Using a sturdy sailmaker's needle, she was stitching together a garment from shreds of freshly killed, uncured animal skins that exuded a fetid stench.

'What are you making?'

'Trousers. For you. I cannot have you frying your bum.'

'You don't cure the skins?'

'Why? The sun and the water cure them. When they cure on the wearer, they suit him better.' She pinched two edges of flesh together, and juice ran down her fingers.

The odour made Maynard's lip curl. 'They smell like death.'

'Aye.' She looked up. 'What else?'

134

The skin covering the doorway was pulled back, and Nau stooped and entered the hut. He carried a wooden chest, with brass handles on either end. A length of half-inch chain lay atop the chest. He set the chest on the ground and shovelled the chain towards the woman.

She looked at the chain and at Nau. It seemed to Maynard that she wanted to argue, but instead she said, 'As you wish.'

'I'll not put in peril threescore people,' Nau said sharply, 'just so you may indulge your ... pet.' He turned to Maynard and slapped the chest. 'Here, scribe. Make order of this. Our assigns will thank you.'

'Where's my son?'

'You have no son. You have nothing. Soon you will *be* nothing, not in this world.' Nau's eyes were cold, giving nothing, encouraging Maynard to look away.

He refused. 'I want to see him.'

'Sometime, perhaps, if he chooses. I will ask him.' He backed to the doorway and said to the woman, 'Get to work, Goody. When you are a whore, you may live like a whore. As long as you are a woman, you will work like a woman.' He left.

Maynard saw the woman's hands shake as she took a final stitch in the hides. Angrily, she threw them into the dirt.

He wanted to say something consoling, but he did not know what. He tried: ' "Goody" is a nice name.'

' "Goody" is no name,' she said. 'It is an attachment, from the old days: "Good wife." My name is Beth.' She lifted an end of the chain. 'Come here.'

She wrapped the chain twice around his neck, stood and fed the free end over the main brace in the roof of the hut, then joined the two ends with a shiny new combination padlock. She snapped the shackle and spun the three little combination wheels.

'Do you really think . . .?' Maynard began.

'He is concerned. Now he need not be concerned. If you try to flee, you must take the whole house with you.'

'Do *you* ever think about fleeing?'

'From what?' she said. '*To* what?'

'This isn't much of a life for you.'

'I have no other.'

'There is more ...' Maynard gestured at the vague beyond.

'We are taught that more is worse, not better.'

'I could tell you ...'

'Aye,' she interrupted, 'and I could listen, and time would pass, and work would not be done, and my reward would be the wrath of l'Ollonois. As Jean-David Nau, he is a man as God made man; as l'Ollonois, he is a creation of the lord of darkness.' She gathered a wicker basket, a short-handled iron hoe, and a crude machete, and she left the hut.

When she had gone, Maynard sat on the dirt floor and listened. He heard the whisper of breeze in the dry leaves, the clicking and chattering of bugs, and raucous complaints of sea birds and, far away, sounds of hammering and sawing and men's voices.

He examined the lock that joined the ends of the chain. It bore no scratches, no signs of tarnish; it was still coated with a film of silicone. He judged that the lock had never been used. Probably, it had been taken from a recently captured boat and stored in its original plastic-and-cardboard container.

The lock mechanism contained a thousand possible combinations. The only one Maynard could surely eliminate was the one Beth had left: 6, 4, 8. He spun the wheels until the numbers read 1, 1, 1. Then he tried 1, 2, 1, then 1, 3, 1, then 1, 4, 1. It was inevitable that eventually he would find the combination, but the search might take days, or weeks, for he could fiddle with the lock only when he was alone, and he had no way of knowing how often, or for how long, he would be left alone.

As he tugged on the shackle after dialling 1, 9, 1, he noticed a tiny hole on the side of the lock. At first, the hole made no sense to him; what purpose could it serve? Then an image crept into his mind, of Justin squirrelling away his birthday money in a strongbox. He secured the strongbox with a combination lock. Unlike the locks Maynard was familiar with – on which the combinations were set permanently by the manufacturer – this one could be set, and changed, by the owner. Maynard recalled Justin poking a slim stylus into a hole on the lock and dialling the last three digits of their phone number. When he removed the stylus, the combination was set at those numbers.

Maynard let suppositions tumble in his head: suppose this lock had changeable combinations; suppose it was, in fact, new, unused, when it was taken from a boat; suppose that these people had found the instructions on the card too complicated to follow and had not bothered to reset the combination.

Still, the manufacturer would have had to set *some* combination of numbers. What was the simplest, the most logical? He dialled 0, 0, 0 and tugged at the shackle.

The lock popped open.

Maynard smiled to himself, pleased by his resourcefulness. He wanted to take off the chain and leave the hut and prowl around the island in search of a vessel on which to escape. No, he told himself. It was too early; he knew too little about where and with whom he was; the risk of capture was too great, the punishment for attempting escape unknown. He didn't know where Justin was. His new knowledge was an advantage, but he should husband it until it could be played for greater value.

He snapped the lock closed and returned the combination to 6, 4, 8.

He crawled over to the chest Nau had left and opened it. It was packed with papers – some old and frayed and yellowed, some joined in packets by twine woven from plant fibres, some crumpled and torn. All were handwritten, and on many the ink had faded to a shadow.

He crawled to the doorway, pulled back the skin, and blocked it with a rock. Dragging the chest into the shaft of light that streamed through the doorway, he sunk his hand into the chest and pulled out a paper. It was a coarse, grainy vellum, brittle and cracked with age. The ink was brown and faint.

It seemed to be an entry from a log or diary, scribbled in haste. But the writer had taken care to observe certain proprieties: 'An account of the events of the day of

September the 7th, 1797, writ in the blood of a quadroon due to the carelessness of the quartermaster, who knocked to bits the inkwell.

'At first light spied a two-masted barkentine and pursued her. Too swift for our sickly vessel. Planking started well at sea, caulked it with beef. Damn nigh sank, but made shore.

'Rum all out. Our company unhappy, somewhat sober, *too* sober. A damn'd confusion among us! Rogues a plotting – great talk of separation – so I looked sharp for a prize, any prize with liquor on her. Took one, a trader with a quantity of rum on board, so kept the company hot, damn'd hot, then all things well again.'

The paper was signed, with a bold flourish, 'l'O. V.'

As he took the papers from the chest, Maynard began to arrange them in chronological order in a circle around him. The earliest scraps, dated in the 1680s, he set on his left; the latest, some written on loose-leaf note paper and dated 1978, on his right. For the moment, he tried to see only the date on each document, but words and phrases caught his eye and compelled him to read.

'Tempest drove a vessel ashore,' said a paper dated 1831 and signed 'l'O. VI.' – Nau's great-great grandfather. 'Bartered with the master for drink. He seemed one of the old buccaneers, a hearty brave toss-pot, a trump, a true twopenny. But he asked sly questions and had a hidden motive, so I put him to the sword and his crew as well who refused to tell their true purpose even under duress. Hizzoner washed his hands of it and said we'd all meet damnation, so I put him to the sword as well after telling him that his talk was not a friend's talk and if he was not my friend he was my enemy, and if he was my enemy I was damn'd if he was going to draw another breath.'

Maynard discerned a pattern to the documents: the more recently they had been written, the less detailed they were, the less careful and less literate. Accounts of ships taken in the 1920s spoke of methods of capture ('... bored a hole in her bilges, packed some powder in and blew her ...'), cargo taken, and number of people killed. By the 1950s, there were simple lists of valuables recovered and prisoners taken. And the most recent account was a small scrap of notepaper on which was written: 'Sporter *Marita*, killed 2, tok 1 aliv. Fruits, rums, etc. Scutld the bich.'

Maynard dug deep into the chest and pulled out what appeared to be several bulky fragments of a single book, worn and thumb-stained pages held together by strips of fragile, flaky leather. He peeled back the leather strips and bent over the faded frontispiece: 'THE BUCCANEERS OF AMERICA,' it said, 'A True Account of the most remarkable assaults committed of late years upon the coasts of the West Indies by the Buccaneers of Jamaica and Tortuga (both English and French), by John Esquemeling (one of the buccaneers who was present at those tragedies).'

According to a barely legible printer's mark, this copy of the book was of the first English edition, translated from the Dutch, and published in 1684.

Maynard had read Esquemeling in a paperback reprint years before. A friend of his, a historian, had touted it as the only comprehensible reliable text about the early days of the so-called Spanish Main, and the fact that the book existed – had ever been written – was testimony to the hardiness and great good luck of the author.

Esquemeling had sailed to the New World in 1666 as a boy apprentice, but as soon as the ship docked in Tortuga, he was sold into slavery. He was bought by the Lieutenant General of Tortuga, whom he described as 'the most cruel tyrant and perfidious man that ever was born of woman'. Esquemeling was beaten and starved, and the only thing that saved him from death was his master's realization that if the boy died, an investment of thirty pieces of eight (an able-bodied seaman's salary was roughly two pieces of eight a month) was down the drain. Esquemeling was sold to a surgeon who fed him, treated him well, trained him in the rudiments of surgery and, finally, freed him in return for a promise that if Esquemeling ever found himself flush he would pay the surgeon a hundred pieces of eight.

Esquemeling decided to become a buccaneer, and for the next few years he served on several ships as a surgeon, a position whose authority and salary were commensurate with the contemporary state of medical science – that is, he was paid almost nothing and served beneath almost everybody. But he had a finely tuned ear and an active pen, and he took upon himself the task of chronicling the age of the buccaneers. He endured disease, battle, treachery, cruelty and ambush and, in 1672, returned to France and wrote his book.

The book was an immediate success, was circulated all over the known world, made Esquemeling a celebrity, and attracted lawsuits from the likes of Sir Henry Morgan, who claimed he was nothing like the brutal, opportunistic, rapacious genius Esquemeling portrayed him to be.

What had initially appealed to Maynard about the buccaneers, and why he had pursued the study of them, was that they were survivors – men of mediocre talent and no great aspirations who had hacked a living from a barren wilderness (a metaphor, Maynard thought, for a lot of us). They had gone on to plague the most powerful nation on earth. Many had died of natural ills, many others had been killed in battle or executed by their enemies, and a few had retired to riches, respectability, and even renown.

They had begun as runaway slaves, abused apprentices, shipwrecked mariners, and escaped convicts, all outcasts – by accident or design – from the civilized world. In the middle of the seventeenth century they established communities on Hispaniola and Tortuga and lived as hunters. They killed wild cattle and cured and smoked the meat on racks called *boucans*. They were known as *boucaniers*, later Anglicized into 'buccaneers'. They bothered no one and, in fact, contributed to the survival of countless ships' companies, for they provided vital supplies – meat, hides, and tallow – in return for cloth, gunpowder, muskets, and liquor.

When a man became a buccaneer, his past was erased. He took a new name, whose source might be in his country of birth (like Bartholomew Portugués or Roche Brasiliano) or in a physical peculiarity (Louis Bad-Ass, who had lost one of his buttocks in a fight, or Port Tack, whose nose had been bashed to one side). They asked no questions of one another, and of the outside world they asked only to be left alone.

140

The kings of Spain, however, had decreed that all trade with the New World must be conducted by Spanish ships. Never mind that the fleets from Spain arrived only once or twice a year, and that when they did arrive they carried pitifully few provisions. Never mind that to follow the letter of the law, the colonists must condemn themselves to life without building materials, clothing, or food. Technically, the colonists were not allowed to grow agricultural produce, make their own shoes, or trade with anybody for anything.

By existing, therefore, the buccaneers were outlaws subject to frequent assaults by the Spaniards, who slaughtered those they could catch and drove off those they could not. In their perverse wisdom, the Spaniards succeeded in depriving their colonists and mariners of a vital source of supplies, and, at the same time, in engendering in the tough, skilled, sea-savvy and wilderness-wise buccaneers an inveterate hatred of Spain.

Unable to survive as hunters of animals, the buccaneers became predators on Spanish shipping. They sailed small, fast vessels that could outmanoeuvre the bigger, slower Spanish galleons. Employing stealth more than force, they used weapons designed for speed, ease of access and close-in efficiency: knives, short-swords and hand-axes that would find the joints in a Spaniard's armour and dismember him while he fumbled to aim his clumsy arquebus.

The buccaneers' reputations spread through Spanish fleets and Spanish colonies like a virus, at first in proportion to the savageries they committed and, eventually, out of proportion to all reality. As one Spanish sailor cried on seeing his ship overrun by wild-eyed, ragtag, drunken, shrieking raiders, 'Jesus bless us! Are these devils, or what are they?'

By all accounts that Maynard had read, the worst of the buccaneers was Jean-David Nau, who took his name from his birthplace, Les Sables d'Ollone, in France. He was a nightmare figure to the Spaniards, worse by far than Henry Morgan. From Morgan there was always the chance of clemency; he was a man of whims. A Spaniard in the hands of l'Ollonois was a man who had only yesterdays.

141

Maynard flipped through the fragments of Esquemeling's book. 'It was the custom of l'Ollonois,' he read, 'that, having tormented any persons and they not confessing, he would instantly cut them in pieces with his hanger, and pull out their tongues; desiring to do the same, if possible, to every Spaniard in the world.'

Further along in the same handful of pages, Maynard found reference to the event that had given l'Ollonois mythic stature. Nau had captured some Spaniards and was trying to extract information from them, information they did not have. And so, Maynard read, 'l'Ollonois grew outrageously passionate; insomuch that he drew his cutlass, and with it cut open the breast of one of those poor Spaniards, and pulling out his heart with his sacrilegious hands, began to bite and gnaw it with his teeth, like a ravenous wolf, saying to the rest, "I will serve you all alike ..."'

Anathema to the Spaniards, l'Ollonois was popular with his own crews. He was reputed to be fearless and just. He adhered strictly to a code governing division of spoils. Most important, he was very successful. A voyage with l'Ollonois was as close as a buccaneer could come to a guarantee of ample booty, to be spent on a memorable orgy in the bar-rooms and brothels of Port Royal, Jamaica.

Maynard guessed that for his chronicle Esquemeling had, perforce, drawn heavily on hearsay; what first-hand authority he had had ended with his departure for Europe in 1672. And other historians, writing from an even greater distance, were more arbitrary and less reliable. The Age of the Buccaneers was said to have ended before the beginning of the eighteenth century. By then, Spain had ceased to be a formidable power in the New World, had become a dinosaur besieged by ferrets of several nationalities. The War of the Spanish Succession, which lasted until 1714, made buccaneering unnecessary: rather than be an outlaw, a captain could ally himself with one side or the other and plunder 'enemy' shipping under the aegis of his chosen sovereign.

After 1714, sufficient order had been established so that a man who raided anyone's shipping could make only feeble claim to noble or political purpose: he was a pirate. And even the fabulous 'golden age of piracy', around which so much romantic fustian had been spun, was slotted into a single decade. By 1724, Edward Teach (Blackbeard), Calico Jack Rackham, Samuel Bellamy and the others were all dead or retired to more pedestrian pursuits.

But now, sitting naked on a dirt floor, chained to the roof of a hut, the 'Trends' editor of *Today* realized that most historians had been egregiously sloppy.

He put the Esquemeling pages aside, stacked the other papers according to date, and continued to read. It did not take him long to find the missing piece; it was in a log kept by the first l'Ollonois until his final voyage.

By the early 1670s, the buccaneers had begun to attack Spanish settlements in Central and South America. They would hold the populace, or the town itself, hostage, exact what ransom they could, then flee to their island sanctuaries. But l'Ollonois' welcome was already thin in most of the buccaneers' refuges. He was a hunted man, and association with him was crime enough to warrant half a ton of rocks on the chest, a bamboo spike through the eardrums, or a dangle from the gallows. Even by the standards of his fellows, l'Ollonois' psychopathic blood lust was considered extreme. One sanctuary was closed to him after he had, in a drunken rage, amputated the arms of a whore who had refused to drink from a fungus-covered cask of wine.

'What they call society,' he had noted in his log, 'has got too pretty for me. I'll have my freedom. I'll be no shopkeeper.' He set sail for an uninhabited chain of islands known vaguely as 'the Caicos'.

'God does not love this place,' he wrote, 'so I shall. What God is said to love gives me grief, and what I love is sin to God. The Spaniards avow that God loves them; if that be so, then God is a fool.'

Maynard realized that there was much about the islands to recommend them to a fugitive from society. They were barren of food, water, timber, and wildlife, so there was no reason for any ship to stop. They were visited only by the shipwrecked, whose possessions and supplies could be confiscated, whose women (if there were any) could be prostituted, and whose lives could be either preserved – should the person have a useful skill – or summarily ended without fear of retribution.

Inhospitable as they were, the islands promised an endless supply of shipwrecks, for they sat between two of the most heavily travelled deep-water passages leading from Cuba, Puerto Rico, and South America into the Atlantic.

'We shall have visitors,' l'Ollonois wrote, 'and those that Nature will not arrest, I shall.'

He took with him twenty men – murderers whose freedom he purchased on the eve of their execution, by bribing the authorities and promising that the men would never again be seen; drunks whom he shanghaied on the docks; teenagers he seduced with assurances of romance and riches; and six kidnapped whores, two of whom turned out to be pregnant and all of whom were diseased. The whores he considered to be as important to his mission as food or gunpowder: he had to maintain a heterosexual community. He said homosexuality was like scurvy. It broke out on long voyages and wrecked the efficiency of a crew.

'If God and I agree on one matter,' his log said, 'it is that we abominate pederasty. A sodomite is worse than a plague. He forms strange alliances, pits man against man, demands favours for admission to his cavities. Such behaviour is to be expected in women. In anything else it breeds confusion.'

On July 2, 1671, l'Ollonois found an island that suited him: 'It lies half way up the archipelago – a wretched islet about a league in length and half a league in width – covered with scrub that might give sustenance to hardy cattle. To the east are trackless shallow banks no vessel can traverse; to the west blue water and a fish-hook cove that will conceal us and give us ambuscade. Everywhere salt marshes and hollows to fashion into cisterns. It may be a merry life, if the whores will cease their caterwauling.'

L'Ollonois had drawn in his log a crude map of the region, and Maynard tried to compare it to his memory of the marine charts. Navidad was missing – Maynard guessed that l'Ollonois had never seen it – and West Caicos and

South Caicos were rough lumps that bordered the Caicos Banks (a field of 'x's, to indicate shallow water). L'Ollonois' island was shaped like a kidney. It was off the air routes, out of the shipping lanes, surrounded (on modern charts) by warnings to mariners to steer well clear.

For more than three hundred years, the island had remained unseen, its people unmolested. No one had ever come here willingly, and, obviously, no one who had come had ever left alive.

If l'Ollonois' life on the island had its merriments – and there was no indication in the log that it had – it was also short. The last entry in the log was dated January 6, 1673: 'I will away at dawn, in the pinnace, with a dozen of the lads. I had thought that life would sustain itself on this hell-hole, but a few necessities are damn'd scarce, to wit – mercury – for all the whores – the damn'd lot! – are poxed; and citrus – Hizzoner's teeth are loose as dice in a cup; and muskets, to replace those with rotten locks; and rum; and even gold, for there are ships I can not take with my tiny company and must barter with; and lastly a few young boys and a healthy girl or two – if any exist on earth! Too many young are dying in the womb or soon thereout, be it pox or what.

'I have left command with my infant son; that is, the speckled harlot tells me it is my son, though her scabbard has fit every sword in the company, but I need a son so I do not quarrel. He is a scrofulous imp and may not last. I have appointed the shaman Hizzoner to be regent – a fine conceit, as if I were king. Well, I am prince, as much as any free man. If the child dies, Hizzoner will rule until I return to poke another harlot. I trust him because he fears me greatly. He will kill to uphold my order, for he knows I would pursue him to the bowels of hell and skin him by bits. Fear is power.'

According to the documents, Hizzoner waited a year before he declared l'Ollonois dead. He then assumed complete, tyrannical command, paying only token obeisance to l'Ollonois' slow-witted son, who bore, as a legacy from his mother, a white syphilis streak in his hair. Hizzoner wrote, and governed by, a covenant.

In 1680 a ship foundered on the inshore reefs. Among the survivors was the daughter of the governor of Puerto Rico, a little girl too young to have been exposed to venereal diseases. Hizzoner declared the girl to be his ward and sequestered her from the attentions of the other buccaneers. To the others, his purpose appeared entirely selfish. It was not.

When the girl was fourteen, Hizzoner impregnated her. As soon as she had borne a healthy boy, Hizzoner arranged the quiet demise of l'Ollonois' son. In an elaborate ceremony, laced with religious and mystical nonsense (a Bible scholar, Hizzoner could find textual justification for virtually any act, however savage or depraved), he decreed that the new baby was the rightful heir to power. He would continue as regent until the boy was old enough to take command. The festivities were fuelled with so much rum that no one found voice to object.

For insurance, Hizzoner had three more children by the girl. Then, bored with her and wearied by the importunate pleas of the randy men, he released her to the company.

Hizzoner hung on until 1690, by which time his first-born – though named l'Ollonois II and assigned lineage from the original – was fifteen. Hizzoner spent his last month drilling the boy on the covenant. When he was satisfied that he could do no more – he had, after all, given the community a new generation of undiseased leadership, as well as a code to live by – he removed his robe one night, went swimming in the sea, and never returned.

Maynard searched through the papers for a copy of the covenant. It was so prominent that he missed it twice: it was not a paper but a roll of parchment, sealed against decomposition by a thick glossy varnish.

'Whereas we are a free people,' the preamble to the covenant began, 'with right to make war or peace on any other people, but whereas we are also a community of men who must have order in their lives, now therefore we establish the following Covenant, and we swear by Almighty God to live by that Covenant, under pain of penalties set forth in each article hereunder.'

The articles followed:

1.

Every man shall obey the l'Ollonois, or in his absence, Hizzoner. Disobedience is a capital offence.

2.

He who shall flee, or try to flee, or keep secrets concerning the flight of others, shall be shot. Attempting to flee is a capital offence.

3.

He who shall attack another member of the Company, without fair warning, shall receive the Cat (thirty stripes). Should his victim die, the attacker shall be whipped unto death.

4.

He who shall lose a limb in battle shall receive 500 pieces of eight; if his life, his assigns shall receive the tenth part of the next rich prize.

5.

He who shall deprive a righteous woman of her chaste treasure without her permission, shall be shot. A righteous woman is a rare commodity, and sullying her is a capital offence.

The first Hizzoner had foreseen the changes time would work on the needs of the community, and beneath the articles he had added an afterword: 'Whereas no man can tell the future, it may become necessary to add to the Covenant. There shall be no deletions: the articles are forever inviolate. Additions shall be known as amendments, and they shall be attached hereunder.'

To the bottom of the parchment was tacked a sheaf of papers – the amendments. There were twelve in all. A few set penalties for offences that did not exist at the time the covenant was written. No individual could own a radio, for instance. The community kept one (all others were destroyed), and it was used only as a receiver. Transmitting any signal at all was a capital offence.

Nor could an individual own or consume any 'pharmaceutical', 'lest the madness overtake the company'. All pills and serums were destroyed, with the exception of penicillin, which was kept by the l'Ollonois and administered to anyone 'who has fire in his water'.

Creating smoke or fire that might be seen by a passing ship or plane was a corporal offence during daylight, a corporal offence with torment at night.

Homosexuals had been admitted to the community, albeit grudgingly, in the middle of the nineteenth century. A young woman brought yellow fever to the island and gave it to all the other prostitutes. In the space of a month, the female population dropped from twenty-six to five, and without legislative relief the surviving five would soon have died from overexertion.

'Whereas all men are now deprived of their natural function,' went amendment number six, 'and whereas their vitality and stoutheartedness are suffering from the deprivation, now therefore be it amended that a rank of catamites shall be established from the finest boys next taken. They shall have all the rights and restrictions of prostitutes, for prostitutes they shall be.'

That the recourse was regarded with distaste was demonstrated by an amendment to the amendment. 'This amendment shall be expunged when the community of females has been revived. Until that time, the catamites shall be catamites and nothing else. He who interferes beyond his function shall be shot. An impudent catamite is a capital offender.'

One of the earliest amendments acknowledged the uselessness of money in the islanders' daily lives. Foodstuffs and liquor were substituted for pieces of eight as compensation for injury and reward for prowess. The prostitutes were permitted to establish their own currency, and they chose delicacies (nuts, olives and candy), lingerie, and fragrances. The various changes in currency were noted on a long list of addenda. At the moment, according to recent notations in the handwriting of the current l'Ollonois, the items most prized were, in order: '1. 6–12 family size, 2. Deep Woods OFF, 3. Cutter (no good for nats), 4. meltin lead, 5. Haiti rum, 6. new guns.'

Why, Maynard wondered, were modern weapons given such low priority? And if they hadn't used money for the last couple of hundred years, what had they done with the money they had got?

But of far more concern to Maynard was an amendment that had been drafted in 1900. Evidently, it had been accorded more importance than most, for it had a title: ABOUT CHILDREN.

Whereas the state of innocence can be said to have been corrupted in all mankind by the age of adolescence, and whereas the loss of innocence brings the birth of wórldliness, and whereas a wordly person is a threat to the community for he has notions and knowledge that call to question (and thus put in peril) the life we cherish, now therefore from this time forward the community shall accept into its number no person over the age of thirteen years. All others shall, upon their arrest, be given present death, for it can be said that their lives have been full led and they can offer to the community nothing but disruption and disunity, agitating, as has proved their wont, for escape and discovery. A child is a hungry diner, whose plate may be filled with proper food for thought; a worldly person's plate is already filled with unwholesome fare.

A shadow crossed the doorway, quenching the light in the hut. The woman, Beth, unlocked the ends of the chain. She removed one end from the roof brace and left the other wrapped around Maynard's neck.

'Stand.'

Maynard stood. She took the hide trousers from the floor and helped him into them. The inside of the hides was still coated with wet blood and a film of fat, and the trousers squished as Maynard hiked them around his waist. Strands of mucous meat dangled against his kneecaps, and a putrid strench rose into his face.

She smeared hog grease on to his chest and back, gestured at the doorway, and said, 'Outside.'

'Where are we going?'

'Tue-Barbe has consented to see you.'

'Who's Tue-Barbe?' His senses had been fogged by pain; the name was like a moth that flitted in the twilight of his memory.

'Maynard Tue-Barbe, who was your son.'

Maynard looked at her. 'Consented? Nice of him.'

'Remember,' she said, jiggling the chain to urge him towards the door, 'the young are honoured here, for they are the future. The likes of you are the past. Dead.'

12

She led him by the chain along a twisting path through the underbrush. As they approached a bend in the path, Maynard heard laughter.

The path dissolved into a clearing. On the right was a rectangular, hogan-like building, eight or ten times as large as Beth's hut. A short, plastic, dime-store Christmas tree stuck out of the sand to one side of the door, decorated with tinsel and fruit rinds and shreds of coloured cloth.

'Where did that come from?' Maynard asked.

'A prize.' Beth increased her pace, eager to reach the other side of the clearing.

There was another burst of laughter, and two young men came out of the building, shoving and slapping at each other. Maynard stopped and stared. The chain tugged at his neck.

One of the men wore a gaudy, flower-print sarong, half a dozen bracelets on each wrist, and rings on every finger. The other man was nearly naked. The white-blond hair on his head was cropped close to his skull. His long, lean body was tan and oiled and hairless. The only clothing he wore was a grapefruit-size black leather codpiece, swollen to the point of bursting.

When the men saw Beth and Maynard, they stopped frolicking.

Beth looked at them and spat in the sand and yanked the chain.

As Maynard was jerked forward, he glanced back and saw the two men return Beth's contemptuous salute.

They came to another clearing, and Beth stopped a few yards before the end of the path. 'Do not pause here,' she said, 'or I will snap your neck.' She lowered her head, hunched her shoulders forward, and stepped into the clearing.

There were eight small huts in the clearing, each tended by a single woman. Two wore diaphanous gauze shifts, through which every detail of their bodies was visible. One wore a long, stained silk shirt and, above the waist, nothing but lipstick, which had been applied to her breasts in circles that made targets of her nipples. One wore a full set of long underwear, and when she saw the passers-by, she turned her back to them, bent over, unbuttoned the trapdoor in the rear of her trousers, presented her bare butt, and released a raucous fart.

One of them laughed and called to Beth, '*That*'s your salvation, Goody? He's a scrawny one.'

Another crowed, 'I'll find you a dog with a better weapon than that.'

'Roche is more formidable dead than that is alive,' laughed a third.

'Your pallet is ready for you.'

'We'll see you here before the new moon.'

Maynard blushed. He kept his eyes on the sand. He did not know that Beth had stopped until he ran into her.

She glared back at the whores, red-faced, furious. 'You cows!' she bellowed. 'I'll die of old age before I join you!' She shot her hand down the front of Maynard's pants and grabbed his balls. 'If this seems nothing to you, it is because you lack the alchemy to make it worthy.'

She removed her hand and dragged him away.

Trotting along behind her, Maynard said, 'How many women are there who aren't whores?'

'Twelve, all wed.'

'And how many men without wives?'

'Perhaps two dozen.'

'Why can't you marry one of them?'

'Married once, a woman has two courses: motherhood or whoredom.'

'Even if you do have a child by ... by me, the child will grow up. You can't be a mother forever.'

'Motherhood is permitted for thirteen years.'

'So after that, you'll have to become a whore anyway.'

'You think you have the answers.' She laughed. '*I* have the answers.'

'You won't be a whore?'

'If I live that long? Never. Who would pay to rut with the elderly?'

'What, then?'

She stopped and looked at him and said earnestly, 'I will be venerable. Sage. Consulted. Respected. Fed. Until the time comes for me to be put to death. I want that. And this' – she pointed to his crotch – 'can give it to me.'

The path ended in a cove entirely protected by limestone cliffs. It was, as the log had described it, a fish-hook cove: to reach open water, a boat would follow a channel south along a natural breakwater, then turn the corner and head north along another breakwater, then finally turn east to reach the opening to the sea.

Several boats were careened on the beach – two pirogues, a derelict Boston Whaler and four pinnaces, with sails furled.

At first, Maynard did not recognize Justin. He stood at the water's edge, flanked by Nau and the boy Manuel. He wore new clothes, a white cotton shirt and leather knickers like Nau's – and, in its shoulder holster, the Walther PPK.

As Beth and Maynard emerged from the path, Nau and Manuel assumed an imperious stance – legs spread, hands on hips. Nau spoke sharply to Justin, who tried, clumsily, to mimic their stance.

Maynard wanted to run to Justin, but Beth restrained him with the chain and walked him slowly down the beach.

When they reached a spot a few yards in front of Nau, Beth

153

stopped and pulled downward on the chain. Maynard did not know what was expected of him, so he resisted. She yanked down, hard, and forced him to his knees.

He looked up at the faces – at Nau's, which seemed to reflect his ancestor's conviction that power is fear; at Manuel's, which shone with precocious arrogance; and at Justin's – nervous, ill at ease, pained at the sight of his father humbled before him.

None of the three seemed to have anything to say, so at last Maynard said softly, 'How you doing, buddy?'

'Okay.' The word caught in Justin's throat. He said louder, 'Okay. How about you?'

Maynard nodded. He could not take his eyes from his son.

Nau nudged Justin, who fumbled for words and said, 'Where are the rest of the bullets for this?' He tapped the butt of the Walther.

'Back at the room. You know that.'

Justin looked at Nau and, in response to another nudge, said, 'Where?'

'In the bureau. Top drawer.'

Justin said to Nau, 'I didn't think he took them on the boat.'

Nau replied, 'I will have them fetched.' He said to Beth, 'That is all.'

She pulled Maynard to his feet.

'No!' Maynard said. 'Let me speak to him.'

'Speak of what?' Nau demanded.

'I'm his father!'

'I have told you ...'

Without thinking, Maynard snapped, 'Fuck your word games! He's my child, and I want to talk to him.'

Nau hesitated. He spoke, tightly, to Beth. 'Control him or I will kill him. I swear it.' Then he turned to Justin. 'Tue-Barbe?'

It took Justin a moment to realize he was being asked if he chose to speak to his father. He nodded uncomfortably.

Nau said to Maynard, 'You read the covenant. You are a worldly man who has no place here. He is ours to mould,

154

not yours. You may speak to him privately this once. Not again.'

Nau walked up the beach, followed by Manuel. Beth paused, not knowing whether to stay or follow. Then Nau motioned for her to drop the chain, and she followed.

Maynard rolled backward off his knees and sat. He patted the sand before him, urging Justin to sit. Justin glanced at Nau for guidance. Tentatively, he sat down opposite his father.

Maynard said quietly, 'Are you really okay? They haven't hurt you?'

'No. I'm okay.'

'We've got to roll with it, do whatever they say. Every day we're alive, we've got a chance. No matter what they want you to do, it's better than being dead. Do you know who they are?'

Justin shook his head. 'They talk funny. I mean, they don't sound like they come from America.'

Quickly, Maynard gave Justin a capsule account of what he had learned. When he had finished, he asked, 'What have you heard?'

'They say I'm never going to leave here. Is that right?'

'No. I'll find a way to get us out of here.'

'They say they're going to kill you. Are they?'

'They will if we don't get out of here first. Everything you hear, think of in terms of escape. Every fact, everything. Think to yourself: can we use it? Will it help us?'

'They told me there's no escape.'

'What did they tell you?'

'There are no motorboats. They don't keep any – what do they call them? – long-legged boats.' Justin tipped his head at the boats in the cove. 'Those are the only boats on the island.'

Maynard looked at the pinnaces. 'If we could sail one of them out into the shipping lanes ...'

'They're guarded, even at night.'

'How long have we been here?' Maynard saw that the question perplexed Justin. 'I slept. I don't know for how long.'

'This is the fourth day.'

'You haven't heard anything else? Anything that could help us? Think.'

'Nothing like what you mean. Just training.'

'Training for what?'

'They say to become a man.' Justin glanced up the beach at Nau, then whispered to his father, 'How can I be a man? I'm only twelve! They must be crazy!'

Maynard smiled. He reached for Justin's hand and patted it. 'What kind of training?'

'They want me to be an armourer. That's why they let me wear this.' He tapped the shoulder holster.

Looking into Justin's eyes, Maynard sensed a flicker of pride, as if, despite himself, the boy was pleased to have been given a measure of manly trust. And Maynard's own eyes must have shown reproach, for Justin looked away.

'Do you keep it loaded?'

'I have to. L'Ollonois says that an empty gun is like a eunuch – all show and no force. What's a eunuch?'

'Take a couple of slugs out of the clip and hide them somewhere.'

'What for?'

'Just in case. You never know when they'll come in handy.'

'L'Ollonois says we have to save every bullet.'

'Justin ... if you listen to him, you *will* be here forever. He's *not* your friend.'

'He says that if someone isn't his friend, he's his enemy, and if he's his enemy, he should be killed. I don't want to be killed.'

'You won't be killed. You're too important to him.'

'Me. Why?'

'I'm not sure, exactly. I think he's worried about the future. Anyway ... tell me where do they keep the guns?'

'Everybody keeps one. L'Ollonois keeps the extras.'

'What are they?'

'Flintlocks and percussions. L'Ollonois has an old M–16, but it's all rusty and doesn't work.'

'There are no modern weapons?'

'No, except for this.' Justin touched the Walther. 'They don't like them, because they can't reload them. Once the bullets are gone, they can't get any more, so they throw the guns away. That's why he wanted to know how many bullets we have for this.'

'What does an armourer do?'

'A bunch of things. Moulds bullets. There are three sizes: pistol, musket, and bird shot. He keeps the arms cleaned and greased – fit, they call it. He fixes them: I'm learning how to take a lock apart and put in a new spring. It's weird.' Justin smiled, sharing the revelation with Maynard. 'If you take care of them, flintlocks last forever. There are only about three moving parts in the whole thing.'

Maynard could not return the smile. 'I wonder what Mom is up to,' he said.

Justin started. 'Yeah.'

'Aren't you curious?'

'Sure. I just ... hadn't thought about it.'

'Think about it.'

Nau called, 'Tue-Barbe!'

Justin hopped to his feet. 'Did your great-great-granddad really kill Blackbeard?'

'No. That was some other Maynard.'

'They say he did. That's why they named me that: Kill-Beard.'

'Well ... don't argue. Roll with it. I'll think of something. Trust me.'

'Okay.' Justin was nervous. 'Gotta go.'

Justin turned away, and Maynard watched him scamper up the beach.

Beth returned and lifted the chain from the sand. Maynard did not notice her; he stared after Justin until he and Nau and Manuel disappeared around a far point.

'He is gone,' Beth said.

'He's just up there a-ways.'

'I mean, he is gone. From you.'

'I know what you mean, but ...'

'The sooner you accept that, the sooner the pain will ease.'

'I'll take the pain.'

She tugged gently, and Maynard followed.

'I have styluses for you,' she said.

'For what?'

'He would have you use the time you have left ...' She stopped, suddenly embarrassed at her bluntness, '... use your time to write a chronicle. Like Esquemeling.'

'Chronicle? You mean copying. I have nothing to chronicle.'

'You will, soon.'

'How do you know?'

'Many things are growing scarce – rum and spray and citrus. Many things. There is talk of eating leather. Soon a prize must be taken. A rich one.'

They passed the whores' encampment, and again exchanged pleasantries, passed the catamites' lodge, and again spat salutes. As they approached Beth's hut, Maynard asked her, 'How much time do you think I have?'

'Oh, a long time,' she said encouragingly. 'I am just now feeling the tiny pains that tell me my cycle is beginning. I would give you a very long time.'

'Really?' Maynard said, counting. 'I'd give me about a week.'

He waited until her breathing slowed and deepened. And then, to be sure, he waited a few minutes more. She began to snore. Her lips moved and her brow furrowed, as she argued with a creature in her dream.

He felt along the chain until he found the lock. He could not read the numbers of the combination, so he crawled to the doorway and pulled back the skin and held the lock up to the moonlight. He dialled 0, 0, 0, and the lock opened.

He timed his movements with the chain to the sounds of her snores. When he was free, he rejoined the ends of the chain, snapped the shackle closed and spun the combination wheels. Somehow, vaguely, he hoped that this would exculpate Beth from having helped him escape. If, in the morning, they found the lock open, they might accuse her of setting him free; if the lock was securely closed, they might attribute his flight to magic, or at least legerdemain, and consider themselves lucky to be rid of him.

He crawled out of the hut and held a finger up to the wind. There was a soft, steady breeze from the north, so he headed south. He had no knowledge of the local tides or currents, but he knew that an offshore breeze would help him float farther away from the island.

He made no attempt to find or free Justin. He was certain that the boy was being kept confined, under guard. Even if he could free him, he did not want to expose him to the risks he himself was prepared to take: to drift alone in the open ocean until he encountered either land or a boat. Justin would be safer here, until he could return with armed help. He had convinced himself that, no matter what he did, Nau would not harm the boy. He had examined every conceivable rationale Nau might use for punishing the boy for his father's escape; none was practical. And from all Maynard had read and observed, Nau regarded violence and brutality as practical tools.

On the beach at the southern tip of the island he found a log of driftwood. He had neither the time nor the means to make a proper raft, but he wanted something with him that would float, something on which he could rest. He pushed the log into the water and tested it with his hand, to make sure it was not rotten or so sodden that it would sink. It was dry and light, and it bobbed briskly.

He walked away from the beach until the water was chest-deep, and then he tucked the log under his arm and let himself float, testing wind and current. If there was a current, it was very weak; the wind was moving him – slowly but perceptibly – away from the island.

He was about fifty yards offshore when, as he paddled with his feet, he felt a searing, stinging sensation in his thigh. Surprised, his impulse was to shout or curse, but he clamped his mouth shut. A jellyfish, he told himself. Or some tiny stinging seabug. He had not been bitten, was not cut or bleeding.

He reached down with his hand and touched his thigh, and suddenly his hand was afire. He grunted in shock and jerked his hand back, and whatever was burning him was dragged across his stomach in tracks of agony.

He spun around, and his chin struck something soft and flimsy, like a balloon, a cloudy white bubble that rocked gently from his touch.

A man o' war.

Reflexively, he flailed with his arms to get away from it, and his flailing snared the skein of toxic tentacles that hung beneath the bubble. He splashed and kicked and smeared the poisonous whips all over his face and chest. It was as if someone was removing his skin with a hot knife.

He struck at the thing with the log and knocked it aside. He struggled for clear water, still choking off the screams that fought to escape his throat.

He was free, and for a moment he thought he might control himself, might continue. But then new lashes raked his back, and more slid between his legs and scraped flame across his inner thighs.

He turned again, frantically, and all his eyes could see was an armada of opaque white bubbles. He was in a field of men o' war.

Now, finally, he screamed. His arms slapped at the water, his feet kicked, and every movement brought new agony.

Shrieking, lurching spasmodically, he churned towards shore. His feet touched bottom; he tried to run. His fingers clawed at his chest, trying to peel away the pain.

He flung himself on the beach and writhed in the wet sand. Movement did not ease the pain, but he could not stay still. He bucked and rolled and twitched like a berserk marionette.

Then something struck him on the chest and pinned him to the sand.

He heard a voice say, 'You bloody fool!'

He thrashed. 'Stay still!' The voice commanded. 'Jackass!'

Was it raining? Liquid was hissing down on him, warm, acrid-smelling. It felt good. Wherever the liquid touched, the pain seemed to seep away.

He tried to speak, but his tongue was too thick to move. A heavy fog spread through his brain.

He heard a new voice, arguing with the first. A man and a woman.

'You were warned.'

'He did not ...'

'He would have ...'

'But he ...'

The voices faded. He was unconcerned, for he assigned the voices to a dream.

A scream. Not his. Another scream. A woman. Why was a woman screaming? Then a scream that went on and on and on.

He sat up and shook his head. The pain was there, but dull now, bearable. The scream did not stop.

He looked to one side and saw Beth. She was staked, spread-eagled, naked, to the sand. Her stomach and chest and legs were crisscrossed with welts. A frail, cloudy bubble – a man o' war 'sail' – lay on either side of her. The tentacles had been draped across her.

When she saw him, she yelled, 'Piss on me!'

'What!?'

'Piss on me! It is the only way! I did as much for you!'

He did as he was told, and soon her shrieks subsided into sobs and whimpers.

Leonard Hiller was feeling righteously indignant, as he always did when a source declined to be interviewed – especially a source who claimed to be a member of the fellowship of journalists. 'What do you mean, Trask said no? Who does he think he is?'

'"No" wasn't exactly the word he used,' said Dena, checking her note pad. 'He said that as far as he was concerned, *Today* could go crap in its corporate hat. *He* didn't say it; his PR man said it.'

'What did you tell him?'

Dena blushed. 'I told him I bet that's how he got off, talking dirty to women.'

'Where's Trask now?'

'Nassau. He's supposed to leave in a day or two. He's going to the out-islands.'

'Tell Miami to get a man over there. I want him aboard that boat. I don't care if he has to charter another boat and chase him down. I want a Trask interview, and I'm not about to give up just because he's being coy. I mean, this is the father of modern media! He quits, and billion-dollar companies get the runs. The most trusted man in America doesn't trust television anymore! Two hundred and thirty million people believe every word out of that man's mouth, and suddenly he doesn't think there's anything worth saying. That is *news*!'

'The *news* is that he wouldn't prostitute himself. These days, that makes him the Messiah.'

'Miami can charter a plane if they have to.'

Dena nodded. 'The man from the Coast Guard called again.'

'What man?'

'About Maynard.'

'Oh, Christ . . .'

'He says he talked to the pilot who flew Maynard and the boy to some island. The next day they disappeared.'

'I told you, he wigged out and went native.'

'The trouble is, he took his son with him.'

'So what?'

'His mother has been on the phone to the chairman's office.'

'How do you know that?'

'They called me. They wanted to know what I knew about it.'

'If the Today Publications Company wants to mount an air-sea rescue operation for him, that's their business.'

'They don't *want* to, exactly. Blair's ex-wife is in the ad business. She has a lot of clients who advertise in *Today*. And all our other rags, too: *TV Week*, *Health & Happiness*, you name it.'

'She's *threatening* us?'

'Not in so many words. But she is . . . eager, let's say . . . to find her child. She's already tried to get the FBI involved.'

'On what grounds?'

'Kidnapping.'

162

'Good God ...'

'She's going to go look for him, and she wants us to help her. I can't say I blame her.'

'I don't *blame* her either. But what am I supposed to do?'

'You were talking about chartering a plane ...'

'Yeah, but ... Okay,' Hiller sighed. 'Call her.'

13

Every day at dawn the pinnaces left the cove, and every evening at sunset they returned, empty. Twice, in frustration, the men attacked and sank native fishing sloops and killed the fishermen, but the victories were so worthless, the rewards so puny – a few bushels of conch, a few dozen spiny lobsters – that they stopped molesting the native boats and steered well clear of them.

The men grew bored and restless and hungry for food more savoury than dried fish and cassava paste. The half-dozen cows had not yet calved, so beef was in short supply, and the few remaining hogs – skinny and tough in the best of times – were stricken with an ailment that swelled their eyes shut, puckered their skin, and made them wobble as they walked. The memory of an outbreak of diarrhoea dehydration was fresh enough in Nau's mind to make him declare any suspect food inedible.

Liquor was rationed. It was a step Nau was loath to take, for booze was an anodyne for discontentment. A drunken rebel was controllable, and he would sleep off his rebellion; a surly, sober rebel thought too clearly, hatched too many intricate plots, and was unpredictable. But the community was running out of alcohol, and Nau's rationale went: better to keep half the company half-lit half the time than to run the risk of having all men sober all the time.

However, the rationing was soon overturned by petition from the whores. The community might suffer politically from total abstinence, they argued, but in the meantime they were suffering physically at the hands of the disgruntled men. Drunk, their customers were malleable; sober, they were impossible. So the whores relinquished their own rations and exacted a similar pledge from the wives, who were better off than the whores only in that they suffered the abuse of but one man. Nau agreed to the bargain and restored the men's traditional rations of a bottle a day.

Maynard's days slipped into a dull routine. In the morning, Beth would wake him and coax him into servicing her. No matter how reluctant he was – and he was always intellectually reluctant, since every act was, potentially, the one that would give life to her body and consequently take life from his – she would employ threats, cajolery, tickles, kneads, and massages until, inevitably, she succeeded.

His feelings for her were equivocal: she had saved his life; he had repaid her by trying to escape and causing her agony, and for this he felt guilty. But her intercession on his behalf had been entirely selfish, and by servicing her he was holding up his end of the bargain, so he felt honourable. Sexual intimacy had begun to breed (if, as yet, nothing else) a measure of fondness: she was demanding but solicitous, inexhaustible but gentle. She was simple and candid and totally absorbed in her crusade to attain her ideal position within her community.

Either by incapacity or intent, she refused to consider a life beyond the island. She claimed to know nothing about her existence prior to arriving on the island, but Maynard was sure that her amnesia was the direct result of an iron determination to block out anything that might interfere with survival and success within the perimeters of local laws and customs. Memories would trigger longings, which would, in turn, trigger fruitless aspirations. Better to have no memories.

She would not permit Maynard to talk about the outside world, except in terms of his family. She was eager to know about his wife – not about what she did or what she wore or

165

where she went, but what kind of person she was: loving or cold, harsh or lenient. And she wanted to know everything about how to raise a child. Always, the conversations returned to that: how she would succeed as a mother. She truly cared for the child that was yet to be, and Maynard found her concern touching.

Once, he asked her to help him escape, to work with him at night building a raft or a boat. He promised to take her with him and Justin, to ensure that her child would be born in the finest hospital, to support her indefinitely.

She responded angrily to the proposal, accusing him of violating a code. He couldn't tell whether her anger was genuine or a manifestation of confusion at the planting of an unwelcome seed in the orderly garden of her mind. He tried to explain that from his point of view, anything was fair if it would save his life. She couldn't blame him for wanting to live. She replied that he was wasting his breath, and she forbade him from raising the issue again.

He decided that her reluctance was based, at least in part, on a profound fear of the unknown. Before he could even hope she would listen to another proposal, he would have to – somehow, subtly – convince her that she could survive off the island.

After what she referred to as 'the morning breed', she would feed him. Maynard had learned never to look at his food, always to hold his breath before he took a bite (thus blocking his sense of taste) and to hum when he chewed, so he would not hear, as once he had, the crunch of a bird's skull between his teeth. If Beth chanced to look away while he ate, Maynard hurried to pluck the insects and slugs from his bowl, but usually she monitored his every bite. She was like a fastidious cat owner, determined to maintain her pet at the peak of health.

They always took a morning walk, watching the shipwrights caulking hulls and sewing sails, the women doing laundry (boiling clothes in seawater) and collecting roots and birds' eggs, the cattle-tender plying his charges with herbs and massages to encourage healthy deliveries, the swineherd – a young man blinded, Maynard was told, when a battery exploded and sprayed him with acid – squatting in the hog yard lamenting the sorry state of his diseased pigs, and Nau and Hizzoner sitting cross-legged on a knoll overlooking the sea, searching for signs of success from their scouts.

Beth took him by the armoury – a hut, always guarded, beside Nau's – only when the children were somewhere else. He begged her to let him see Justin, even from a distance or from hiding, but always she gently refused. He is gone, she would say, he is a new person. Maynard's elliptical arguments – one went: 'If I'm dead and he's a new person, he won't see me and I won't recognize him, so what's the harm?' – were met with a silent smile.

Most of the day he spent chained to the roof of the hut (the combination lock had been replaced with a key lock), writing, dipping a sharpened quill into a bowl of fish blood (for richness of colour) mixed with berry juice (for permanent set) and scratching the saga of the l'Ollonois line on to a roll of brown wrapping paper acquired, he assumed, from some unlucky vessel. The writing was drudge work, but it gave him relief from his otherwise ceaseless pursuit of a way to escape.

He thought he had thought of everything, and everything he had thought of amounted to either fantasy or suicide. All his options began with him getting loose from the chain around his neck. That he could do, either by picking the lock or, if he had to, by dismantling the hut and lugging the chain with him. Stealing a boat was unlikely, and if he succeeded he still could not be sure of freeing Justin. If he could get a boat and Justin and some water, he could poke holes in the other boats and render them temporarily useless, then put to sea. But he had seen how quickly a damaged boat could be repaired, and how expert these men were at reading winds and tides. He would be caught before he had gone a mile.

His plan had to be perfect, for he could not risk failure. He would not be given another chance; he would be killed instantly. The prospect of his own death was bothering him less and less; he had almost accepted his end as imminent. But his end would spell Justin's, too – not a physical demise, but the end of opportunity, condemnation to a life barren of promise. Maynard had no designs on immortality for himself, would not be chagrined to leave the world no better a place than he had entered. But he didn't like these sentiments in himself: he wanted to want immortality, wanted to want to change the world. And most of all, he wanted Justin to have the chance.

Now and then, he thought of praying, but he felt like a wretched hypocrite. It was the same impulse he had felt as a child: 'Dear Lord, if you'll let me pass this exam (or get this date with Susie, or whatever), I swear I'll . . .' As soon as the crisis passed, prayer was forgotten.

What *would* he do if he got away? How would he change his life? He didn't know. He would appreciate it more, that was for sure, would treat every minute as something precious – not something to be preserved, safely, for its own sake, but something to be filled with experience and learning. He had lost his capacity for wonder; he would try to regain it, and to keep it alive in Justin. But all those thoughts were safe and easy. He had first to confront the hard one: how the hell was he going to get off this island?

He had debated trying to get to the radio in Nau's hut. If, as he had read in the covenant, there was a penalty for transmitting signals, that must mean that the radio was capable of transmission. But, supposing that he could co-opt the guard – and what, he thought amusedly, could he offer the man? – whom could he be sure of reaching? What would he say? One possibility was to send an SOS to all ships, giving longitude and latitude (which he would have to guess). Another was to place a call to the Miami or Nassau marine operator. But to reach across five hundred or a thousand miles of open water and changing weather, that would have to be one formidable radio, powered by a bank of batteries.

Always Maynard's musings ended with the faint hope that someone might be looking for them. When he found himself wallowing in that hope, he knew it was time to give his brain a rest. Nobody would be looking for him because nobody cared very much what happened to him, a thought that

168

was mildly depressing but not at all surprising. He had no commitments, and no one had any to him. His disappearance would anger Hiller, to whom it would be an inconvenience, and annoy a couple of editors of other magazines who were expecting him to deliver freelance pieces. Otherwise, no one would miss him, which didn't particularly bother him. But the fact that it didn't bother him, bothered him. He decided that, by God, there is more to life than surviving, and he laughed at himself for deciding that now.

Their one chance was Devon. By now, she would be frenzied. She would have demanded the mobilization of the militia, placed calls to the White House, and would be hectoring Hiller to distraction. Maynard's worry was that all her flurry would generate no action, until it was too late.

At the end of the day, Beth would bathe Maynard in the ocean, feed him, and take him for another walk.

One evening, they found Nau sitting alone on a cliff above the cove, watching two of his pinnaces duel for puffs of breeze that would bring them home. Beth flicked the chain, to urge Maynard along, but he resisted. Nau heard the clink of the chain and turned around.

'Just passing,' Beth apologized. 'We'll be gone.'

Maynard expected Nau to nod curtly and turn his gaze back to the sea. Instead, he said, 'How goes your scribbling?'

'A little more every day.'

'And now you know all there is to know about us.'

'Hardly. I know a few of the "whats" – what to do, the way you got here, what you live on – but I don't know any of the "whys", like why you stay, why you do what you do, why no one has found you.'

'Too many questions, the middle one first: we do what we do to live. Life is staying alive. Why has no one found us? We take great care. No one comes to us; we go to them.'

Maynard gestured at the two pinnaces. 'None of them has ever struck out on his own, tried to escape?'

'Rarely, and never successfully. Each man is watched by another, and in each boat there is one man – at least – whose

169

life is mine several times over. But it is not an issue. What would they escape to?'

'The unknown. For all they know, it may be better than this.'

'There is no unknown. They know what is there. They have been taught. Some – Tue-Barbe will be one – have recollections, but time allows us to cast them in their true light.'

'*What* do they know is out there?'

'Governments of crafty rascals and damned villains, half dedicated to preserving their own suet and the other half to throwing them over so they may purvey their own villainy. Misery, hunger, drones who serve queens they know not. Thus it has been since the beginning, and thus it shall be.'

'What do you have here? Misery, sickness, drudgery ...'

'... freedom ...'

'To do what? Kill people?'

'Kill, kill, kill ... why does death so concern you? A mountain explodes and thousands die; a river overflows and thousands die; nations war on each other and millions die. Those are accepted as nature's way. But an administrative death' – Nau drew a finger across his throat – 'raises the hackles of the righteous, while in fact it is as natural as the others – a clean, quick, sure way of excising a sore, a vital surgery. He who ignores a festering wound, and trusts it to sort itself out, poisons the whole. Cut it out and burn it closed and be done with it.'

'I can't accept that,' Maynard said.

Nau laughed aloud. 'Said the chancre to the surgeon, "I can't accept that. 'Tis the unkindest cut of all." What you can accept, or cannot accept, is of no concern to me. Or to you. It will be done.'

'What purpose will it serve?'

'We will be rid of you, shed of an annoyance or, worse, of an agitation.'

'And of a chronicler,' Maynard said hopefully. 'You need a chronicler.'

'Not one whose mind is deep-poisoned, whose ways are set. If I need one, I will teach one.'

'How long do you think all this can last?'

Nau shrugged. 'A day, a year, an age. Who knows? They say it ended three hundred years ago, but it did not.'

'It will.'

'Of course. And when it ends, it ends. I am a simple man and I have a simple charge, as did my father and as will my son: to keep one generation alive.'

'How old is your son?'

'I have no son.'

'Then how ...?' Maynard's words were throttled by a tug on the chain.

Nau smiled at Beth. 'It matters not, Goody.' He said to Maynard, 'I had a son. His mother died bearing him – the best of all signs, for it meant that all her strength, not just a part, had gone into the body of the child. He was killed in an engagement.'

'How old was he?'

'Ten. He was being readied for ...'

'Ten? At *ten* he was fighting?'

'Surely. At thirteen he would be a man. He fought well but not cautiously. He was too eager to please. So he died.'

The pinnaces slid, one after another, into the cove. Nau rose and stretched his legs. 'I have been giving thought to something,' he said. 'I need not ask you; I need not tell you. But I think it might give you pleasure, so I will tell you.'

Reprieve, Maynard thought, and he said, 'Please do.'

'When you have done your job for Goody, and have been sent on your way, I think I shall adopt Tue-Barbe. I think he has leadership within him.'

Maynard stood, stunned, unable to speak.

Nau patted him on the shoulder. 'I thought that would please you,' he said, and he walked down the hill toward the cove.

A noise jarred Maynard awake in the darkness. It was a horn, a hollow, mournful monotone that he imagined as similar to the sound that summoned Biblical armies to battle.

171

Beth was already up. Hurriedly, she wrapped the chain around his neck and motioned him to the door.

'What's ...?'

'The hunt. Go!'

'At night?'

'Go!' She kicked at him. 'A tenth of this one is mine. I'll not be late.'

She trotted along the paths, and he followed her footsteps.

Night was almost over; between bushes he could see patches of twilight dawn. He heard coughs and wheezes and muttered curses and the crackle of branches breaking, as other people ran along other paths.

They arrived at a clearing, and Beth slowed to a walk. The other women halted at the edge of the clearing, but Beth – evidently because she had a stake in the proceedings – was permitted to advance, and to take Maynard with her.

Nau stood before his hut, with pistol bandoliers across his chest and cutlass and dirk at his belt. Beside him stood Hizzoner and before them Manuel and Justin. A flashlight was stuck in the sand, facing upward, and the beam reflected fear and excitement from Justin's eyes.

A huge pot sat at the centre of the circle, and when all the armed men were present, Hizzoner stepped forward and poured gunpowder from a powderhorn into the pot. 'Drink,' he said stirring the brew, 'so ye each may have the strength of ten, so ye may bring honour to the company and to yourself, and so ye may fear no evil. Amen.'

Solemnly, each man dipped into the pot, using a cup or a hat or his hands. The men coughed and sputtered and laughed and slapped each other on the back and drank again.

Nau urged the two boys forward. Maynard saw that Manuel knew what to expect: he held his breath and splashed the liquid into his face. He choked, and his eyes watered. To Maynard's surprise, Manuel drank a second time, as if he also knew that he would need the courage the liquor offered.

Maynard hoped that Justin would look at him before he drank, for he wanted to exchange a smile or a wink. Partly,

172

he wanted to give the boy support and encouragement; mostly, he wanted to reassure himself of the strength of the bond between them.

But Justin did not look at him. He cupped his hands and dipped them and swallowed all he could, before his gag reflex took hold and sprayed liquid in a fine shower. The men laughed, but Justin did not blush. He drank again, and this time he kept it all down.

The men cheered. Nau clapped Justin on the back, and Justin smiled proudly.

A knot formed in Maynard's stomach, and his ears felt hot.

'Goody,' Nau said to Beth, 'this will be your legacy from Roche. May it be rich.'

'It cannot *but* be richer than *he*, l'Ollonois.' Beth laughed and drank from the pot. A shudder passed through her shoulders, and she coughed. 'God love the innkeeper! My guts cry out, brimstone!' She laughed and drank some more.

'Now you, scribe,' Nau said to Maynard. 'You do not want to face this day without fire in your belly.'

As Maynard bent over the pot, he glanced at Justin. The boy was smiling at him. Maynard smiled back, and winked. Then he saw that Justin's eyes were glazed, his smile frozen, his gaze fixed not on his father but on some distant, private vision.

Maynard drank. He swallowed slowly, squeezing the liquid down his gullet in a thin stream. It burned his throat, spread a web of warmth through his chest, and landed in the pit of his empty stomach like a rain of lava. Its stringent aftertaste was of rum and raw alcohol and sulphur.

Nau held up his hands, commanding silence. A few of the men darted to the pot for another draught, then returned to their ranks.

'We have word of a ship rich-laden,' Nau said, 'coming under sail from the sou'west. Her cargo is unknown, her crew a baker's dozen. She is surely armed. If any man among you would withdraw, let him speak.'

A chorus of 'No!' was followed by more laughter, more quick trips to the liquor pot.

'The shares will be as always, with this exception: Goody Sansdents will take the tenth part, of her choice, before the spoils are divided. Any man who holds back from the company will suffer present death.' Nau put a hand on the shoulder of each of the boys. 'To each of the lads will go a half-share, for to them will fall the task of firing the prize.'

Manuel grinned. Justin's vacant smile did not change.

'You're not taking *him*!' Maynard shouted, pointing at Justin.

'Aye, scribe, and you too!' Nau smiled. 'He must learn his surgery, and you must chronicle it. Goody, you and the scribe will ride in Hizzoner's pinnace. The boys will be with me. And now,' he raised his voice to the company, 'let us prepare. If our number be small, our hearts are great, and the fewer persons we are, the more union and better share in the spoils.'

Nau's last statement was spoken with a lilt that suggested to Maynard that it was a ritual, and when Nau was finished, Hizzoner stepped forward and continued it.

'Bow your wretched heads,' Hizzoner said. 'O Lord, sail with us on this day, for we go forth to trials we know not of. Keep firm our hearts and strong our arms, for what we do we do in Thy name, through Jesus Christ our Saviour. Amen.'

The benediction over, Nau said, 'Fire your furnaces, lads, get damned hot, for this will be a day like the old days.'

Each pinnace carried six men. The boys were extra, as were Maynard and Beth. They sat amidships, before the mast, where they could be watched from fore and aft and where no reckless movement, no sudden shifting of weight, would pose a hazard to the stability of the tippy boat.

The commander was in the stern, at the tiller. His second – in Maynard's boat the second was a stubble-faced young man who had filed his canine teeth into fangs and whom Maynard had heard called Jack the Bat – crouched between the thwarts and tended the sail. On the bow thwart sat a

174

marksman. A long-barrel, full-stock Kentucky rifle rested in brackets beside him. Cubbyholes had been carved in the bow, and in these he kept his powder horn, his bullets and spare flints. The other men sat by the four oars. Each man had a pistol, a hand-axe, a cutlass and a dagger. They were drunk but quiet, disciplined enough to know when they had fuelled themselves to the proper pitch.

They rowed out of the cove. In open water the sails were raised, and the pinnaces glided noiselessly before the gentle wind. The sun had risen behind them; flecks of gold flashed on the grey ocean.

Nau's boat led the way. Maynard looked at the backs of the men, and he could pick Justin's out – straight and tense – by the shoulder-holster strap that crossed his shirt.

The island had receded behind them to a grey-green smudge on the horizon, when Nau whistled. His second dropped the sail, and the seconds in the other boats did as well. There were no other boats on any horizon.

They waited, hunched over in the pinnaces, listening to the lapping of the water against the wooden hulls and to the occasional splashes as fish broke water in flight or pursuit. The sun rose higher and hotter, and Maynard felt his back beginning to burn.

'You have any grease with you?' he asked Beth.

'No.' Beth pushed a finger into the flesh atop Maynard's shoulder. The skin paled in a circle, then flushed pink again. 'Jack-Bat,' she said, 'pass the grog.'

Jack the Bat grumbled and pulled a stoneware jug from the bilges. Before he passed it to Beth, he uncorked it and took a long pull on it and said, 'When you gonna ripen up, Beth? Damn waste of grog.'

'Soon, Jack-Bat, soon,' She poured the liquor over Maynard's shoulders and rubbed it into his skin.

'Give him a drink, Goody,' said Hizzoner. 'The fire within will keep the fire without.'

Maynard sipped from the jug. His back still stung, the skin was still hot and tight, but now he had something else on which to focus his attention: the embers glowing in his stomach.

The jug was passed around the pinnace and returned to the bilges.

Nau whistled and pointed, and heads turned to the south-west.

'By the gentle Jesus,' Hizzoner said. 'That is a noble vessel.'

At first, Maynard could see nothing but the horizon. Then a pinpoint seemed to break the grey line, and gradually, as slowly as the hand of a clock moving from one minute to the next, the pinpoint stabilized and became a speck, a blemish, on the surface.

'A schooner,' Nau called. 'A fine, robust bitch.'

Maynard squinted, but still the boat was an indistinct speck.

'You'll sup tonight, lads,' Nau said. 'What'll you have?'

'Beef!' answered someone.

'Rum!' said another.

'Peaches for me!'

'Solomon Grundy!'

'Aye, that's it,' Nau said, laughing. 'A plate of Solomon Grundy would sit sweet. Hotten up, lads, and stow your jugs and say your honours and check your arms. There's them that will sup with us and them that will sup with the devil, and nothing in between.'

The jug was passed again, and stowed. In the bow, the marksman loaded his Kentucky and lay it across his lap. In the stern, Hizzoner threaded pitch-soaked pieces of twine through his braided pigtail. Seeing Maynard eying him quizzically, Hizzoner said, 'Does this bring back memories, scribe?'

'Memories of what?'

'This was Teach's trick. It abashed all but your forebear.'

'What did?'

'You'll see.'

The sails were raised, and the little boats were sailed in circles, awaiting the arrival of the schooner. It was a mile or so away, but its lines were clear: two masts, a full suit of sails, a sleek black hull. The schooner moved along smartly, using every breath of wind, its bow slicing the sea. It was at least a

176

hundred feet long. Maynard could not imagine that the pinnaces would be able to intercept, let alone overtake, this juggernaut.

Hizzoner called to Nau, 'Who will be the fox?'

'Yourself. I will be the poor fisherman, too ignorant to see the approach of doom. You will be wiser, for you will save yourself. He will think highly of you, until you are up his bum.'

Hizzoner pushed the tiller to the right, bearing away from the other pinnaces, which continued to wander in lazy disarray directly in the path of the oncoming schooner.

The schooner was so close now that Maynard could hear the rush of water along its hull, could see the name *Brigadier* painted in gold letters on the bow. Men stood at the rail, and two, forward, were shouting at the pinnaces and waving them away from the schooner's path. Aft, the helmsman was visible at the wheel. A klaxon sounded, but the pinnaces did not disperse: they kept a close circle as the schooner bore down on them.

Hizzoner's pinnace was off to the side. The bow of the schooner passed twenty yards away, a massive black wall that swept by and shouldered off a mountain of water.

'Now!' Hizzoner shouted.

The oars shot out on either side of the pinnace. The sail fell in a heap, and Jack the Bat swiftly lashed it to the boom. The oarsmen pulled, and the pinnace surged forward. The marksman stood in the bow.

The schooner was already beyond them; there was no way they could catch it.

And then Maynard saw the rudder turn, and the schooner fell off the wind. To avoid the three other pinnaces, the helmsman had, at the last possible instant, turned hard to starboard. The sailing rhythm of the big boat was broken, and for a moment it wallowed.

The man behind the marksman jammed his head between the marksman's legs and steadied him with his shoulders. The marksman raised his Kentucky, pulled back the hammer, and sighted along the barrel. The pinnace was bobbing in the schooner's wake, the bow rising and falling and

177

yawing in the troughs. As the bow rose, the marksman held his breath, and at the apex of the rise – when, for an unmeasurable fraction of a second, the bow hung motionless – he pulled the trigger. There was a click as flint struck steel, a hiss as the spark-ignited powder in the pan burned through the touch-hole, and a boom and a flash of flame and a puff of smoke as the gun went off. The marksman staggered, caught his balance, and craned to see if his shot had been true.

On the schooner, the helmsman's hands flew away from the wheel and seemed to claw at the chips of bone that exploded from his skull. He fell out of sight, and the wheel spun crazily to the right. The schooner pitched and rolled and slid farther off the wind. Ripples of luff fluttered in the sails.

'Pull, lads!' Hizzoner called, and the oarsmen swept their blades deep into the rolling seas.

Hizzoner shouted, 'Regard, scribe!' and Maynard turned. Hizzoner was touching the flaming wick of a rusty Zippo lighter to the pitch-soaked twine in his pigtail. Each piece burned with a greasy, smoky flame, surrounding his head with a mantle of fire. Hizzoner grinned. 'Truly a creature of hell, eh?'

Maynard looked to Nau's pinnace, which was creeping along the leeward bows of the schooner, its oarsmen heaving frantically to avoid being crushed by the advancing black hulk. As Maynard watched, a small red pennant was run up Nau's mast.

Hizzoner saw the pennant, too, and he shouted, 'The *jolie rouge* is up, lads! Pull, and ye shall have gizzard to feast upon!'

'What's the flag?' Maynard asked Beth.

'The *jolie rouge*? No quarter.'

'I thought he never gave quarter.'

'It gives the lads heart.'

The pinnace was within a few feet of the schooner's stern when, on unspoken signal, the lead oarsman shipped his oar and passed it forward to the marksman. The marksman raised the oar like a harpoon and drove it between the schooner's rudder and sternpost. The rudder froze, and, immediately, the schooner settled into a slow, easy roll.

The men were screaming now, shrieking savage, incoherent imprecations against the enemy, the deity, the sea and each other. They flung themselves on to the schooner's rudder and, like spiders, scampered up the stern and over the railing.

His hair afire, his eyes alight, a dagger between his teeth and an axe in his hand, Hizzoner stepped on Maynard, leaped out of the pinnace, and yelled, 'We have made a covenant with death, and with hell we are in accord!'

There were screams from the schooner, and cries of fear and sounds of running feet and a few shots.

'Come along,' Beth said. She tossed the free end of the chain to Maynard, hiked up her skirts, and jumped on to the rudder.

'Me?'

'Come, or they'll kill you where you sit.' She pointed off the stern of the pinnace. Another pinnace was blocked from access to the rudder. From the crowd of yelling, cursing faces a knife appeared, spinning end over end. Maynard ducked, and the knife stuck and quivered in the rudder.

Maynard wrapped the rest of the chain around his neck, jumped on to the schooner's rudder, and climbed. His hands slipped, his feet skidded, his fingernails clutched at bolts and ridges and cracks in the hull. Inch by inch he climbed.

The afterdeck of the schooner was a mêlée of running, shouting men. The helmsman lay at Maynard's feet, the back of his head a puddle of grey and red.

Two others of the schooner's crew lay on the deck, one nearly decapitated, the other leaning against a gunwale and staring, with vacant wonder, at a mess of exposed viscera.

Crouching to avoid stray bullets, Beth pulled Maynard forward.

Nau came aboard amidships, paused at the railing, and helped the two boys aboard. As soon as Manuel's feet hit the deck, he scampered away, dodging, stopping, looking, ducking – a weasel, Maynard thought, searching for prey.

Justin was stiff with fear. Nau bent and spoke to him. Justin took the Walther from the holster, chambered a round, and stepped gingerly forward.

Maynard saw Manuel flatten himself against the deck-house. Slowly, with infinite care and patience, his fingertips pulled from his pocket a garotte: two wooden handles connected by eighteen inches of thin wire. He was stalking something – Maynard couldn't see what – and his senses had obliterated all extraneous sounds and movements. His body moved fluidly, silently, his feet seeming not to touch the deck as he advanced.

A woman rounded the far corner of the deckhouse. Looking backward, fleeing, panicked, she did not see Manuel until he sprang upon her and wrapped his legs around her waist. And, even then, she probably didn't see him, for before she could turn her head he had whipped the garotte around her neck and snapped it tight.

Maynard saw her eyes bulge and her tongue pop out of her mouth, and then she fell, with Manuel on top of her, leeching the life from her.

Nau's second shouted and pointed upward. A long-haired young man in tattered denim shorts was climbing the rigging – a mad hopeless flight. The second drew his pistol and pointed at the climber, but Nau slapped his hand away. He knelt beside Justin.

'No!' Maynard yelled. Beth yanked on the chain, to silence him.

Nau smiled and said, 'Surgery, scribe.'

Maynard watched, helpless, as, with two hands, Justin followed Nau's guide and pointed the Walther at the climbing man.

'Squeeze,' Nau said. 'Slowly squeeze.'

Justin nodded and closed one eye and pulled the trigger. The Walther jumped in his hand. The bullet whined through the schooner's rigging, and the climber ducked.

Nau murmured to Justin and cupped his hand under Justin's. Maynard heard him say, 'When you are ready.'

This time there was no whine, only a *thuck* as the bullet struck flesh. The climber touched his chest, and blood seeped between his fingers. He fell forward, his body upright and graceful. His chin caught on a stay; his feet swung beneath him – a high-wire artist about to execute a difficult somersault – until his chin cleared the stay; and then his body fell horizontally, laid out as if for burial, and thudded on the roof of the deckhouse.

'Tue-Barbe!' cried Nau.

'Tue-Barbe!' echoed his second.

They slapped Justin on the back and praised him and called his name. The boy's face rouged, and then he smiled and then was gleeful. He hopped from one foot to the other; his arms flapped. He was seized by a fit of hyperkinetic delight.

Maynard watched and felt sick, remembering the last time he had seen his son so seized: when Santa Claus had left a kitten for him under the Christmas tree.

There was still an uproar forward, belowdecks, and Nau and his second and the other men left Justin and raced to the hatches in the bow.

Justin walked to the deckhouse and climbed on the roof and stared down at the man he had killed.

'Come.' Beth pulled the chain, eager to go forward and begin picking through the spoils.

'In a minute,' Maynard said. 'Please.'

She hesitated, then gave Maynard the chain and went forward alone.

Maynard approached the deckhouse. 'Justin ...'

The boy did not turn.

Maynard heard footsteps, running, beneath him. They stopped, and started again, but he paid no attention. 'Justin ...'

The deckhouse door flew open in Maynard's face, and a man – panting, slashed, and bloody – backed on to the deck. He held an M–16 rifle. He looked up and saw Justin and raised the M–16 to his chest.

Maynard threw his shoulder into the door. It caught the man in the back and knocked him off balance. The M–16 fired once.

Justin spun and crouched, the Walther raised. The man

181

stumbled, regained his footing, and swung the M–16 upward.

Maynard jumped on him. He coiled the end of his chain around the man's neck, jammed the last links to the deck with his foot, and pulled as hard as he could on the rest.

The man dropped the rifle. He scratched at the steel links that were already cracking his windpipe and bluing his skin. Maynard pulled until his arms ached and his temples throbbed and he saw the man's pupils dilate and his eyeballs flutter and roll backward.

Then he untangled the chain from the man's neck and leaned, exhausted, against the deckhouse.

Justin smiled.

Still gasping and looking at the dead man, Maynard said curtly, 'What are you smiling at?'

Justin just stared.

'Give me the gun, buddy. Enough is enough.' Without looking up, Maynard raised his hand, expecting the pistol to be placed in it.

'Justin . . .' he began angrily, 'I said . . .' He raised his eyes, and all he could see was a little black circle surrounded by a plug of black metal.

Justin was holding the Walther not four inches from his father's head, pointing it half an inch above the bridge of his nose and directly between his eyes.

Behind the pistol, out of focus, Maynard could see Justin's face, twisted into a crooked smile.

Maynard fought to keep his voice from cracking. 'Justin . . .'

'I am Tue-Barbe!'

Maynard's eyes focused on Justin's – glistening, unwavering, feral, their pupils as big as raisins. The boy was drunk.

'All right. Tue– . . .'

'They tell me you're dead.'

'Not yet, but . . .'

The flash of the explosion blinded Maynard, and the sound hammered at his eardrums. When he could see again, the barrel of the Walther had moved a few inches to the right, over his shoulder.

Justin laughed, a soprano cackle, and slid off the deck-house roof and sprinted forward. His laughter hung in the air behind him, a toxic melody.

Maynard was alone on the stern. The noises forward had subsided; now there was just the voices of Nau's men and the sounds of cargo being shifted and crates opened and a strange faint buzz that, for several moments, Maynard could not identify.

His mind separated the sounds, discarding the familiar and isolating the strange: it was the drone of a motor, very far away, barely audible, erased by any closer interruption. He shielded his eyes and searched the horizon, but there were no boats. The buzz seemed to be growing slightly louder, but he couldn't be sure.

He squinted into the sky and looked everywhere but straight at the sun, where his eyes could not tolerate the brilliance. The sky was empty. Then something flashed, like a spark of a star. He looked again, cupping his hands around his eyes and forming tiny peepholes with the joints of his fingers, blotting out the blinding aura and allowing him to scan the sky near the sun.

Again the flash, and this time Maynard's eyes locked on it, a silver gnat against the yellow-blue carpet: an airplane.

He looked for something to signal with, a reflector, a mirror, a shard of polished steel. His feet struck the body of the man he had strangled. His chain. He held the links up to the sun, but they were rust-spotted and dull, and they did not glitter. A wristwatch. He dropped to his knees and turned the body over and fumbled with the shirt cuffs. The man wore a watch, but the band of plastic and the watch itself was covered with a waterproof rubber case. He searched the pockets for a coin, a jack-knife blade, a lighter. He tore open the man's shirt, hoping to find a medallion or dog-tags, and there, dangling from a slender chain, was a gold-plated razor blade, one of the ritual tools of the cocaine fraternity. He unfastened the chain and held the razor blade to the sun.

Devon had been sitting in the co-pilot's seat for nearly five hours. Her rear end hurt, and with every bounce of the plane she worried that her bladder might burst. They had descended the entire length of the Bahamas chain, flying low over every sparsely populated island, making two or three passes over the out-islands of the Turks and Caicos group, and had seen nothing remotely encouraging. They had one more island to scout, Great Inagua, and then they would head back for Miami.

She wasn't even sure what she was looking for, what would be worth landing beside and exploring: an isolated encampment, perhaps, or a solitary boat anchored in a hidden cove. She had no idea what Blair had in mind when he absconded with Justin from New York. They might be in Tahiti by now. But her search had to start somewhere, and when the *Today* people had offered to let her ride along in their chartered plane, she had accepted without question.

She was convinced that the *Today* stringer in the seat behind her had no more confidence in the success of his mission to find Trask than she had in hers. She didn't know much about boats, but she knew enough to conclude that it was a waste of time to look for Brendan Trask this far south: there was no possible way Trask could have sailed so great a distance in so few days. Suppose that somehow – miraculously – they did find Trask: what then? Granted he was supposed to be an amiable fellow, and certainly he appreciated journalistic enterprise, but why should he be expected to put up with being dive-bombed by somebody from Miami? This stunt wasn't worthy of *Today*: it was *National Enquirer*-type shenanigans, and she wouldn't blame Trask for telling the reporter to get stuffed.

The pilot dipped the starboard wing, beginning a right turn, and amid the vast expanse of blue, Devon suddenly saw something flash.

'Down there,' she said to the pilot.

'What's down there?'

'I don't know. It looks like somebody's signalling.'

The pilot righted the plane, then dipped the left wing so he could see from his side. 'Looks like a party boat. Some dame's checking her make-up in a mirror.'

'Take us down there,' Devon said. 'I want a closer look.'

'That's not Trask's boat,' said the reporter. 'Let's go home.'

'Take us down there!' Devon ordered.

The pilot shrugged. 'Whatever you say, lady.'

The plane was coming. It was still far away and very high, but it was coming. They had seen his signals. Maynard continued to tip the razor blade in and out of the sun's rays, aiming the flashes at the oncoming plane.

Something struck Maynard between the shoulders and threw him across the deck. He waited, eyes closed, for the blow that would end his life.

'On your feet, scribe,' said Jack the Bat. He jerked his head toward the plane. 'Visitors.'

Maynard had been knocked down by the deckhouse door, flung open by Jack the Bat's charge from below. As he got up, he saw Jack the Bat drag the body of the strangled man to the gunwale, prop him up and lay the M–16 across his lap. As a final, cosmetic touch, Jack the Bat raised one of the corpse's knees and rested one of the already stiffening hands upon it.

Jack the Bat moved the body of the man on the deckhouse roof. Although the blood had begun to settle in the body, and the skin to grey, the man looked reposed. Jack the Bat scooped a hat off the deck and plopped it on the dead man's face. 'Pleasant dreams,' he said, folding a lifeless hand over the bullet wound in the chest.

'Cover that one.' Jack the Bat pointed to the helmsman.

A canopy, designed to protect the helmsman from the sun was folded back against the stern. Maynard drew it forward and over the helmsman's body, careful to leave a clutching hand exposed.

'Now come.' Jack the Bat jammed the last body against the port gunwale and covered it with mops and buckets. Then he sat on the deckhouse roof and patted the spot beside him. 'Sit on your chain, scribe.'

Maynard piled the loose end of his chain on the deckhouse roof and sat on it.

Jack the Bat put his arm around Maynard's shoulders – a chummy gesture if Jack the Bat's hand had not gripped the coil of chain around Maynard's neck and if he had not said, 'Move your head so much as a twitch and I'll kill you.'

The altimeter read a hundred feet, and it was still inching downward. The black hull of the schooner sped toward them.

'Low enough?' the pilot said with a smile.

'Fine,' said Devon.

The reporter yelled, 'You're gonna hit the goddam thing!'

The pilot laughed.

Devon leaned forward, trying not to blink, her eyes scouring the deck of the schooner.

Two men were on the deckhouse, apparently in a drunken embrace, and others lounged around the deck.

'Tough duty,' said the pilot as the plane zoomed over the deck. 'Lie around on your ass and drink rum all day.'

'What are they doing?' asked Devon. 'They're in the middle of nowhere.'

'Trading with the spades for lobsters. Those are native boats alongside.'

The reporter looked back. 'You see that guy asleep? He had a rifle in his lap.'

'Can't be too careful out here. Guys'll rip you off for the shine on your shoes.'

The pilot pulled the stick back, and the plane climbed and turned for Great Inagua. 'Satisfied?' he said to Devon.

'No, but I don't know what more we can do.'

14

There were five survivors of the schooner's crew – four men and a woman, all young, all dressed in faded denim shorts – and they were herded aft by Nau's second, a full-bearded man named Basco Tom. Basco was furious. He held a blood-stained cloth to his cheek and glared venom at the woman.

The survivors were scared and confused, but they did not yet know they had reason to despair.

Nau stood in the stern, flanked by the boys and Hizzoner. Beth had stationed Maynard to one side while she examined each article of cargo brought up from the hold.

The men loaded the pinnaces with cases of food and liquor, tools, clothing, kitchen utensils, weapons and flashlights. That which they didn't recognize – certain appliances, machines, medicines – was left on the deck for Nau to dispose of. That which experience told them was useless – food mixes that required milk or eggs, paint, cleansers and frozen foods – was thrown back into the hold.

Beth supervised the loading like a dockmaster, ordering her share to be put in Hizzoner's pinnace, making sure that she got '6–12' bug spray and not the Cutter, squeezing melons, sniffing meats, debating between peaches and pears, and finally settling – profligately – on a case of each, and even modelling baubles of jewellery for herself.

'Wounded, Basco?' said Nau.

Basco pressed the cloth to his cheek. 'Vixen bit me.'

'Did you abuse her?'

Basco smiled and raised the middle finger of his right hand. 'I took her measure, l'Ollonois.'

'You know the law on meddling with a prudent woman.'

'If she be righteous, why I'm the Pope.'

One of the survivors said, 'Where are you taking us?'

Nau looked at him and replied evenly, 'You'll be going home, lad.'

The survivors were relieved. They exchanged glances and secret smiles. 'Where you guys from?' said one. He looked at Nau and Hizzoner and Maynard. When he received no reply, he went on, 'You sure tricked the shit out of us, I'll give you that.'

They don't know Maynard thought. The place stinks of death; there are bodies all around them, and they still don't know.

Nau said to the five, 'Which of you is the master?'

A young man stepped forward. 'I am.'

'What's your cargo?'

The young man gestured at the cases on the stern. 'You got it, man.'

'That's provender, not cargo.'

'What's provender?' Emboldened by the certainty that, after whatever minor reprimand, whatever insignificant humiliation, they would be set free, the young man affected a slight swagger. He smiled at his friends. 'I mean, what are you, the heat?'

'Your cargo.'

'You're lookin' at it, chief.'

Nau tipped his head at Basco, who grabbed the young man's hand, slapped it down on the gunwale and, with a swipe of his cutlass, amputated the little finger.

The young man pulled his hand back and looked at it. 'Hey, man ...' The hand was as before, except that instead of five fingers, now there were four, and where the fifth had been all that remained was a pulpy nub of bone. 'Hey, shit ...'

Maynard saw the colour drain from the man's face, saw him weave as if a last, unneeded drink had suddenly taken hold. 'Your cargo.'

'I'm gonna bleed to death!'

'You'll be home before that can happen. Don't try my patience, or your journey will be paved with misery.' Again Nau tipped his head at Basco.

This time Basco grabbed the girl, but she struggled and pulled away from him, and before he could catch her she screamed, 'No.'

'Your cargo, lady.'

'It's down there!' She pointed to the hold. 'Under a lot of shit.'

'And it be . . .'

'Coke, hash . . .'

Nau didn't understand. He looked at Hizzoner and Basco, but they didn't know, either.

'Drugs,' Maynard volunteered, shaking his head.

'Medicines, scribe?'

'No, drugs. You know . . . like narcotics. Drugs.' Maynard reached back in his mind and found the word used in the covenant. 'Pharmaceuticals.'

'We will see it.' Nau dispatched two of his men below.

Hizzoner said, 'The Doctor's purse . . .'

'Ah, yes.' Nau addressed the woman. 'Tell me, lady, where be your ship's purse?'

'What?'

Maynard said, 'Cash.'

'I don't know.' She nudged the wounded man, who was staring at his bleeding hand. 'Dingo, where's the cash?'

'Huh?' The man seemed to resent having the contemplation of his stump interrupted. 'You want a couple bucks?'

'He wants the fucking cash, man!' She shook his shoulder. 'Where is it?'

'Only got a few bucks,' the man said blankly. 'It's in my bunk.'

'We didn't make the drop yet,' the woman apologized to Maynard.

Maynard felt ridiculous. The woman was using him as an

189

interpreter. He wanted to tell her that he was a prisoner, too, to warn her. But the information would have been useless, the warning pointless.

'The cargo was to be sold,' he said to Nau. 'Until then, they have little money.'

This Nau understood. He nodded to Hizzoner. Hizzoner drew breath, preparing to orate, but the woman interrupted. 'We can make a deal. That coke is worth a shit-pot.'

Nau said to Maynard, 'The woman has a foul tongue.'

'She wants to make a bargain with you.' Maynard saw no harm in speaking for the woman. He sensed that she, alone among the survivors, had begun to recognize the imminence of death. To stall for her would be a small kindness. 'Their freedom in exchange for their cargo.'

'Indeed!' Nau laughed. 'A generous bargain. I have their ship, their cargo and their persons. What can they offer me that I do not have?'

There was no answer. Justin broke the silence: 'Be done with it!'

Nau smiled. 'Aye, Tue-Barbe. Talk wastes breath.' He cued Hizzoner.

Hizzoner began to speak, gazing reverently at the heavens waving his arms, ostensibly addressing the survivors but, in fact reciting a litany of justification. It was a time-worn speech, and one, Maynard was certain, that Hizzoner altered only slightly from one delivery to the next.

'The crimes you have committed are known to you and to God, but crimes they are and punishment they carry, and they who commit them are threatened to have their part in the lake which burneth with fire and brimstone, which is the second death, Revelation 21:8. See Chapter 22:15.' All this Hizzoner delivered in one breath, and as he gasped for more fuel, he looked at the survivors, expecting to see signs of repentance, or at least of fear. All he saw was stunned perplexity.

Hizzoner continued, as the first plastic bags of cocaine were dragged on to the deck.

'Words which carry the terror with them, that considering your circumstances and your guilt, surely the sound of them

190

must make you tremble; for who can dwell with everlasting burnings? Chapter 20:14. As the testimony of your conscience must convince you of the great and many evils you have committed, by which you have highly offended God, and provoked most justly his wrath and indignation against you, so I suppose I need not tell you that the only way of obtaining pardon and remission of your sins from God is by a true and unfeigned repentance and faith in Christ, by whose meritorious death and passion you can only hope for salvation.'

While Hizzoner droned on, Nau pointed to the heap of bags of cocaine and said to Maynard, 'What is that for?'

'It changes your mood. It's like ... well, like rum, sort of.'

'Does it give you courage?'

'No.'

'Then what purpose does it serve?'

'It makes you feel good. That's what people say.'

'Do you drink it?'

'No. You sniff it.'

'Sniff it? Snuff?' Nau sliced open one of the bags and scooped some of the white powder on the blade of his knife. He sniffed deeply and waited for something to happen. He shook his head and, derisively, spat on the deck. 'Into the deep with it,' he said, and the men began to pitch the bags overboard.

'Hey, man,' protested one of the survivors. 'That's like throwin' fuckin' *money* away.'

'Silence!'

Hizzoner stopped in mid-exhortation.

'Proceed, Hizzoner,' said Nau, 'but give more sail to it. You'll kill these unfortunates with tedium.'

'Tedium!' Hizzoner was offended. 'I prescribe the way to salvation. Is that tedious?'

'The way you tell it, it's everlasting. Proceed.'

'Had your delight been in the law of the Lord,' Hizzoner went on, 'and had you meditated therein day and night, Psalms 1:2, you would then have found that God's word was a lamp unto your feet and a light to your path, Psalms

191

119:105, and that you would account all other knowledge but loss, in comparison of the excellency of the knowledge of Christ Jesus, Philippians 3:8, who to them that are called is the power of God, and the wisdom of God, 1 Corinthians 1:24, even the hidden wisdom which God ordained before the world, Chapter 2:7. You would then have esteemed the Scriptures as the great charter of heaven, for in them only is to be found the great mystery of fallen man's redemption, and they would have taught you that sin is the debasing of human nature, as being a derivation from that purity, rectitude and holiness in which God created us, and that virtue and religion, and walking by the laws of God were altogether preferable to the laws of sin and Satan; for that the ways of virtue are ways of pleasantness, and all their paths are peace, Proverbs 3:17.'

The last of the bags of cocaine splashed into the water and fell in line with the others being carried south by the swiftly moving tide. The chain of white dumplings bobbed for a hundred yards behind the boat.

Nau tapped his knife, impatiently, on the railing.

Hizzoner noticed him and said, 'I arrive.'

'None too soon.'

'If now you will sincerely turn to Christ Jesus,' Hizzoner told the survivors, 'though late, even at the eleventh hour Matthew 20:6–9, he will receive you. But, surely, I need not tell you that the terms of his mercy are faith and repentance. And do not mistake the nature of repentance to be only a bare sorrow for your sins, arising from the consideration of the evil and punishment they have now brought upon you; but your sorrow must arise from the consideration of your having offended a gracious and merciful God. But I shall not pretend to give you any particular directions as to the nature of repentance: I consider that I speak to persons whose offences have proceeded not so much from not knowing, as sighting and neglecting their duty. I only heartily wish that what, in compassion to your souls, I have now said to you upon this sad and solemn occasion, by exhorting you in general to faith and repentance, may have that due effect upon you, that thereby you may become true penitents.'

'Judas priest!' Nau erupted. 'As the boy begged, be done with it!'

'It becomes you ill,' Hizzoner chided Nau, 'to call upon the arch-traitor for relief. It was he who, when faced with just such a decision, when salvation and damnation were warring for his soul, chose to—'

'I know what he did! Be on with it!'

'Yes ... well ...' Hizzoner harumphed. 'And now therefore, having discharged my duty to you as a Christian, by giving you the best counsel I can, with respect to the salvation of your souls, I must now do my office as a judge. It is the sentence of this court, for the court is where the judge sits, even if the judge stands but does not sit, and even if he stands at sea, that you ...' He stopped. 'What are your names?'

'Who cares what be their names?' Nau roared. 'Call them Willy and Billy and Millie!'

'That you, Willy and Billy and Millie ... and Willy and Billy again, for you are five ... that you shall be presently rendered dead, dead, *dead*!'

Maynard looked at the survivors. The wounded man seemed not to hear, or, if he heard, not to care; he was hypnotized by his hand. Two of the other men were incredulous; they shuffled their feet and eyed each other and muttered things like, 'Hey, man ...' and 'C'mon, chief ...' and 'Hey, let's cut the shit ...'

But the woman knew, and believed, and was hysterical. She screamed.

Nau said, 'Basco ...'

Basco stepped forward, grabbed the woman's hair and slit her throat.

Without waiting to be told, Justin pulled the Walther from its holster and shot the wounded man in the chest. The man fell without a sound. As he slumped to the deck, Justin aimed at him again, but Nau stayed his hand.

'Add not insult to injury. He's done. Besides, bullets are precious.'

Swiftly, with three efficient slashes of his cutlass, Basco dispatched the others.

Maynard stood at the stern, trembling with horror and outrage. He said to Nau, 'You've made a monster of him.'

'A monster? Not at all. An engine. A job to do must be done. Do you weep for these five? for *these*?' With his toe, Nau nudged one of the still-twitching bodies. 'What's the loss?'

'For them? No, but I should. I weep for my son.'

'Aye, that's a loss. But take comfort: your loss is our gain.' Nau spoke to Manuel. 'Put her down.'

'Fired?'

Nau scanned the sky, looking for the airplane. 'No. Put her down easy. Show Tue-Barbe how it's done.'

The boys ran forward and disappeared down an open hatch.

The pinnaces were loaded above the gunwales; they had only an inch or two of freeboard. If the sea had not been calm, they would have been swamped.

Three pinnaces stood off. The fourth, Nau's, stayed tethered to the schooner's stern, awaiting the boys.

The schooner lay perfectly still in the water. As Maynard watched from fifty yards away, the bow began slowly – barely perceptibly – to sink. After a few moments, the stern, too, settled slightly. The boys appeared on deck, scampered aft, shinned down the rudder and tiptoed on to Nau's over-loaded pinnace.

The schooner seesawed – sinking first by the bow, then by the stern, then by the bow again – until, when the decks were almost awash, either something substantial shifted below or a compartment refused to surrender its air, and the balance in the hull changed and the stern rose out of the water and the bow knifed downward with a reptilian hiss.

When the schooner was gone, there were a few residual noises – or perhaps they were not noises but sensations that reverberated through the water and the wooden hulls of the pinnaces, feelings of cracking and crushing and splitting.

Bubbles rose and burst where the schooner had been. The sea had swallowed and digested it, and the surface was normal again as the schooner had never been.

194

'Set your sails, lads!' Nau called, 'and wish for a fair westerly. There's rum to drink and whores to dandle!'

It was twilight when the pinnaces reached the cove, and half the men had a headstart on tomorrow's hangover. Jack the Bat had finished his jug of rum-and-gunpowder and was at work on a bottle of hundred-proof vodka, borrowed ('on account', he insisted) from Beth's share of the booty. Over and over, he sang a song that had only two lines: 'Hey boys, up go we, Molly's caught her skirts on the manzanilla tree.' Nau's second fell out of his pinnace while lowering the sail at the entrance to the cove. He was unable to swim, and he kicked and thrashed until someone threw him a line and then – to the merry guffaws of the rest of the crew – proceeded to pee on him as he was towed towards shore.

A Boston Whaler was beached in the cove, and a man stood beside it, waiting. In the near-darkness, Maynard did not recognize the man: all he saw was a white linen suit, with the trousers rolled up to the knees. Then he heard the man call, 'Well done, Excellency! If it were done when 'tis done, then 'twere well it were done quickly.'

Windsor.

'Say hey, Doctor!' Nau cocked his arm and threw something at the shore. 'Your purse. Poor perhaps, but all she had. And what have you brought me?'

'Powder – two kegs – and medicine to cleanse your wretched persons.' Windsor picked up the purse and put it in his pocket.

The pinnaces were run up on to the sand, the cargoes unloaded on to the beach.

Justin and Manuel walked a pace behind Nau as he approached Windsor.

When Windsor spotted Justin, he said cheerfully, 'Now there's a lad. Give me your name again, boy.'

'Who he was is gone,' said Nau. 'Now he is Tue-Barbe.'

'A fine name. So, Tue-Barbe, how goes the battle?'

'Fine, sir,' said Justin.

'He is worthy,' Nau said. 'Time will come, he and Manuel will vie for leadership.'

195

'Top shelf. Survival of the fittest. Keep the line pure.'
Windsor surveyed the cargo being stacked on the beach. 'She
was rich. I thought so. Their talks with the mainland
suggested it.'

'Aye, but a worthless cargo. Drugs, the scribe called
them.'

'Who?'

Beth had led Maynard out of the pinnace and stationed
him on the beach while she supervised the separation of her
share.

'The scribe.' Nau pointed at Maynard.

Windsor crossed the beach to Maynard and examined
him, unbelieving, as if suspicious that Maynard was a practical joke. All he said was, 'Why are you alive?'

'Hello to you too.'

'I tried to save you, but you were pigheaded. Now you
should be dead.'

'Well ...'

Windsor said to Nau, 'Why is he alive?'

'It's a tangled web,' Nau replied. 'I'll unravel it for you
over a glass.'

Windsor insisted, 'He should be dead! That's the
way.'

'That he will be, and before long. He knows it, we know it,
it is a fact. Meanwhile, he scribbles for us.'

Windsor did not argue with Nau. He whispered to
Maynard, 'I don't know how you did it, but whatever it is,
it's finished. Believe me.'

'You're threatening me?' Maynard smiled. 'Please ...
don't bother.'

'Just believe me,' Windsor repeated. He turned away.

Maynard took a guess. 'You worried I'll contaminate your
laboratory?' Windsor halted. 'This is your perfect society,
isn't it?'

'Not yet,' Windsor could not stifle a smile. 'There are more
things in heaven and earth, Mencken, than are dreamt of in
your philosophy.'

'Come, Doctor,' Nau called. 'Your jug is full and your
dandelion is lonesome.'

Beth fetched a crude wheelbarrow from the underbrush, and she and Maynard loaded her goods aboard and pushed them back to her hut. Sounds of celebration were carried on a fresh breeze throughout the island: shouts and laughter, squeals and curses, bottles breaking and bodies stumbling through the bushes.

'Sounds like a real blowout,' Maynard said as they stacked cases and cartons and mesh bags in the hut until there was barely enough room to squeeze by one another.

'Warming up for council.'

'Council?'

'We'll go by and by. We've another business first.'

He looked at her, expecting an explanation, but all he saw was a peculiar sad smile that he could not interpret.

When all the goods were stored, she said, 'What rum pleases you?'

'I don't know rums.'

'You must have a favourite.' She pointed at the cases. 'Vodka rum? Whisky rum? Gin rum? Rum rum?' She waved her hand proudly. 'I have them all. I am rich. Roche would die a second death to see how rich I am.'

'Whisky rum.'

Delighting in the role of munificent hostess, Beth tore open a case of scotch and presented Maynard with a bottle. For herself she took a bottle of vodka. She opened hers and gestured for him to do the same. Then, 'Wait,' she said. With her fingernails she scraped the dirt floor of the hut and uncovered a key. She unlocked Maynard's chain, unwrapped it from his neck and cast it aside. 'There,' she said.

The muscles in Maynard's neck and shoulders felt suddenly elastic and alive. Gingerly, he touched the skin the chain had abraded raw. 'Thank you.'

She nodded. 'Drink.'

'Why ...?'

'Why drink? Because ...'

'No. Why ... that?' He indicated the chain.

'No reason.' She shook her head, but she wouldn't look at him. 'You are to be trusted.'

'All of a sudden?'

197

'You would have me replace it? No? No! Be quiet and drink.'

They sipped from the bottles. The liquor, neat, burned on the way down and then pooled warmly in the stomach.

'You have brought me good fortune,' Beth said.

'That's something, I guess.'

'It is too bad.'

'What is?'

She gestured, vaguely, at the world. 'Everything.' She took a long pull on the vodka bottle. 'But ... that is the way.'

Maynard sipped and said, 'You know what? The way is a pain in the ass.'

Beth laughed. 'Well perhaps ...'

'You know,' Maynard said carefully, hoping not to sour her mood, 'My offer still stands.'

'What off—?' Beth knew. 'No. It is too late.'

'Why?'

Beth shook her head, dismissing the thought, and set her bottle on the floor. 'Come.'

'Where to?'

'Come. I told you: other business.'

She took his hand and led him to the beach, where she bathed him with, it seemed to him, extraordinary tenderness.

They started back up the beach, but halfway to the underbrush she stopped and said, 'Here.' She dropped to the sand, dragged him down beside her, clamped her mouth on his, and rode him with a fierce intensity. Then, breathing heavily, she touched his face and said softly, 'You have been good to me.'

There was nothing in her words to distress him, but the flat finality in her voice made his heart race.

They walked along the dark paths, following the now-concentrated din of revelry. They came to the edge of a clearing, and Beth paused and peered ahead, as if checking for ambush.

'What are you worried about?' Maynard asked.

Beth held a finger to her lips and said, 'Ssshhh.'

198

She dashed across the clearing, and Maynard, following, saw the empty catamites' lodge.

They came to the clearing where the prostitutes lived, and again Beth paused warily before crossing.

They continued silently along the path. Suddenly, from the underbrush, an enormous man bulled his way on to the path and blocked their passage. He was roaring, drooling drunk. He staggered across the path, stumbled into a bush, righted himself, and swiped viciously at the air with his cutlass. 'Stand', he cried.

'Stand yourself, Rollo,' Beth said, 'if you can.' She seemed neither frightened nor alarmed, but resigned to an unpleasantness.

The big man weaved and squinted at them. 'However many ye be, have a glass with me or I'll have at ye with my hanger!' He waved his cutlass at them.

'Let us pass, Rollo.'

'Ye'll not pass until ye've drunk to my honour.' He reached behind a bush and dragged on to the path a case of Kahlúa. He knocked the neck off a bottle and held it out to Maynard. 'Drink. To my honour.'

'No, thanks.'

Rollo bellowed and lunged at Maynard. Maynard sidestepped and, as Rollo passed, punched him in the kidney and knocked him to his knees.

'A fine blow!' Rollo said as he lurched to his feet. 'Rattles my guts. Now,' he wiped the neck of the bottle on the seat of his trousers, 'drink or I'll have at ye again.'

Maynard glanced at Beth, who said, 'Pacify him.' So Maynard sipped from the bottle and passed it to her. She sipped and muttered, 'Your honour,' and returned the bottle to Rollo.

Pleased, Rollo said, 'My honour.' He drained the bottle and pitched the empty into the shrubbery. Then, giggling, he removed the case from the path and tottered back to his hiding place, to await the next passers-by.

'How long'll he play that game?' Maynard asked as they continued along the path.

'Till he topples. He's harmless enough.'

199

'Harmless! He was joking?'

'Oh no. He'd kill you sure enough, but if you drink with him, he's a cub.'

They walked on, toward the sounds of celebration. 'Suppose he did kill somebody,' Maynard said.

'Rollo? He has.'

'What happens to him?'

'Happens?'

'There's no punishment?'

'If it is a child, yes, that's butchery. He wouldn't. But a grown person ... that's a fair fight.'

'Suppose he ambushes him.'

'Anyone who can't defend himself against a reeling sot like that ... he's no loss.'

The company was gathered in the clearing before Nau's hut. The brim-full rum pot, surrounded by ruptured cases of various liquors, stood in the centre, simmering over charcoal embers. Drunken men and women were sprawled everywhere. As Beth led him into the clearing, Maynard stepped over a pair of grunting, sweating, copulating bodies.

Jack the Bat, clad only in a pair of rubber boots, sat in the sand with a half-dressed whore in his lap. Jack the Bat was weeping copiously, and as Maynard passed he heard him say to the whore, 'But Lizzie dear, I've always loved you! You're my heart's desire.'

'There, there, Jack,' the whore replied, stroking his neck. 'I can't run away with you. Where would we run to?'

'I'll build you a cottage at the end of the island. Make me happy!' Jack the Bat blubbered. 'Say you will.'

'There, there, Jack. Have another drink and we'll have another go, and you'll feel better.'

Hizzoner leaned against a tree stump, sucking on a bottle of brandy and offering catechism to a sleeping whore. He asked questions, and, receiving snores in response, pronounced learned answers to himself. 'Yes, you could become Magdalen,' he said thoughtfully. 'But a question of theology remains. Is it enough simply to stop taking pay for your services, or must you stop rendering them altogether? If you give them away, are you Magdalen or Samaritan? Or wanton? I must consult the Scriptures.' Hizzoner consulted the brandy bottle, and rambled on.

Nau sat in front of his hut, alone, drinking rum from a pewter chalice. His eyes monitored the behaviour of the company, but he did not interfere – not when voices rose, curses were exchanged, bottles broken. Evidently, his presence was sufficient to maintain a certain order.

'Ah, scribe,' he said when he saw Beth and Maynard. 'Come to chronicle the downfall of Rome? It's rare we have a day worth celebrating thus.' Nau noticed that Maynard was not tethered. He spoke sharply to Beth. 'Where is his leash?'

Beth bent down and whispered to Nau, who smiled and nodded and said pleasantly to Maynard, 'Come sit by me, then, and share a glass.'

Maynard put a hand on Beth's arm. 'What did you tell him?'

'Only ...' Beth looked away. 'Only that you are trustworthy.'

Maynard sat down. Nau filled the chalice and passed it to him. 'You might have been a trump, in another time.'

Maynard drank. Behind him, in the hut, he heard a slap and a giggle and a high voice squealing, 'Oh, you rogue!' He raised his eyebrows at Nau.

Nau chuckled. 'The Doctor is having his way.'

Windsor's voice, petulant: 'You're a nasty tease, and I won't have it!'

The sound of another slap came from the hut, and then a sigh.

Suddenly, Nau seemed to sense something wrong amid the crowd, as if an undrawn line had been crossed. A voice yelled in anger. There was a slap, and a cry of genuine pain.

'Hold!' Nau commanded.

The crowd quieted. Basco Tom was on his feet, his dagger poised above a cowering whore.

'Basco! Leave it!'

'I'll cut her, l'Ollonois. You'll not stop me.'

'No,' Nau said evenly, 'I'll not stop you.'

The crowd waited.

Basco prepared to strike.

'But as you cut,' Nau said, 'Bid farewell to your hand. I'll have it off myself.' He stood and took a knife from his belt.

Basco paused.

'Lay on,' said Nau. 'Cut her. It will be a costly cut, but you're a man who knows the worth of things. If a cut's worth a hand, so be it.'

Basco said, 'She offended me.'

Maynard saw the muscles in Nau's back relax.

'It must have been a mighty offence.'

'It was.' Basco was responding to Nau's sympathy. 'I offered her good value to see her naked, but she refused.'

The whore, too, felt the tension ebb, for she spat in the sand and said, 'Good value! A stinking kiss and a tin of peas!'

'It's fair value! I had no designs to touch you.'

'I'm a prostitute, not a picture! A *man* doesn't feast only with his eyes!'

Nau said to the whore, 'What do *you* deem a fair value?'

She got to her feet and dusted off her smock, prepared to negotiate. 'Well, seeing that I'm not in the business of window-shopping, I offered him proper feast. And all I asked . . .'

'All!' Basco shouted.

The whore continued primly, 'All I asked was his pretty locket.'

'Too dear for an ogle.'

'I promised more than an ogle.'

Nau said, 'What locket?' There was a new, sharper edge to his voice.

Basco's expression dissolved into dread. 'Nothing. It's nothing. I was in error.'

'No great prize,' said the whore. 'A pretty little thing . . .'

'What locket?' Nau held out his hand.

Maynard saw Hizzoner stir from his religious reverie and rise to his feet.

'A bauble,' Basco said, smiling lamely. 'A trinket.'

'I'll have it.' Nau's hand was still extended.

'Of course!' Basco stopped at the rum pot and dipped his cup. His hand shook as he raised the cup to his lips.

He stood before Nau and reached into his pocket, but there his hand froze: Nau had the barrel of a pistol pressed against his forehead.

'Leave it.' Nau glanced to the side. 'Fetch it, Hizzoner.'

Hizzoner dug into Basco's pocket and came out with a double-barrel percussion Derringer.

'Well!' Nau said.

Now Basco was terrified. 'The locket's in there! I swear!'

'I'm sure. And well protected, too.'

Hizzoner found the trinket and passed it to Nau. It was not a locket, but a gold ankh on a gold chain.

'How long have you had this?'

'Years! A keepsake.' Basco's eyes were crossed, focusing on the pistol barrel.

'How long have you had this?' Nau repeated.

'I swear ...'

'How long have you had this?' A third time, as if following a tradition.

Basco knew very well what was happening. Sweat poured down his face.

Maynard looked at Basco and knew – analytically, matter-of-factly, without shock or chagrin – that man was dead. Whatever Basco had done (Maynard assumed theft) had been heinous enough by itself, and Basco had compounded the offence by lying, not once but three times. Maynard had become so inured to carnage that he wondered only how, not if, Basco would die. And, he noted idly, a new part of his brain, or of his humanity, must have atrophied, for he no longer even cared about not caring.

'The drink, l'Ollonois,' Basco said. 'The battle ...'

'You took this from the woman,' said Nau. 'That is why she bit you.'

'I ...'

Hizzoner said, 'He kept a secret from the company.'

'A trinket!'

Nau said, 'We were boys together, Basco.' Then he pulled the trigger.

The top of Basco's head exploded in a shower of splinters, and he fell to the sand, an uncapped bottle.

Nau put the pistol back in his belt and tossed the ankh to the whore. Two men dragged Basco's body out of the clearing.

Slowly, arduously, like a steam locomotive pulling away from a station, the revelry regained its momentum.

Nau refilled his chalice, sipped from it, and passed it to Maynard. 'How would you write that, scribe?'

Maynard shrugged. 'Another death. Here one minute, gone the next. That's how you treat it, isn't it?'

'Basco was a friend.'

'Were you sad to kill him?'

'I will miss him, but it had to be done.'

'There's no forgiveness, even for friends.'

'No. Forgiveness is weakness. Weakness becomes a crack; a crack becomes a rent, and soon there is a riot. They expected no less from me.'

There were footsteps behind Maynard, and he heard Windsor say, 'I heard shrill notes of anger, and mortal alarms.'

Windsor stood in front of the hut, cinching his trousers. He had a half-empty bottle of scotch under one arm. His face was flushed, his eyes glassy. He was followed by the lithe blond catamite with the black leather codpiece. The catamite posed in the doorway, smug and narcissistic.

'Basco has gone home,' Nau said.

'The crime?' Windsor sat in the sand.

'The covenant,' Hizzoner explained.

'Ah,' Windsor nodded. 'Most serious.' He drank from his bottle.

'I might not have known,' Nau said, and in his voice there was a touch of rue, 'if he hadn't been squabbling with that.' He gestured contemptuously at the whore, who had removed her blouse and was admiring how precisely the ankh fell between her breasts.

'He died for *that*?' the catamite sniffed. 'My! he *was* a man of meagre taste.'

'Be quiet, Nanny,' Windsor said.

The whore had heard—if not the words, the tone and the direction. 'Say again, capon,' she challenged.

'Hear *her*,' said the catamite. 'Hide your dreary dugs dearie, before they've dug another grave.'

'Nanny ...' Windsor cautioned.

'Hey, pullet,' the whore crowed, 'what's stuffing your pouch tonight? Mangoes?'

There was laughter, especially raucous from the other whores, and the catamite blushed.

'Look, ladies, how he reddens!' continued the whore. 'He sprouts a coxcomb, but that's as close to a rooster as he'll ever be!'

Another whore called, 'I bet his pouch is full of eggs.'

'Aye,' chimed a third. 'He lays himself.'

Outnumbered and outvolleyed, the catamite burst. Vaulting Windsor, he screamed, 'Bitch!' and sprinted into the clearing and slapped Basco's whore across the mouth.

Her lip split against her teeth. She raised a hand to wipe blood from her mouth.

The catamite kept his eyes on the raised hand, ready to defend against a punch. He didn't see her other hand ball into a fist, her thumb extended, her long, pointed thumbnail drive, with all her weight behind it, deep into his navel and gouge at his backbone.

He shrieked and tumbled backward, and she followed him down, stabbing with other nails his plucked armpits.

He lashed out with his legs. A knee hit her in the temple and knocked her off him. He rolled on top of her and gnashed at her breasts.

The crowd laughed and cheered. The whores were partisan, but the others were neutral: they applauded each telling blow, each new draw of blood, and they roared equally unbiased approval at the loss of the whore's nipple-tip and the catamite's earlobe.

'Worried, Doctor?' Nau said. 'Your dandelion loses his petals.'

'He's all sinew,' Windsor replied. 'She's no match for him.' From his jacket pocket Windsor took a box of bullets and placed it on the sand in front of Nau: a wager.

Maynard recognized the box: he had hidden it in his bureau drawer at Chainplates.

Nau reached into a small leather pouch he wore around his neck and removed a sapphire earring, which he set beside the box of bullets.

Windsor noticed Maynard's quizzical expression, and he explained, 'Something has to be saved out, else there'd be no games. It all shakes down eventually.'

The catamite and the whore were at a standstill, their hands and legs locked, teeth snapping at air.

'A draw? Hizzoner said.

'No!' cried a voice from the crowd.

'Break it, then.'

A man staggered to the centre of the clearing and aimed a kick at the catamite's head.

Dodging the kick, the catamite lost his grip on one of the whore's hands. Her fingernails raked his face. He rolled free, and she sprang after him. He fended her off with a flailing punch to the chest.

'How long have you been part of this?' Maynard asked Windsor, as they watched the sweating, bleeding bodies wrestle in the sand.

Windsor's eyes did not leave the fight. 'Thirty years. My boat broke down, and I swam ashore here.'

'They let you live?'

'They never caught me. I saw them first. I was about to seek their help, but there was something, a feeling, an aura – I credit my background in anthropology for recognizing it – that told me they were not the sort to welcome visitors. So I swam away.'

'You *swam* away?'

'Floated. I killed a pig and stopped up his bum and his mouth and used him as a float. For two days I floated on him, and then the sharks got him, and for another day I swam. A conch boat picked me up.'

'But when you got to shore, how come they didn't send someone back here?'

'I kept my counsel; I never opened my mouth.'

'*What?*'

The combatants were on their feet now. Blood streamed from bites on the whore's breasts and from scratches that

206

crisscrossed the catamite's chest and back. The whore screamed and charged. The catamite yanked at her hair, deflecting the charge. A patch of scalp came away in his hand.

'A handful of pain, Nanny!' Windsor shouted. 'There's a lad!'

The whore ducked and charged again. Her claws tore away the leather codpiece. Two lemons fell to the sand, and the crowd erupted in catcalls and guffaws.

The enraged catamite lashed wildly at the whore, who danced nimbly away, pointing derisively at his small shaven genitals.

'He's bought it now,' said Nau.

'No, sir! Behold!'

Keeping his distance from the whore, the catamite delicately poked his testicles up inside his groin and tucked his penis between his legs.

Nau was amazed. 'It's gone!'

'See Achilles hide his heel!' Windsor laughed.

The whore tackled the catamite, rooting for his vulnerability.

Windsor drank from his bottle and said to Maynard, 'They fascinated me. Either they were some exotic religious group, in which case they had a right to privacy, or – and I didn't dare dream this – they were ... well, what they are. I knew what would happen if I told the authorities. In a week, they'd have been extinct: civilization's solution would have been to save them by extinguishing them, and these people would have cooperated by fighting to the death. Oh, a few might have survived, the children, to be reprogrammed. They'd be actuaries now, or salesmen, free to be the same as their fellows, free to worry about auto loans and pyorrhoea.'

'How did you join them?'

Windsor smiled. 'Carefully. I approached them as I would the Tasaday or the Jivaro or any other anachronistic society. I stood well at sea and sent things ashore on the tide: rum and powder and – silly of me, but I had no way of knowing – glass beads and costume jewellery. I always sent a message along, professing friendship, explaining that I meant only

207

well, assuring them that I alone knew they existed. When they finally permitted contact,' – again Windsor smiled – 'l'Ollonois told me that for a year I had driven them crazy. They never saw me, couldn't catch me. In the end, they agreed to speak to me – in the ocean, armed boat to armed boat – only because they were fearful that I would become discouraged and expose them.'

A surge of outrage welled in Maynard's chest. It was a hot feeling, and welcome. 'Do you know how many lives your little experiment, your fascination, has –'

'Tush!' Windsor ignored the rebuke. 'When civilization has blathered itself into oblivion, these people will still exist. Everything is reduced to the simplest, most basic, incontrovertible virtue: survival. Morality, politics, philosophy, all aim to that one end. And that's the only end worth aiming for.'

'Survive . . . to do what?'

'Survive to survive. Never forget, Mencken, that beneath it all, man is an animal. Civilization is fur. These people are shaven; they are true to their nature.'

As he said this, Windsor had looked at Maynard, but now his attention snapped back to the fight, drawn by an anguished wail from the catamite.

The catamite lay on his back, curled up, his hands clamped to his bleeding crotch. The whore crouched over him. Her fingernails dug into the flesh surrounding his pharynx.

The catamite looked at Windsor and raised a hand to him, pleading.

'Doctor?' Nau said. 'He's yours.'

Windsor grimaced at the devastated wreck. 'He is not pretty,' he said, and he shook his head and turned away.

The catamite's scream was throttled by the whore's claws.

Maynard felt bile rise in his throat.

The cut-and-battered whore paraded around the clearing, triumphantly twirling the leather codpiece above her head, grinning in acknowledgment of the crowd's applause.

As he watched the catamite's body being dragged away, Maynard said, 'An expensive party.'

'Two? Expensive?' said Nau. 'No. Many battles cost more.'

Maynard had not seen Beth leave the clearing, so he started when he saw her appear from the darkness and walk, with measured pace, to the centre of the clearing. She had changed into a clean white linen robe and had oiled her skin and hair. She looked demure, virginal. She stood silently by the rum pot, hands clasped in front of her, eyes downcast.

'Hold!' called Nau. 'Be still.'

The whore sat down, and the crowd noise subsided.

'Goody Sansdents has a statement.'

Beth raised her eyes and said, 'No longer am I Goody Sansdents. I carry a Maynard child.'

An appreciative whoop rose from the crowd.

Nau saluted Maynard. 'You have done your work.'

Maynard's fingers touched the raw skin of his neck. He knew now· why there had been a sadness, a tenderness, to Beth's lovemaking, why Nau had permitted his chain to be removed, why he was suddenly 'trustworthy'.

Hizzoner patted Maynard's shoulder and said, 'Journey's done, lad. Take thine ease; eat, drink, and be merry.' Routinely, he added, 'Luke 12:19.'

Windsor picked up the thread. 'Thou fool, this night thy soul shall be required of thee. Luke 12:20.'

'God is in heaven,' Hizzoner responded to Windsor, 'and thou upon earth: therefore let thy words be few. Ecclesiastes 5:2.'

'When?' Maynard said dully.

'Tomorrow,' replied Nau.

'The Lord's day.' Hizzoner nodded. 'A good day to die, for He is resting and will attend to your welcome.'

'How?'

'Quickly,' Nau said. 'As you choose, for this is surgery, not retribution. But for the moment,' – he passed Maynard the chalice – 'give thought only to revelry.'

Maynard wet his lips, but he could not drink. Fantasies of elaborate, impossible escapes flashed through his head, and though he knew, realistically, that he had no hope, he was unwilling to signal complete surrender by drinking himself into a coma that death would only deepen. Besides, for all he knew they were right: death might be an adventure, and there was no point in starting a new adventure smashed.

The rum pot was refilled and reheated, and drinking resumed with an active fervour which suggested that a gold star awaited the first to reach unconsciousness.

Hizzoner opened a new bottle of brandy and took it back to his tree stump, where he slapped his companion awake and embarked on a new course of religious instruction.

Windsor lay back and sucked on his scotch bottle and contemplated the stars.

Beth filled a stoneware jug with rum and sat on the ground, occasionally rubbing her stomach and smiling. She refused to look at Maynard – reluctant, perhaps, to mar happy thoughts of her future with reminders that Maynard, who had given her that future, had no future of his own.

Nau drank less hastily that the others, and every few seconds he glanced into the darkness.

'Expecting someone?' Maynard asked.

'Aye. The capstone of a successful day.'

A moment later, they heard footsteps on the path and turned to see the two boys enter the clearing.

Manuel led the way. He wore a white shirt and clean white trousers and, around his neck, a gold coin on a gold chain.

Justin following, was dressed like a dauphin. He wore a doublet of lavender velvet, white satin knickers, silk stockings, and silver-buckled black leather shoes. An ivory-handled dagger was stuck in his belt. The little finger of each hand bore an emerald ring. He was a perfect period piece, except for the shoulder holster slung under his left arm.

Justin's hair was swept back and tied, and a ribboned pigtail had been pinned on to it. His manner was self-consciously regal: he carried his head high, and, as he crossed the clearing, he looked at no one but Nau.

'Hear me!' Nau said.

What little chatter there was, faded, and all that remained were faint sounds of snoring and, from a clump of bushes, retching.

'I had a son and he died,' Nau announced. He was

210

drunker than Maynard had thought: his head seemed heavy, and every time it tipped slightly it unbalanced Nau's stance, forcing him to compensate with a half-step forward. 'I would have taken this one as my second son.' He let a hand flop on Manuel's shoulder. 'But he's got Portugee and zambo and a rightful stew of others in him, so if he is to lead it will be by conquest. This one' – he clapped his other hand on Justin's shoulder – 'I therefore take now as my son, to share the burdens and the benefits and . . .' He forgot his words. 'And . . . the rest.' Nau staggered, and steadied himself on the two boys. 'But I predict the day when this Manuel and this Tue-Barbe will have at it for the office. Who will win? The better, and that is as it should be, for the strong must prevail.'

Unbidden, Hizzoner proclaimed from his place by the tree stump, 'One generation passeth away, and another generation cometh, but the earth abideth forever.'

'Well said.' Nau took a gold-chain pendant, larger than the one Manuel wore, from his pouch and hung it around Justin's neck.

Justin smiled a complacent half-smile, almost a smirk of *noblesse oblige*.

You insufferable little twit, Maynard thought, and he had consciously to restrain himself from leaping to his feet and, as his last mortal act, punching his child in the mouth.

'And so the time has come,' Nau said, taking Justin by the hand, 'to become a man.' He led the boy among the slumbering bodies, stopping here to examine a countenance, there to squeeze a thigh. 'Here,' he said finally, and with his toe he prodded a whore awake. 'Up, lady. You've work to do.'

The whore stirred and coughed.

'Take this lad and teach him the use of his weapon.'

Snorting and spitting and grumbling, the whore struggled to her feet. 'I'd be more lively with a night's sleep.'

'I say be lively now.'

The whore took Justin's hand. 'Come, boy.'

'When next I see him, he'd best be no more a boy.' Nau turned to Manuel. 'Go with them. That sow is like to sleep before her duty's done.'

211

As Manuel passed in front of Maynard, he glanced Maynard's way, and in the glance Maynard read Manuel's intention that Justin should never reach the age of leadership.

One by one, they fell asleep. First Beth, who passed out while draining the last drops from her stoneware jug. Then Windsor, whose bottle slipped from his hand and gurgled empty on his chest. Hizzoner launched a statement about the Kingdom of Heaven, which sank in snores. Finally Nau, who crawled for the shelter of his hut but succumbed with his legs sticking out through the doorway.

Maynard had listened for sounds of wakefulness, but there were none.

He was alone and free. He could leave the clearing and go to the cove and take a boat and sail away. No. There would be a guard on the boats. He could make a float, then, and float away. Something was wrong; it was too easy. Perhaps they wanted him to try to float away, perhaps they thought – in some perverse solicitude – it would be a kindness to let him float away and drown. After all, they had said he could choose his own death. No. They couldn't take the chance that he might survive. It was possible. Windsor had.

It was something else. Maybe they knew he wouldn't leave without Justin. But what was to stop him from taking Justin? Not the whore. Manuel? Maybe, but Manuel could be taken unawares and quickly silenced. Did they think he wouldn't kill Manuel? Were they counting on him being restrained by his 'worldly' code of ethics? He hoped that was the case. It would be a pleasure to show them how well they had corrupted him.

He would get Justin and go to the cove. If he could kill the guard and take a boat, he would; if not, they would go to a far end of the island and make a raft – of something, anything – and cast themselves adrift. Maynard wished he could tell time from the stars, for he would have liked to know how much time he would have before daylight, before discovery and pursuit.

He crawled to the edge of the clearing, where Jack the

212

Bat's trousers hung from a bush. There was a knife in a sheath threaded on to the belt, and Maynard took it.

When he was well away from the clearing, walking silently – careful to avoid snapping dry branches – in the assumed direction of the prostitutes' lodges, Maynard stopped and cut a length of vine to use as a garotte, if Manuel could not be otherwise subdued, or as bonds to tie Manuel or the guard stationed by the pinnaces.

He rounded a bend in the path and saw the prostitutes' lodges. He stopped and held his breath, searching the darkness for Manuel. The clearing was empty, the lodges dark and silent.

He sprinted across the sand to the nearest lodge and stood outside, listening. It was empty, as were the second and the third. As he crept along the wall of the fourth lodge, he heard heavy breathing and Justin's voice, angry, 'Well? Now what?'

In response, a snore.

The click-*click* of a bullet being chambered into an automatic pistol, then Justin's voice, menacing. 'Wake up, damn your eyes! I'll blow your head off!'

Maynard was shocked by the icy resolve in Justin's voice, but he didn't have the luxury of contemplative reaction: he couldn't let a bullet explode in the still night. He swept the curtain away from the door and threw himself into the hut, reaching for Justin's hand.

As he fell and knocked the pistol away, his eyes photographed the dim vision of his son's bare bottom nestled between the fleshy thighs of the snoring, stuporous whore.

'What?' Justin cried. 'Who . . .?'

Maynard put a finger across his lips. 'Ssshhh! It's me.'

Justin did not try to keep his voice low. 'What are you *doing*?'

Maynard read the confusion in the boy's voice, but there was outrage, too.

The whore stirred.

'Ssshhh! Let's go.'

'Let's *what*? If you think . . .'

A form filled the doorway, throwing the hut into utter

213

darkness. Maynard was knocked backward. The length of vine was ripped from his hand. He heard Justin try to scream, then gag and choke and slip to the ground.

Manuel, gasping for breath, knelt over Justin and removed the vine from around his neck.

'What are ...?'

'Pick him up,' Manuel ordered Maynard. 'Follow me.'

'Is he all right?'

'He'll sleep, but not for long.'

'He was frightened.'

'He would have cried out.'

'... confused ...'

Manuel found the whore's linen shift, tore off the hem, and tied it around Justin's mouth.

'You don't have to do that,' Maynard said. 'He was just ...'

'Call it what you will. *I* won't take the risk. Pick him up.'

Maynard obeyed. Justin was limp and unwieldy, like a sack of oranges, but light enough to carry easily over the shoulder. 'Let's go, buddy,' he murmured. 'Dad's gonna take you home.'

Maynard followed Manuel along the dark paths – trusting him, first, because he had no choice but also because Manuel's motive was obvious and selfish and therefore credible: pure ambition, unalloyed by any outside conflicts. The earlier and more simply competition could be eliminated, the smoother would be Manuel's accession to the l'Ollonois leadership.

When they reached the beach, Manuel did not hesitate: he trotted directly to the pinnaces. He motioned for Maynard to lay Justin in the nearest boat.

Justin's eyes were closed, his breathing regular.

'No guard?' Maynard whispered.

Manuel pointed to a dark heap, spread-eagled on the sand.

'Did you kill him?'

'You did,' Manuel said. 'If anything goes wrong, you did everything. You killed the guard and stole the boy and

214

bashed me in the head. They'll find me in the whore's lodge, crying about my terrible pains.'

'Fair enough.' Maynard leaned against the pinnace, to push it into the water. Then he noticed that though the sail was rigged and furled, there were no oars in the boat. 'I'll need oars. I'll be all night trying to tack out of this cove.'

'There,' said Manuel, and he ran along the beach toward a teepee of stacked oars.

Maynard turned away from the boat, to meet Manuel halfway.

In an instant, Justin was up and sprinting for the underbrush.

Maynard turned at the sound and yelled at the sight. 'Justin!' He took a few, frantic running steps, then stopped.

He saw the gag wrenched off and cast away, and he heard Tue-Barbe's cry, 'Alarm! Alarm! Alarm! Alarm!'

The cry echoed in the cove.

As he promised he would, Manuel ran for cover. Passing Maynard, he paused long enough to say, 'Fool!'

'I thought I knew ...' His despair had no words.

'Go yourself.'

Maynard looked up, but said nothing.

'If you stay, take that knife and stick it in your belly. Anything you do to yourself will be better than what we will fix for you.'

Maynard watched Manuel until he disappeared into the darkness. Then – unsure of himself, confused but suddenly afraid for his own life – he picked up a pair of oars, threw them in the pinnace, and pushed off from the shore.

As he rounded the first turn in the cove and reached the shelter of the breakwater, he heard distant voices. He leaned into the oars, pulling with desperate strength.

He reached open water and saw a flashlight beam playing, over his head, on the outboard breakwater. He rowed north for about fifty yards and turned another corner, putting a new barrier between himself and any searching lights.

The voices were louder now, more distinct. They had reached the cove.

He raised the sail. The wind was fresh from the southeast,

215

pushing him northwest into deep ocean water. As long as it held fresh, he had a chance of keeping his lead.

The little pinnace hissed swiftly through the water; tiny waves tapped against the wooden planks in the bow. He brought the sail close in. The boat heeled over, and the tapping of the waves on the bow grew sharper, more urgent.

Then, suddenly, the bow seemed to settle in the water. The boat's motion lost its crispness. The waves no longer tapped against the bow; they splashed, sluggishly, sloppily. From the darkness forward came a gurgling sound.

Maynard cleated the sheet and used its tail to lash the tiller. He moved forward on his knees, and immediately he felt water rising in the boat. He groped blindly for the leak; if the hole was small, he could plug it and bail the boat and keep sailing.

His fingers probed beneath the bow thwart, and felt a rush of sea water. The bow planks had separated, all of them. He withdrew his hand. His fingertips were sticky. He held them to his nose: molasses.

Manuel had covered all his bets: he had scraped the caulking from the bow and replaced it with molasses. Even if Justin had not fled and raised the alarm, even if he and Maynard had not been pursued, the pinnace was guaranteed to sink, with wind and tide pushing them into the open ocean.

Maynard looked toward the island: in the moonless dark all he could see was a faint pale strip of beach. He dived overboard and swam for shore.

15

Michael Florio stood on the bridge of the Coast Guard cutter *New Hope*, nursing a cup of coffee and gazing idly at the crowd of children who had gathered on the dock since first light to gawk at this great war machine that had slipped into South Caicos during the night.

Florio was tired and annoyed – tired because he had had almost no sleep since leaving Florida two days before, annoyed because he was convinced he was on a fool's errand.

There was no reason to believe that Brendan Trask was anything but safe. He had not been heard from in several days, but his silence was hardly cause for alarm: he was aboard a large, well-stocked, fully crewed motor-sailor with transatlantic capability, and he had said – publicly – that he had no intention of contacting anybody. He had not filed a float plan, but that was a rule observed more often in breach than compliance.

The weather had been calm and clear. There had been no significant thunderstorms – not even any of the routine, brief but violent local tempests – that might have jammed or garbled a radio distress call. And if the boat had sunk, there would certainly have been news of her by now, for she carried a dinghy, towed a Boston Whaler, and had strapped to the deck four pushbutton-launched, self-inflating liferafts. All

217

the auxiliary craft were equipped with powerful transmitters that pulsed unmistakable signals on marine and aviation distress frequencies.

But the world was evidently unwilling to believe Trask's declaration of retirement. What he said on televison was universally accepted, but when he said he didn't want to speak on television any more, there had to be an ulterior motive. He could not be permitted to escape without explanation – or, at least, without observers to capture his words of wisdom and to chronicle the twilight of his extraordinary career. It was almost as if the public and the media resented him, felt they had made him a star and they alone should determine when he would fall from orbit.

And so, when days had passed without word from, or sight of, the Most Trusted Man in America, the public – enamoured of conspiracy, thirsty for melodrama – had demanded proof that Trask was alive and well. Unsubstantiated rumour had changed the public's perception of his voyage: it had begun as a sailing trip, but now it was a disaster.

They want reverse news, Florio thought. They want a headline that says: 'Trask Okay'. That's like a headline saying: 'No Plane Crashes Today' or 'Tiffany's Not Robbed'.

Someone at *Today* Publications had called a couple of congressmen because one of their stringers had flown over a big sailboat and couldn't state positively that it wasn't Trask's boat. The congressmen had called somebody in the Pentagon. Then someone at Trask's network, which still hoped to negotiate for his return to duty, called the Secretary of Defence.

A friend had alerted Florio at 2.30 in the morning, and he had immediately called his commanding officer and volunteered to lead the search. He argued that he was the only officer with both sea experience and up-to-date knowledge of boat disappearances, and his request had been granted. But now, after forty-eight hours of aimless, fruitless cruising, he was ready for a change of clothes and a night's sleep.

The captain of the *New Hope*, a young lieutenant named Mould, climbed to the bridge and stood beside Florio, taking deep, therapeutic breaths of cool morning air.

'You look awful,' Florio said.

Mould nodded. 'The goddam sound man did it again. At the dock, for chrissakes! This time he fell in it.'

The network had pulled strings and got permission to send a television crew on board the ship, to record the epic search for the missing anchorman. The correspondent, Dave Kempe, was a slick, leisure-suited New Yorker, but arcane union regulations had prescribed that the crew itself – cameraman, sound man, lighting man – be recruited from Atlanta. None of the three had ever been to sea. The cameraman's hobby was mountaineering, the lighting man kept bees, and the sound man's avocation was hypochondria. He was short, bald, rotund, and at least sixty. By his own account, he was afflicted with corns, sciatica, gas, angina pectoris, sinusitis, seborrhoea and what he called nerves. It was impossible to tell which of his ailments were fancied, but since leaving Florida he had added to his catalogue of ills chronic – volcanic – seasickness. And as if subconsciously intending to force others to share his misery, he refused to go outdoors even to puke.

'He won't take a pill,' Mould said. 'Says it might react with his other medicine.'

'Why don't you fly him out? The guy who brings the water can probably get him on a plane.'

'He says he won't go. Doesn't want to lose the overtime.'

Florio shook his head. 'Dumb bastard's gonna rupture something.'

Ahead, on the bow, two seamen slopped water on the deck and began their matutinal swabbing. A third seaman removed the canvas cover from the .50-calibre machinegun mounted beside the bridge and oiled it with a rag.

Florio looked at the machinegun. 'When was the last time that was fired?'

Mould hesitated before saying, 'Not under my command.'

'Bullshit, Lieutenant.' Florio smiled. 'Flying fish are targets too sweet to pass by.'

219

The seaman oiling the gun grinned.

Mould blushed. 'Well ...'

A leaky, decrepit tank truck rattled along the dock and stopped, and the driver got out and passed a hose to a seaman below.

A policeman with a clipboard disembarked from the other side of the truck. He was sleepy-eyed and rumpled and having trouble being officious. He consulted his clipboard, cleared his throat, and spoke to the bridge. 'Purpose of visit?'

'Water,' said Mould. 'Have you heard anything ...'

'Weapons?'

'What?'

'Are you carrying weapons?'

Mould exchanged glances with the seaman, who continued to rub the barrel of the machinegun. 'Um, y'see friend ...'

'All weapons must be placed in bond with the constable.'

'We'll be here ten more minutes.'

'I can order a search of the vessel.'

'Is that so?'

'Any weapons?'

Mould looked at Florio. 'No.'

'Very well. Any narcotics or prescription drugs?'

'How many questions have you got?'

'Twenty in all. I can order your vessel impounded.'

Mould whispered to Florio, 'I'm gonna tell him to fuck off.'

'I wouldn't,' Florio said. 'Someday – God knows how – it'll get back to Washington, and some enemy you didn't even know you had will find a way to kick your ass with it.' A buzzer sounded. 'Talk to the man. I'll get it.'

Florio walked to the front of the bridge, pressed an intercom button and said, 'Bridge.'

'Got a bullet from Miami,' said the voice of the radio operator. 'Trask just pulled into Annapolis.'

'Annapolis?'

'Generator froze up on him. They told him it'd be a month before they could fix it in the Bahamas. He figured he could get home and back before then.'

220

'Okay. Thanks.' Florio laughed.

When the water was loaded and paid for, and the ship made ready for sea, Florio said to the policeman, 'You ever see an American around here, a skinny guy with a kid?'

'People come and go. He on a boat?'

'No. He came in on the plane that crashed.'

'Prob'ly long gone.'

Mould was looking at a chart of the Turks and Caicos group. 'Do I really have to go south before I can turn north?' he asked the policeman.

'How much you draw?'

'Nine feet.'

The policeman chuckled. 'Man, you try to take nine feet across them banks, you gonna be there for *ever*. There's six feet at the highest high tide, and nobody live out there to pull you off.'

The *New Hope* left the dock and steamed south, along the edge of the Caicos Banks.

'When I retire,' Florio said, 'I'm gonna get a boat and come down here and spend a summer shipwrecking. Those banks are supposed to be loaded with Spaniards.'

'Is that what that guy did?' Mould asked.

'What guy?'

'The one you asked about, the one with the kid.'

'No, he came down here to look into a story for *Today* and poof! Gone.'

'*Today*? Good riddance. It's one of those bastards got us sent off on this asshole jaunt.'

Maynard lay, half buried in dirt and brush, on the top of the hillock that overlooked the cove. He had crawled there in the darkness, had arrived and buried himself just as the sun was beginning to peek over the horizon. It was, perhaps, foolhardy of him to return so close to the community, but he had concluded that to hide away from people would be suicide. He would not know how or when or where they planned to look for him; capture would be inevitable. So he could not wait. He had to overhear and anticipate and

221

actively evade until he could decide how to trap and subdue Justin, how to steal a boat (this time without Manuel's help), how to escape with enough lead so he would not be overtaken, how to ... The questions were endless, the answers nonexistent, but he was confident that, given time, he could formulate a plan.

His best hope for time was that he would be given up for dead.

There was no wind. The bugs had been bad since first light, and as the morning warmed they grew more ferocious. Maynard plucked some berries from a bush by his head and mashed them into a paste that he smeared on his face. He didn't know what was in the berries – sugar, for all he knew – but the paste provided a shield against the tiny gnats. He watched the cove, and listened.

Nau and Windsor and the two boys waited in the cove as Jack the Bat and Rollo rowed a pinnace to the beach. Aboard they had the mast and sail from the pinnace Maynard had abandoned.

'He could sail,' Jack the Bat said as he beached the boat. 'He might have made it if she hadn't sunk under him.'

'Where is he?' asked Nau.

'Never saw him. I 'spect he went overboard and slipped under.'

Windsor said, 'You didn't see him at all?'

'No. It was dark as a hog's ass. But we looked when light came. He's not out there.'

Nau was satisfied. 'He's gone, then.'

'No!' Windsor shouted. 'He's here.'

Maynard saw Windsor stab a finger at the ground, then wave his arm at the hillock. Reflexively, Maynard ducked his head, as if avoiding an extrasensory detector in Windsor's wave.

Don't believe it, Maynard thought. Why would I come back here?

'Why should he return?' Nau said. 'He was not mad; he did not seek pain.'

'You have his child,' said Windsor.

Nau paused, pondering. He put his hand on Justin's

222

houlder. 'This was his child no longer; he knew it. This is
Tue-Barbe.'

Justin smiled and repeated, 'Tue-Barbe.'

'We are many,' Nau said. 'He is one and weak and ...'

'And an enemy. You must find him and kill him.'

Nau said to Justin, 'You are excused.'

'No,' Justin replied. 'I can hunt.'

Maynard heard Justin speak, and for a second he regret-
ed having returned to the island, only to be hunted down
nd killed by his own child. But he forced away his rage: As
ong as he was alive, he would not accept the loss of his son.

'All right, Doctor,' Nau said. 'We will gather the company
nd sweep for him. We will begin with the rocks beyond the
ill' – he pointed directly at Maynard – 'and sweep the island
lean. If he is here, we will find him, even if he has used
vizardry to shrink to the size of a new-born piglet.

Nau ordered Rollo to remain with the boats, then led
Windsor and the boys away from the cove, inland.

In a few moments, Maynard heard the hollow sound of the
orn, calling the company together. His plan – such as it
vould ever be – had to wait: now he must run, hide, avoid the
earchers. They could not cover the whole island. There had
o be a cave or a ditch or a treetop they would overlook.

He heard footsteps and voices, heading north toward the
ip of the island where he had come ashore. He waited until
ll the sounds had faded, then brushed the sand and dirt off
is body, crawled away from the lip of the hillock overlook-
ng the cove, got to his feet and ran south. He still had Jack
he Bat's knife with him, and he clutched it as he ran.

The searchers were practised and thorough. They coated
he island like a brushfire, missing nothing. They walked
ide by side, strung out from one shore of the island to the
ther. Their pace was set by the slowest member: if someone
ad to stop to shake a tree or lift a rock or pick apart a pile of
rush, the others waited. Nothing would filter through the
eine.

They flushed birds and rats and lizards, driving every-
hing before the search.

Maynard stayed ahead of them, but just far enough so

223

they could neither see nor hear him. He did not want to rush blindly to the south end of the island, for that would trap him in a cul-de-sac from which the only escape would be by wading or swimming out on to the banks, where he would be a conspicuous, solitary target. He took care to examine every bush, every hut, every hole in the ground.

The searchers made no effort to be silent. They stamped their feet and slashed the bushes and called out to one another. They were entirely confident of success.

Maynard backed against the clearing where the armourers worked. Barrels of gunpowder were stacked inside lean-to. Broken muskets and pistols were arrayed on a work bench for repair. Maynard quickly assessed and rejected all possible hiding places in the clearing, and he moved on.

As he crept along a path, he heard Nau's voice behind him, instructing: 'First, look for signs of fresh digging. See any mound, and scattered earth, stick your cutlass in it. Well?'

Justin's voice: 'None.'

'Good. Now we overturn every barrel, upend the table run a sword through every bush.'

Maynard's mind was soaking up every bit of information he heard; all of it might be helpful. As he came to the next clearing, he was aware that what he had just heard had added several minutes to his life. It was the clearing where the company had gathered last night – the charcoal embers were still smouldering beneath the rum pot – and on the far side there were two fresh graves: Basco's and the catamite's. Sand and dirt were dug and scattered and heaped everywhere. It would have been tempting to add one more small pile to the general mess. The surprise would have been as bad as the pain when – curled and suffocating in the blackness – he would have felt the probing sword.

He moved on, past the catamites' clearing and the prostitutes', past the latrine and into Beth's clearing. Beyond was the sea.

As the voices drew nearer and were more distinct, they were also more concentrated, for the island narrowed sharply on this end, drawing the searchers together, closing the bag.

Maynard chose. He cut a hollow reed. He would walk into the sea and lie underwater on his back and breathe through the reed while he tried to paddle away. They would probably see him, and if they saw they would pursue, and if they pursued they would catch him, and if ... to hell with it. He took a step toward the open beach.

Then he heard the horn – two blasts, urgent, like a warning. Two more blasts. A pause. Two more.

At first he thought they had seen him, and he prepared to dash for the water. But the voices suddenly receded, back toward the north.

Cautiously, keeping away from the paths, peering through the underbrush, he followed.

'A vessel.'

'Where?'

'Sou'west, making nuth'ard.'

'What is she?'

'Big.'

Nau's voice: 'To the boats!'

Windsor's: 'You can't leave it now!'

Nau, angry: 'Stop your tongue or I'll cut it for you!'

Maynard could see nothing, but he heard people shouting and running for the cove. He returned to Beth's clearing and crept to the edge of the beach and looked off to the south.

The boat was two or three miles away, but the bow wave that curled and flashed in the sun told Maynard that she was big and fast – too big for a sports cruiser, too fast for a commercial fisherman. It was the colour of the hull, as gradually it took shape against the blue-green water, that raised a clot of hope in Maynard's chest: Coast Guard white And, on the bow, a wide red chevron. The boat was heading north, keeping seaward of the banks, and from the speed she was making she was not sightseeing.

Maynard's impulse was to run out on to the beach and wave, but a moment's reason condemned the impulse. The ship's course would bring it past the island half a mile offshore, at least. The watch on the bridge would be keeping his eyes on the reefs, not the land. There was a chance that Maynard could wave or flash something or cause enough movement to catch the watch's attention, but the odds were too long and the cost of failure too high: once the ship had passed, it was gone. He had to send a signal that could not be ignored.

He ran back along the paths, making too much noise, recklessly confident that everyone on the island had gathered at the cove. When he drew near the cove, he slowed and crept through the thickets.

He stopped and listened to the sounds from the beach. The pinnaces were being prepared for sea. He was about to step forward, to try to see the beach, when he heard Nau's voice.

'*She*'d be a prize!'

Maynard froze. The voice was only a few feet away, on the other side of a fat bush. He bent his head and peered through the leaves. Nau and Windsor were sitting on the hillside, watching the boat through a brass telescope. If Maynard had taken his intended step, he would have stumbled upon them.

Windsor put down the telescope. 'It's a warship!'

'Aye. Robust, too. What would be her cargo?'

'No cargo.'

'But munitions.'

'Not worth the risk.'

'But the vessel is. Would she not make a fine flagship?'

'Don't make jokes.'

'I don't joke,' Nau said.

'Then it's fool's talk.'

'It's what, Doctor?'

Windsor retreated. 'You're a man of courage. A courageous leader does not expose his men to certain death.'

'Surprise lessens certainty.' Nau raised the telescope. 'A *fine* flagship!'

'You don't want a war with the United States government.'

'They wouldn't war on phantoms.'

226

Windsor started to argue further, but Nau cut him off. 'Rest your mind. She's firing both barrels; she'll be gone before I could get to her.'

'Unless she stops,' Windsor said.

'And why should she stop? To jolly on the beach?'

Maynard tried to see the ship; underbrush blocked his view, but he could hear the throbbing growl of the big diesel engines. He guessed that the ship was a mile away, moving at, say, twenty knots. He had three minutes.

He backed away from the thickets, turned, and, watching his footfalls to avoid dry branches, moved inland.

The signal would not be a sound: the engine noises would drown out anything less than an explosion. It had to be visual. A fire. A big fire, preferably smoky. He had no matches.

He came to the clearing littered with the debris of last night's celebration: bits of clothing, cases of liquor, half-empty bottles. A wisp of smoke curled up around the rum pot; the embers beneath were still hot, but he saw nothing that would ignite quickly, spectacularly. He didn't need a campfire; he needed a conflagration, like those pictures of Newark burning during the riots.

Riots.

His head had found the answer, and now his hands worked efficiently. He grabbed a bottle of rum, nearly full, and a piece of cloth. He soaked the cloth in rum and jammed it in the bottle neck. On his knees beside the rum pot, he scooped sand away until he found glowing coals. The tip of the cloth ignited instantly. He jumped to his feet and ran.

The engine noise was louder; the ship must be abreast of the island.

He ran into the clearing where the armourers worked. A woman was there, and she saw him and screamed, but he barely noticed. He ran toward the lean-to where the powder barrels were stacked, cocked his arm and flung the burning bottle and then pitched face forward into the sand and covered his head with his hands.

He heard the bottle break, and, for an agonizing second, that was all. His mind shrieked, 'Burn, you bastard!' There

227

was a whoosh as the rum went up, a brief moment of indecisive hissing, then a deafening, painful, concussive *whump*. His skin burned, his ears rang with clashing bells.

He got up and staggered into the underbrush and picked his way toward the cove.

16

'You don't want to take a rifleman?' Florio said.

'I have this.' Mould pointed the a .45 automatic in a holster at his belt. He stood in the bow of a motor launch that hung on davits over the side of the *New Hope*. A sailor was in the stern, at the wheel, and another sailor, amidships, held the launch away from the side of the ship. The rest of the launch, which was designed to carry twenty-five people, was covered with canvas sheets lashed from gunwale to gunwale. 'Besides, if anybody survived that explosion, they won't be in a mood to argue.'

Florio shrugged. 'It's your party.'

Mould signalled for the launch to be lowered. The boat hit the water on an even keel, and the cables were detached from steel eyes bow and stern.

Dave Kempe, the television correspondent, called down to Mould, 'Make it snappy, will you? We'll miss our flight.'

Mould ignored Kempe and said to Florio, 'You might check the first-aid stuff. I don't know what we've got for burns.'

Florio waved and started down the ladder from the bridge.

On a perch in the bow, Mould guided the helmsman through the break in the reefs. From the sea, the entrance to the cove was invisible, and twice the launch passed it by. On the third pass, Mould saw a slim channel of blue water between breakwaters. The helmsman throttled down, almost to idle, and the launch inched into the cove.

'Somebody's here,' said Mould, pointing to the pinnaces.

'What kind of boats is that?' asked Pincus, the midships sailor.

'Run her up on the beach, Gantz,' Mould said to the helmsman. 'You stay with the boat. Pincus and I'll have a look around.'

Gantz nudged the bow of the boat on to the sand and shut off the engine.

'Sure don't sound like nobody's here,' said Pincus. 'Man it's so quiet it's noisy.'

Gantz said, 'Whatever it was went off, probably blew 'em all to ratshit.'

A sound turned their heads toward a small hillock overlooking the cove.

A man stood, waist-deep in the underbrush at the top of the hill, weaving drunkenly, waving his arms, trying to speak. As they watched, the man moaned and fell forward, his arms spread as in a swan dive. He hit the hillside, somersaulted, rolled and skidded down to the sand on the opposite side of the cove from the launch.

Mould and Pincus jogged around the crescent beach. The man lay on his back with his feet in the water. He wore crude, knee-length shorts and nothing else. His body was scratched and bruised.

Pincus said, 'Is he alive?'

'Sort of. Look at that: his hair's singed. He must've been right next to the explosion.'

'He sure don't eat much. Can't weigh more'n a hundred fifty.'

Pincus bent to pick up the man, but Mould stopped him. 'Leave him. No point in moving him till we have to. There may be a litter on board we can carry him with.' Mould returned to the launch. 'You better come too, Gantz,' he said. 'If there's one, there's probably more—to bury if nothing else.'

'There's a path up there,' Pincus said.

In single file, they left the beach.

The path they followed snaked through the underbrush, seeming to lead nowhere. The only sounds were their footsteps and the hum of bugs.

They heard the clink of glass, and a woman's voice, singing softly to herself.

The path opened into a clearing. A woman was gathering bottles in a burlap bag. She was filthy and dishevelled. She wore a formless grey dress.

'Hello,' Mould said.

The woman looked up. She did not seem surprised or upset or happy; her face was blank.

'How many people were hurt?'

The woman didn't answer. There was a sudden movement in the bushes.

Pincus looked to the edge of the clearing and said, 'Shit, Lieutenant!'

The clearing was ringed with armed men.

Mould's fingers twitched at his holster.

'Touch that,' Nau said, stepping forward with a pistol in his hand, 'and your journey's done.'

'Who are you?'

'Your captor. You need know no more.'

'Just what the hell ...?'

'Shut your mouth.'

Windsor said, 'L'Ollonois, I beg you, don't do this.'

'And you shut yours, Doctor. It's flapping too much.' Nau spoke to the boys. 'Take the clothing from that one and that one.' He indicated Mould and Pincus. 'Bind them well. The other leave be. He'll come with us.'

'Listen ...' Mould began, but before the word could leave his mouth, a knifepoint was pressed under his chin, forcing his head back.

Nau said to the company, 'I want every man. We'll stack his boat with men like logs. That will be the fox. Any extras will be poor fishermen and will follow in the pinnaces.'

While Mould and Pincus were being stripped, Nau ordered the women to fetch and pass liquor among the crew. He chose Mould's clothes for himself, and told Jack the Bat to wear Pincus's.

Mould and Pincus were bound back to back, and the tail of the binding vine was looped around their throats and pulled tight.

The men drank heavily and laughed at Jack the Bat and jeered at his threats of violent retribution.

'We are prepared,' Nau said. 'If our number be small, our hearts are great. And the fewer persons we are, the more union and better share in the spoils. Hizzoner . . .?'

Hizzoner recited his ritual prayer, and Nau ended the ceremony with: 'Fire your furnaces, lads, get damned hot, for this will be a day like the old days.'

Maynard rolled over, and tasted the sand and salt water. His ears had not stopped ringing, but now other sounds infiltrated the ringing. Impelled to survive, he crawled for shelter in the underbrush. He had barely covered himself when the first men arrived on the beach and began to load the grey launch.

He remembered the launch. It had had two or three men in it, and he had tried to warn them. Had he said anything before he blacked out? Were they leaving without him? Why were the men in uniform working *with* Nau's people? Then he saw that one of the men in uniform was Nau.

The men were loaded into the launch one by one, prone atop one another, and as each section of the launch was filled, the canvas cover was replaced and strapped down.

'For the last time, l'Ollonois,' Windsor said, 'don't do this.'

'And for the last time, Doctor, stop your tongue!'

'No healthy animal seeks extinction!'

'I agree,' said Nau, and with a stroke so spasmodically swift that it resembled an electric impulse, he drew his knife from his belt and backhanded it across Windsor's throat.

The knife had returned to Nau's belt before Windsor was fully conscious of what had happened to him. A sliver of red appeared on his neck, and darkened and drooled. He raised a hand to his throat, opened his mouth and closed it again, and sat down on the sand.

'Sit there and die, Doctor,' Nau said, and he turned away.

232

'Jesus!' Gantz said. Jack the Bat pushed him toward the launch.

The company resumed loading the boat, but Justin seemed paralysed. He could not take his eyes from Windsor, who was rocking back and forth.

Watching from across the cove, Maynard could tell that Justin was profoundly shocked. He was not sure why: the boy had seen so much death that one more should not affect him. Maybe, Maynard thought, it was that this was the first time he had seen someone die whom he had known before, in real life, and thus it was the first time death itself was real to him.

Justin looked at Nau. All he said was, 'But ...'

Nau took Justin's arm. 'Come, Tue-Barbe. What's done is done. Surgery was called for, and it has been performed.'

Maynard saw Justin resist Nau's pull – for only a second, but resistance was unmistakable – and again he felt a surge of hope.

Windsor tumbled sideways, wheezed and died.

Hizzoner was the last to board the launch. He threaded pieces of pitch-soaked twine through his pigtail, hoisted the hem of his robe and – with the delicacy of a damsel stepping over a puddle – climbed aboard and lay down. The canvas cover was lashed over him.

'Jack-Bat, take the bows,' Nau said. 'I will take amidships. And you' – he pointed at Gantz – 'take the helm. If you cock a finger out of order, if your tongue once trembles, I will serve you like I served the doctor. Agreed?'

Gantz said, 'You're the boss.' He started the engine and backed the launch away from the beach.

Four men remained. They boarded a rigged pinnace and followed the launch out of the cove.

Maynard waited in hiding until he was certain no one else was coming down to the cove. Then he crossed the crescent beach, dropped a paddle in one of the pirogues, pushed the boat into the water, and hopped aboard.

He heard a noise behind him, a whisper of clothing and footsteps on wet sand. He spun, with the paddle raised before his face.

233

Beth stood on the beach. 'Goodbye,' she said.

Maynard ducked, expecting to see a pistol raised and pointed at him. But Beth's hands were empty.

'Whatever happens, I expect I will not see you again.'

Maynard put down the paddle and smiled wanly. 'Not alive, anyway.'

'Good fortune, then.'

Maynard nodded. 'You too.' He dug the paddle into the water and pulled for the mouth of the cove.

'What do you see?' asked Dave Kempe.

'She's riding low in the water,' Florio said. 'Loaded down with something.' He braced his elbows against his chest to steady the binoculars. 'Looks like he's got a couple of kids aboard.'

'What is this, Be Kind to Natives Day?'

'Mr Kempe,' Florio said, as patiently as possible, 'this *is* a government vessel. We do have a responsibility.'

'Not to these people.'

Florio looked through the binoculars again. 'They *are* kids. Why don't you shoot some film of them? Make a nice story.'

'What ... Tom Sawyer marooned on a desert island?' Kempe paused. 'It might at that. Maybe we'll salvage this disaster yet.' He started down the ladder, calling, 'Schussman! Get your camera!'

Florio leaned over the side of the bridge and said to a seaman, 'You might's well lower your davit cables.'

The launch came alongside and wallowed in its own wash.

Looking down, Florio saw the helmsman, Gantz, his face pasty white. 'What's wrong?' he asked, but Gantz did not reply.

The other men had their backs to the ship as they snapped the davit cables into the eyes.

The winches whined; the launch rose.

The two boys looked tense, worried, their hands tucked under their arms. From one of the canvas covers, a braceleted forearm protruded.

'Are those *bodies* under there?'

The television crew, camera rolling, shoved their way to

the railing as the launch reached deck level.

'What the hell ...' Florio started down the ladder.

Canvas covers flew back.

Something slammed into Florio and knocked him cartwheeling off the ladder. The perplexing vision that followed him into darkness was of a man whose head was engulfed in a halo of flame.

The sounds of gunshots slapped across the water, and Maynard felt them slap his ears. There were screams, too, but from this distance they sounded faint and innocuous.

The launch and the pinnace were on the leeward side of the ship. Maynard paddled to windward, to stay out of sight.

He had no specific plan. If Nau and his people were killed, then he was saved. If Nau won, well ... he was no worse off on the ship than he would have been on the island. They wouldn't think to look for him on the ship. If they scuttled it with him on board ... he couldn't think that far ahead.

The shooting stopped. In all, no more than a dozen shots had been fired.

Maynard grabbed the ship's anchor chain. He tied the pirogue to one of the chain links, to keep it from drifting to leeward into view from the ship, and shinned up the chain and peeked through the chain port. The forward deck was empty. He slithered up on to the deck and crawled beside a bulkhead, where he rested.

He heard footsteps below, and scraping noises, as if things were being dragged across the metal decks. Then there was laughter, and Maynard knew how the battle had ended.

In corroboration, Hizzoner's voice intoned from the stern, 'The crimes you have committed are known to you and to God ...'

Grasping with his toes and fingertips, Maynard scaled the sloping face of the wheelhouse, slid over the top of the bridge, and dropped soundlessly to the bridge deck.

'... so I suppose I need not tell you,' Hizzoner went on, 'that the only way of obtaining pardon and remission of your sins from God is by a true and unfeigned repentance and faith in Christ ...'

There were scuppers on the bridge, and Maynard could look through them down on to the afterdeck of the ship.

Two bodies were jammed into a corner. One was a pudgy bald man in a dark business suit, the other younger, handsome, in a tan leisure suit.

Nau and the two boys stood in the stern. Rollo and Jack the Bat and the other men were loading food and weapons and ammunition into the launch and the pinnace.

Hizzoner's sermon was directed at a knot of six men by the port railing. Two were civilians, four wore Coast Guard fatigues. A seventh man, an officer, lay on the deck behind the others. He was alive, but he had been shot in the hip, and he pressed a handkerchief to the hole to stem the bleeding. Maynard looked hard at the officer, for he was sure he knew him.

'If now you will sincerely turn to Christ Jesus,' Hizzoner said, 'though late, even at the eleventh hour, Matthew 20.6-9, he will receive you.'

He's coming to the end, Maynard thought. His eyes searched the bridge. Did they stow weapons up here? Did they carry weapons on board? He knew nothing about military ships. He stared at a canvas-covered piece of machinery mounted on the side of the bridge.

'I only heartily wish that what, in compassion to your souls, I have now said to you upon this sad and solemn occasion ...'

A machinegun.

Maynard crept to the farthest corner of the bridge and hauled himself over the side. He edged his way around the bridge superstructure until he found a foothold on a narrow ledge beneath the machinegun.

The pinnace was directly in front of him. The men loading it had their backs to him, but if one of them turned around, he could not help but see Maynard.

Maynard unclipped the gun cover from the bulkhead and slid it off and set it on the wheelhouse roof.

The gun was enormous. He had seen photographs of these big .50s, but he had never had his face close to one: it was like sighting down a cannon. A box of ammunition was

236

ttached to the side of the gun. He prayed it was full, for he idn't dare open it to look. One hand reached for the cocking ver; the other found the trigger. He held his breath, yanked ack on the slide, and let it go.

The shots came so fast that they were not distinct: they vere a belch. In less than five seconds, the men in the innace and the men loading it were dead or twitching on the eck. Without removing his finger from the trigger, Aaynard swung the gun to the right. Rollo died in the assing spray. Jack the Bat took a step backward and was unched overboard by two bullets in his chest. Hizzoner quashed down in a heap of bloody robes.

Nau backed into the corner and held the two boys in front f him. He reached under Justin's arm, took the Walther rom the holster and held it to Justin's temple.

Maynard pointed the machinegun at Nau's head and said, Put it down.'

Nau smiled. 'No, thank you.'

'I'll kill you.'

'Me, yes. This one' – he nodded at Manuel – 'yes. But this ne' – he jammed the Walther hard against Justin's temple – no. You won't. You should; *I* would. But you won't. And if I lie, this one dies with me.'

Maynard looked at Justin, and he saw a frightened little oy.

He was positive he could put a bullet between Nau's eyes efore Nau could pull the trigger and kill Justin. It was lmost certain. Almost.

'You're right; I won't,' Maynard said. 'So where are ve?'

'I will take the lads ashore. You will wait here for the ight. Some time in the night, I will make a passage with my eople. Tomorrow, you will come ashore and fetch your nen. I will not harm them. You have my word.'

'Your word isn't worth shit.'

'True,' Nau laughed. 'But you have no choice.'

'You'll leave the boy, too.'

'I should tell you yes, but you know I cannot. I need him nore now than before.'

237

Justin's eyes widened and pleaded with Maynard.

Maynard said, 'I might as well shoot him myself.'

'Not so. Better to have the knowledge that he is alive and well, free and merry.'

Maynard hesitated, stymied. 'All right.'

'No!' Justin screamed. 'Dad!'

'Roll with it, buddy,' Maynard said.

'No!' Justin tried to wriggle free, but Nau wrapped his arm around the boy's throat and dragged him to the railing.

Nau told Manuel, 'Take the helm.'

Manuel looked up at Maynard, and in his eyes, too, there was a plea.

The launch was directly beneath Maynard's perch on the bridge. As the machinegun was mounted, it could not point straight down into the launch.

Nau saw that the big gun was no longer a threat to him, so he shoved Justin ahead of him into the launch.

Maynard didn't think about what he was going to do, didn't debate alternatives or weight risks. He jumped, and as he sprang through the air he pulled Jack the Bat's knife from his waist.

Nau heard the rush of air, or sensed the falling body, for he turned and looked up and tried to aim the pistol.

Maynard landed on Nau's shoulders and stabbed wildly, blindly, savagely, as Nau – grunting and cursing – tried to shake him off, pitching the pistol away to free both hands.

Nau stumbled, and Maynard rode him down beneath two forward thwarts. He stabbed again, and this time the knife caught between two of Nau's ribs and would not come free.

Nau writhed on to his back, tearing the knife from Maynard's hand and jamming Maynard beneath him.

Nau staggered to his feet and towered over Maynard. His chest and neck were pocked with blue puncture wounds; streams of blood crisscrossed and joined in a flow that dripped to the deck. The knife was wedged to its hilt, between the bottom two ribs on the right side. Nau grasped the knife hilt with both hands and wrenched it free. Leering at Maynard, he said, 'Not yet, scribe.' Bubbles of blood popped between is lips. 'I am a free prince. I will say when.' He raised the knife.

Maynard tried to back away but he was trapped, stuffed between the two thwarts.

Nau's eyes swelled and bugged; his lips curled back in a snarl. He held the knife over his head – like an Inca priest before a sacrificial altar – and screamed, 'Now!'

The arc of the knife flashed in the sunlight.

Nau plunged the knife into his own groin and ripped upward. Viscera oozed through the tear in his shirt.

He toppled to the right. His shoulder hit a thwart, and he rolled on to his back. The spring binding him to life snapped: the pupils of his eyes dilated, and, like a balloon suddenly released by a child, his chest squeezed out a squeaky, final blast of breath.

Maynard's eyes left Nau and found Justin, rigid in the stern of the launch. He said weakly, 'Hey, buddy ...'

Justin's eyes filled with tears. He walked aft and knelt down and took his father's hand.

AUTHOR'S NOTE

The literature on the buccaneers and pirates is vast, in both fact and fiction. In the course of preparing *The Island*, consulted scores of books, and while I have endeavoured to avoid any resemblance to real characters, I have tried equally hard to be faithful to historical reality.

Four books were particularly helpful: *The Buccaneers of America*, by John Esquemeling (New York: Dover Publications, Inc., 1967); *The Funnel of Gold*, by Mendel Peterson (Boston: Little, Brown & Co, 1975); *A General History of the Pirates*, by Captain Charles Johnson (London: Philip Sainsbury The Cayme Press, 1925); and *Pirates, An International History*, by David Mitchell (New York: Dial Press, 1976).